D0007416

WIRED

ALSO BY ROBIN WASSERMAN

Skinned

Crashed

Hacking Harvard

The Seven Deadly Sins series

WIRED

ROBIN WASSERMAN

Simon Pulse
NEW YORK LONDON TORONTO SYDNEY

This book is a work of fiction. Any references to historical events, real people, or real locales are used fictitiously. Other names, characters, places, and incidents are the product of the author's imagination, and any resemblance to actual events or locales or persons, living or dead, is entirely coincidental.

SIMON PULSE
An imprint of Simon & Schuster Children's Publishing Division
1230 Avenue of the Americas, New York, NY 10020
First Simon Pulse hardcover edition September 2010

For information about special discounts for bulk purchases, please contact
Simon & Schuster Special Sales at 1-866-506-1949 or business@simonandschuster.com.
The Simon & Schuster Speakers Bureau can bring authors to your live event.
For more information or to book an event contact the Simon & Schuster Speakers Bureau
at 1-866-248-3049 or visit our website at www.simonspeakers.com.
Designed by Mike Rosamilia
The text of this book was set in Adobe Caslon.
Manufactured in the United States of America
2 4 6 8 10 9 7 5 3 1
Library of Congress Cataloging-in-Publication Data
Wasserman, Robin.
Wired / by Robin Wasserman. — 1st Simon Pulse hardcover ed.
p. cm.
Sequel to: Crashed.
Summary: Lia is back at home, pretending to be the
perfect daughter, but she has become the public face of the mechs,
devoting her life to convincing the world that she and others like her
deserve to exist, until shocking truths are revealed,
forcing her to make a life-changing decision.
ISBN 978-1-4169-7454-3
[1. Science fiction.] I. Title.
PZ7.W25865Wir 2010
[Fic]—dc22
2010010237
ISBN 978-1-4424-0951-4 (eBook)

For my parents, Barbara and Michael Wasserman,
who did everything right.
(Though I never did get a puppy.)

WIRED

All moveables of wonder, from all parts,
Are here—
. . . .
The Bust that speaks and moves its goggling eyes,
The Wax-work, Clock-work, all the marvellous craft
Of modern Merlins, Wild Beasts, Puppet-shows,
All out-o'-the-way, far-fetched, perverted things,
All freaks of nature, all Promethean thoughts
Of man, his dulness, madness, and their feats
All jumbled up together, to compose
A Parliament of Monsters. . . .

—William Wordsworth

Humans are machines of the angels.

—Jean Paul

NO MORE SECRETS

Just make them love you.

This is not real.

"This is real," I said, because the voice in my head ordered me to say it.

Because machines follow orders, and I am a machine.

This is not me.

"This is me," I said. Because I was programmed to lie.

You see everything, but you get nothing.

"What you see is what you get," I said, and I smiled.

You see: Perfect lips drawn back in a perfect smile. Perfect skin pulled taut over a perfect body.

You see: Hands that grasp, legs that stretch, eyes that understand.

You see a machine that plays the part she was built to play. You see a dead girl walking. You see a freak, a transgression, a sin, a hero. You see a mech; you see a skinner. You see what you want to see.

You don't see me.

"So it doesn't bother you, millions of people watching your

every move?" the interviewer asked. She was sweating under the camera lights. I wasn't. Machines neither sweat nor shiver; we endure. This interviewer had a reputation for wringing tears from all her interview subjects, but in my case it would be easier to get a toaster to cry. So something else was needed. Extra feeling from her, to make up for my lack. Shining eyes welling with liquid, rosy cheeks at opportune moments for anger or passion, a shudder for effect when we passed through the really gory parts: the aftermath of the accident, the uploading of spongy brain matter into sterile hardware, the death and reawakening. I had to admit her act was better than mine. But then, pretending to be human is easier when you actually are.

"You don't feel like you need to put on an act for us? Keep something private, something only for you?"

Artificial neural synapses fired, and electrical impulses shot through artificial conduits, zapped artificial nerves. My perfect shoulders shrugged. My perfect forehead wrinkled in the perfect approximation of human emotion.

"Why would I?" I said.

It had been fifteen days. Fifteen days of posing and preening under their cameras, mouthing their words, following their orders. Burrowing deeper into my own head, desperate for some hidden refuge that their cameras couldn't penetrate, somewhere dark and empty and safe that belonged only to me.

Widen eyes.

Tilt head.

Smile.

"After all, I have nothing to hide."

Day one.

"The commands will feed directly into your auditory system, and it'll sound like the voice is coming from inside your head," Ben said, giving the equipment one final check like the perpetual employee-of-the-week I knew him to be. BioMax's best mender of broken mechs—mender, fixer, occasionally builder, but, as he was always careful to clarify, not doctor. Doctors tended to real, live orgs, and Ben fixed broken-down machines who only looked human. These last six months, every single thing in my life had changed and changed again, everything except for Ben, who was a constant: same tacky flash suits, same waxy hair, same plastic good looks. Same fake-modesty shtick, as in *Aw, shucks, I'm no one important, no one to be afraid of, certainly no one who'd keep secrets from you and manipulate you and blackmail you and hold the power of life and death over your remarkably lifelike head; I'm just a guy, like any other, so you can call me Ben.* "Some people get disoriented by the voice—"

"I'll be fine," I said flatly. I'd had voices in my head before. One of the many perks of being a machine: the potential for "improvements." Like a neural implant that would let me speak silently to other mechs, and hear their voices in my head. Like infrared vision and internal GPS and all the other inhuman modifications I'd had stripped away when I moved back in with my org parents and my org sister and pretended to return to my org life. Like I could close my eyes, make a wish, and suddenly be *organic* again, suddenly be the living, breathing Lia Kahn that had gotten into that car a year ago, pulled onto the highway, slammed into a shipping truck, and been blown into a million burned, bloody pieces.

"I want to make sure you understand how everything's going to work," call-me-Ben said, always pushing. "Once things start, we're not going to have a chance to talk like this."

"What a shame."

He ignored me. "So if you have any questions, it's best to ask—"

"If Lia says she'll be fine, she'll be *fine*." That was Kiri Napoor, director of public relations and my own personal liaison to the BioMax powers that be. She caught my eye and winked, Kiri-speak for *I know he's lame; just go with it.*

Kiri was my watchdog, assigned to make sure I kept both feet on the company line. When they'd first told me about her, I'd imagined a female version of call-me-Ben, some puffbag of hot air with a tacky weave and skin pulled watertight from one too many lift-tucks, a nag who would follow me around all day, tattling back to her BioMax overlords every time I opened my mouth. Instead she turned out to be *Kiri*, with her sleek purple hair, perma-smirk, impeccable taste (retroslum shift dress paired with networked boots flashing mangarock vids, that first time I saw her), and enough of a punk twist to make her look cool without even trying.

"You say you want to help the mechs," she'd said, that first day. "So I trust you to do that. I'm not here to spy on you; I'm here to help you."

It was pretty much the same line call-me-Ben had been feeding me ever since I'd signed on to the BioMax cause. But when Kiri said it, something in her voice suggested she thought as little of the corp as I did, and felt the same about the crap spewing out of her mouth. Then she'd kicked call-me-Ben out of the room, telling him that from now on if he wanted to bother me, he'd have to bother her first. That sealed the deal.

Kiri was the only reason I'd gone along with this stupid idea to begin with. It had been hers, which meant it couldn't be all bad. At least that's what I'd let myself believe when she talked me into it.

Guesting in a vidlife meant wiring myself with micro-cams and mics, ensuring that anyone who wanted could track my every move. Worse, it meant playing whatever part my audience wanted to give me. The perfect blend of scripted melodrama and absolute 24/7 reality, that's how they had advertised it when vidlifes first started popping up. Your favorite characters mouthing *your* lines, dosing on *your* favorite b-mod, hooking up with *your* choice of guy, running their lives by your rules and ruining their lives for your personal entertainment.

I told myself that it wasn't any different from what I'd been doing for the last six months as BioMax's poster child for the happy, healthy mech, doing what they told me to do, saying what they told me to say, bowing and scraping for board meetings and press conferences and legislative committees, dangling on their strings. I'd started because my father had asked me to, and I was still playing nice, honoring the letter of our bargain—I got all the credit I needed to help Riley, and my father got his daughter back. Or at least a reasonable simulacrum thereof. But once I'd made the obligatory appearances he'd asked of me, I stuck around. I'd always been good at acting the part, and at least this time the act would be for a good cause.

Baby steps, that was the plan. Persuade the orgs that the mechs offered no threat, meant no harm. That we were just like them. That we were young and foolish—yet also mature. Carefree, yet responsible. Predictable, yet prone to petty spats and parties like the orgs our age. It meant walking a fine line, and singing different songs to different audiences. Kiri customized the sober lectures I delivered to boardrooms, the grinning idiot I made myself into for pop-up ads, each persona carefully crafted to suit its circumstances—irrelevant, apparently, that none of them suited me.

The vidlife took the act one step further. We would offer them proof—24/7, in living color—that I was no more harmless and no less vapid than your average rich-bitch wild child. We would sucker them into caring about my fights and flings, sacred pacts and romantic treasons, and without realizing it, they would come to believe that *I* cared, that *I* felt. That I was, in my petty melodramas of daily life, no different from them. Or at least no different from the other people they watched on the vids. There were those at BioMax who couldn't understand how acting a part would convince anyone of anything about the "real" me—but they were the ones who didn't watch vidlifes. Those of us who did knew the shameful truth: No matter how much you *knew* you were watching live-action puppets play out the fantasies of the masses, the more you watched the vidlifers, the more you believed in them. That was, after all, the whole point of the vidlife: to forget the fantasy and accept the reality. To ignore the distinction between "reality" and "real."

"Ready?" call-me-Ben asked.

I nodded, and he exchanged a cryptic set of gestures with the vidlife rep, then gave me a thumbs-up. That was it. *This* was it.

Nothing seemed different. Nothing *felt* different. The buzzing of the micro-cam hovering over my shoulder could have been a fly.

Just make them love you, I reminded myself, waiting for something to happen. Preparing myself to be bright and sparkly, harmless and irresistible, to be the old Lia Kahn, the one who didn't run on rechargeable batteries. *We're the same people we used to be*, I'd said at meeting after meeting, lying through my porcelain teeth. *We're perfect copies of our old selves. We're exactly like you.*

The voice, when it finally spoke, was inflectionless and personality-free.

There's a party at the Wilding, the voice said. From what I'd heard, there was always a party at the Wilding. The club ran full speed from dusk till dawn and round to dusk again, the dancers and dosers locking themselves in a nonstop fantasy. *Find something to wear and check it out.*

"You know what?" I said brightly. "I feel like dancing. Maybe I'll go find myself a party."

And without waiting for a response, I skipped out of the bunkered office, already mentally running through my wardrobe, wondering what would be suitable for the Wilding, wondering what the voice would make me do once I got in.

Wondering who would be watching.

Day three.

Mechs don't get tired. We don't, technically, need to sleep. And obviously there's no need to eat or drink or rest our legs from hour after hour of whirling beneath spinning neon lights, arms twirling, head thrown back, bass-pumping music shaking the walls, floor undulating beneath our feet, bodies on bodies pressed together, sticky, sweaty, salty flesh grinding against flesh, and in the center, me. Seventy-two hours at the Wilding, watching dancers flow in and out, like jellyfish washing up on the beach, then dragged out again by the rising tide, ragged and desiccated by their hours in the sun. Except here in the Wilding there was no sun, no hint of anything that might mark the time passing, or the daylight world beyond its midnight walls.

It turned out the Wilding had only one rule, anything goes, which was good for me since I'd heard one too many stories about mechs trying to slip into org-only clubs and getting the shit pounded out of them. But here the wasted masses were too lost in their dancing, their shockers, their threesomes and foursomes, their licking and tonguing and whipping, to notice what I really was, or to care.

"You need a guy," Felicity shouted in my ear, with a giggle that sounded almost sincere. Everything she said sounded almost sincere—the same went for Pria and Cally, the other two vidlife regulars who'd swept me into their circle as soon as I stepped into the club. The fly cams buzzing over our heads glowed as they came within range of one another, and on cue the lifers laughed and shrieked, stroked my hair, whipped me in wild loops across the packed dance floor, and didn't seem to care that I was a mech—which of course only meant that their characters didn't care, and they were playing their parts.

Cally grabbed my shoulders and kneaded her thumbs into the synflesh. "Definitely need a guy," she agreed. "You're way too tense."

"I'm just tired," I shouted back, my body still rippling in time with the music, arms, legs, hips on autopilot as we bobbed on the synthmetal waves. "Don't you ever get . . . tired?" I didn't mean tired of dancing. And they knew it.

"Never," Felicity said, twirling in place. Her red hair furled around her head like a cloud of fire.

"But don't you ever . . ." I chose my words carefully. No mention of cameras or privacy, nothing that would burst the delicate vidlife bubble. ". . . feel like a break?"

"Break from what? This is life." Pria giggled. She threw her arms in the air, where they flickered and whorled like ribbons in the wind. She'd been vidlifing for two years without a day off, and I wondered if she even knew the difference anymore. What would she do if the voice in her head went silent and left her on her own?

"Come on, pick someone," Pria urged me. She twisted me in a slow circle, her pointed finger hopping from a weeper with huge biceps and teary hangdog eyes to an albino blond to an artfully scruffed guy, bare from the waist up and dosed out on Xers, who happened to be a dead ringer for Walker, my org ex. Not going to happen.

"Look, I already have—" I stopped, reminding myself that for these fifteen days Riley—or, more specifically, Riley-and-me—did not exist. No one wanted their vidlifers tied down, at least not with an outsider, and certainly not with another mech, a random from a *city* who'd never been to a club and, if he had, would have spent the night sitting in a corner, still and silent as his chair. It would be different if

Riley had agreed to go on the vidlife with me. It might have been an appealing novelty act, he-and-she mechs, a matched set ready and willing to show off how anatomically correct—how lustful, how passionate, how *human*—the walking dead could be. But Riley never would have agreed to something like that, so I hadn't asked.

Him, the voice in my head decided for me, as my eyes settled on a punkish banger a few years older than me, his spiked hair tipped with metal studs, silver bangles ringing both arms from wrist to elbow. The silver decals striping his neck marked him as a skinnerhead, one of those fetishists who claimed to crave eternal life as a mech—but didn't crave it enough to actually cut open their brains and download them into a computer. Covering yourself in mech-tech was the newest trend, at least among those who weren't trolling the streets looking for a mech to bash, and sometimes—fine line between love and hate and all that—among those who were. This loser clearly considered himself on the cutting edge. Someone out there on the network apparently thought that made him my perfect match. *Go for it.*

It didn't take much.

My come-hither glance was rusty, but it got the job done. Or maybe it was the pinpricks of golden light at the center of my pupils, the dead mech eyes flashing under the neon strobes, the taunting glimpses of synflesh beneath the on-and-off transparent material of the flash shirt. What skinnerhead could resist a skinner?

I love Riley, I thought, as the skinnerhead began to grind his hips against mine.

But: *Tell him you want him*, the voice in my head commanded.

"I want you," I breathed. The skinnerhead smiled like a wolf.

He pressed his left hand—nails coated in metallic silver, of course—to my bare shoulder. His fingers spidered down my back, and I hoped it was too dark for the cameras to see my face. He twisted me around, pressing his sweaty chest against my back, his groin against my ass, and wrapped his arms around me, one hand cupping my breast, the other squeezing my waist, his lips at the curve where my neck met my shoulders, breathing in my artificial skin.

Riley and I had talked about this. We'd discussed the obligations, weighed pros and cons, set boundaries. But boundaries were hard to specify in advance. No nudity, fine. But what about a skirt that barely covered the curve of my thigh, what about silver-tipped fingers creeping beneath the netsilk, what about legs tangled in legs . . . arms encircling chests . . . what about lips?

It's just an act, I had said, we had agreed, I reminded myself now. *Means nothing.*

His lips were on mine. Sucking. Slobbering. His tongue in my mouth, something wet and alien, probing soft places it didn't belong. I counted to ten. Ignored the squishing and smacking sounds, focused on the music. Counted to twenty, closed my eyes as his tongue slurped down my chin, up my cheek, explored the caverns of my ear, his body still grinding against mine, slow, slow, slow even as the music gathered strength and speed, a hurricane of beats. We were the calm at the center. I counted to thirty. Thought about the big picture, the message it would send, another divide between mechs and orgs crumbling to the ground, another thing we had in common: desire, need, want. Thought about the computer that was my brain and the body that was only a body, mechanical limbs woven through with wires, fake nerves that let me feel but made nothing feel real. Counted to forty, and his tongue had no taste, because I couldn't taste; his hair, his neck, his sweat had no smell, because I couldn't smell. I counted to fifty, and when his lips moved down my breastbone to the dark shadow beyond, I threw my head back and tried to smile.

And then I got to sixty and pushed him away, so hard that he stumbled backward, wheeled his arms for balance, and toppled into a klatch of lip-locked vamp-tramps. "Can't spend it all in one place!" I shouted, and let the crowd fill the spaces around me, so by the time he got to his feet, I was gone.

"Let's talk about the Brotherhood of Man." The interviewer flashed a saccharine smile. "Unless it's too difficult for you."

I shook my head. After two weeks in the vidlife, "difficult" had taken on a new meaning; this didn't qualify. "I'm here to talk," I said. "About whatever you'd like."

"We all know the story of how the Brotherhood began," the interviewer said, then immediately disregarded her own words by regaling us with the gory details: the Honored Rai Savona's noble quest to preserve the sanctity of human life, his abdication of the Faither throne in favor of a small, grass-roots, antiskinner organization that helped the poor, fed the hungry, and, incidentally, advocated for the eradication of those of us with artificial blood running through our artificial veins. As the interviewer moved onto the "tragic downfall" portion of events, the vidscreen behind her flashed images: kidnapped mechs strung up on poles at the altar of Savona's temple, the "mysterious" explosion at the edge of the temple complex, the destruction of a facility that was never supposed to have existed in the first place—and then the final image, Savona's right-hand man standing before the adoring masses, apologizing for the transgressions of the supreme leader. Promising a kinder, gentler Brotherhood under his new kinder, gentler leadership. Auden Heller, the best weapon the Brotherhood had against the skinners, because his ruined body, his artificial limbs and dented organs, were all permanent reminders of the damage we could wreak.

"Lia, how did it *feel*—"

I steeled myself, waiting for her to ask me about Auden, though she'd been told he was off-limits.

Or about Riley, who had burned in the explosion but was back now, a different body but the same mind, containing an exact copy of all the memories of the previous Riley, every memory but the memory of how he died. Every mech had an uplinker, and we used them daily to upload a copy of our memories to a secure server, just in case. But unless you were uploading at the moment your body was destroyed, that memory would be gone.

"—when Brother Savona came out of hiding and surrendered himself to BioMax?" she concluded. Then she leaned forward, as if—misinformed about my technical specifications—waiting for waterworks.

"I was surprised."

"Because you were among those who believed that he'd died in the explosion?"

Sure, we'd go with that.

I nodded, wishing I were free to answer honestly. The only surprise was that a cowardly nut job like Savona would deposit himself on BioMax's front doorstep and beg for judgment. The only thing I *felt* was disappointment that he was still breathing.

"And how did you *feel*"—insert predatory smile here—"when corp security operations officially pardoned him for any role he may have played in the unpleasantries at the temple?"

BioMax had released its own official account of "the unpleasantries," one in which Brotherhood fanatics had nearly slaughtered a building full of their own, not to mention a handful of innocent mechs. (Of course it was the *mechs* who had nearly massacred all those orgs. But that kind of truth was counterproductive, and so we all kept our mouths shut.)

"You have to weigh Brother Savona's past behavior against his expressed willingness to repair the damage." The script had been easier to memorize than it was to choke out. "Brother Savona's voice obviously has a wide reach, and now that he's had his revelations—"

"You're referring, I assume, to his statements expressing regret for the way he treated the skinners, and his pledges of tolerance? You believe he means what he says?"

I believed that there was nothing anyone could do to Savona now that BioMax had decided he made a better savior than he did a martyr. He'd signed back on to the Brotherhood as an unofficial consultant—right-hand man to his former right-hand man—and the rest of us were supposed to forgive and forget.

"We prefer to be called mechs," I told the interviewer. "'Skinner' is derogatory." Out of the corner of my eye, and just beyond the camera's sightline, I saw Kiri raise a hand in silent warning.

"Of course," the interviewer said. "I'm sorry. I didn't mean—"

"I know." No one ever *meant*. "And to answer your question, Brother Savona and Brother Auden have a message of tolerance and equality that I'd like to think we can all believe in. All I want is to show people that mechs are no different from anyone else—we're regular people. If the Brotherhood can help get that message out, then I'm all for it."

"You're a very big-hearted girl," the interviewer said.

I could have reminded her about the wireless power converter nestled where my heart should be. But I didn't.

Day seven.

Halfway there.

Not going to make it.

"You skank!" Cally shouted, and launched herself at Pria.

"Not my fault you couldn't give him what he wanted!" Pria screeched, squaring off to face the charging blonde. She crouched and grabbed Cally around the knees, flipping her head over heels. Which put Cally in perfect position to gnaw on her thigh.

Pria went down.

Hands clutched at tangles of blond hair, yanked. Violet nails raked across pale skin. They hissed, they slapped; teeth were bared, backs were arched, saliva was sprayed. There was some very unladylike grunting. Soon the two interlocked, writhing bodies rolled across the mansion's marble floor, a monstrous eight-legged beast.

Sometimes these fights ended at the hospital; sometimes they ended in bed. (Or in the closet, the pool, the shower, the rug—any and every conceivable surface.) Whatever the audience wanted.

Now, the voice commanded. *Tell them.*

"You're both brainburned," I said. "You want to kill yourselves over Caleb? Go for it." The voice gave me the storyline, but—usually—I made up the words myself. A miniature measure of freedom in my zombie life. "You know who'll really love that? Felicity. Because then she gets him all to herself."

The writhing creature froze, then separated itself into two discrete bodies again, every eye, ear, and molecule trained on my next words.

"Of course, she's already got him," I said.

"That bitch!"

"That skank!"

"That tramper!"

"I'll kill her."

"Not if I kill her first."

"I'll kill *you* first, if you try that."

The truth: Felicity had never touched Caleb. I didn't know if I was lying because I wanted him for myself, because I wanted Cally or Pria for myself, or because I wanted trouble. The voice would tell me, soon enough, and then that would be the new truth.

The fight temporarily over, and Felicity marked for death, we were free to move on to more pressing concerns.

"Mini or maxi?" Pria demanded, hanging the two dresses over her curvy frame. "There's a rage at Chaos tonight and we are *there*."

"Maxi," I said. "Definitely." Because that day I was supposed to be hating on Pria, and the billowing black and white gown made her look like a pregnant cow.

"That's *my dress*!" Cally spit, grabbing it out of her hand.

Pria looked clueless, but only for a moment. Then her face transformed—narrowed eyes, tensed muscles, slight upturn in her puffy lips. A masterful dose of pure spite. "So what if it is?" she snarled. "Looks better on me, anyway."

It's your *dress,* the voice decided.

So that's what I said.

Then I added the part about the pregnant cow.

And then I was on the ground, with my hair in Pria's hands and my artificial flesh beneath her nails.

Good luck breaking the skin, I thought, gifting her with a light sucker punch that would give her plenty of material for the cameras.

It had been made clear to me that the audience loved a fight.

Especially when the skinner lost.

"Every skinner—I'm sorry, mech—has an understandably conflicted relationship with the Brotherhood, but I think it's safe to say that yours is more conflicted, or certainly more *complicated,* than most," the interviewer said. "After all, its current leader, Auden Heller, is a former classmate of yours, isn't that right?"

You know it's right, you disingenuous bitch.

I should have known better than to believe Kiri when she said the interviewer had agreed to my terms. Easy to declare a subject off-limits when you're backstage—so much the better to launch a sneak attack once the cameras are rolling.

I smiled.

"Yes. We were in school together for about ten years."

"And you were close?" she said.

"Briefly."

"Until that day at the waterfall—"

"I don't talk about that."

"That's understandable," she said, sounding sympathetic. She patted my knee.

I let her. I even let her regurgitate the story of the waterfall, and how Auden had nearly died trying to save me, the skinner who didn't need saving. My fault, and so—in his mind, and the minds of the Brotherhood's brainwashed masses—the fault of every skinner.

"It must be *so hard* for you," she said. "I'm sure you wish you could talk to him, apologize for everything that's happened. Is there anything you'd like to say to him now?" she asked, eyes hungry. "Anything at all?"

I wasn't about to ruin everything by exploding on camera. Two weeks of misery were *not* going in the garbage just to give myself the luxury of self-pity. Or privacy. I'd given the latter up for fifteen days, and the former up for good. But I couldn't play along.

I glanced off camera. Kiri's lips were moving, and, like a ventriloquist's dummy, the interviewer began to speak. "Looks like we're out of time," she said, stiffly. I was surprised the sweat running down her face didn't harden to ice. "It's been a pleasure to have you with us. Please come again."

I smiled like I meant it. "Anytime."

Maybe I was the better actor after all.

Day fifteen.

"You survived." Kiri swept me off as the interview ended. That was code for *You didn't screw up.* I didn't know whether she meant the interview or the whole two weeks; I was too tired to care.

One more night and I was free.

I couldn't thank her for the save—not without revealing her interference to the vidlife audience. So I just raised an eyebrow, and she mirrored the gesture with her own. *You're welcome.*

"She wanted me to talk about myself," I chirped. "What's better than that?" Code for *I know I'm already dead . . . but kill me now. Please.*

"Ah, the Lia Kahn we all know and love," she said. "Sure you're not too tired to hit this gala tonight?"

A star-studded night with the crème de la crème of high society, pretending not to notice that the crème was made with soured milk? We both knew there was only one acceptable response.

"Me? Miss a party? As if."

No one told me the party was underwater.

A transparent bubble sucked us below sea level. The orgs were intrigued, pressed against the clear walls, watching fish meander by and algae lick at the glass. This was all new to them, an adventure. But I'd stroked through the deep; I knew what it was like to lose myself in the silent dark of the water.

I knew what was hiding beneath the ocean's surface—I'd seen the dead cities and their bloated bodies, and I knew that only algae and jellyfish could survive in the bath of toxic sludge. But the transparent dome was surrounded by an elaborately fake ecosystem, sparkling water clear enough to show off rainbow coral reefs and fluorescent schools of fish. It was the perfect match for the garish undersea spectacle that lay *within* the dome, synthetic algae undulating from the floor, sparkling lights floating in midair, stars hung so low you could flick them with a finger and watch them float across the room, as if we were all buoyant, gravity temporarily suspended. Holographic reefs and ridges projected from every surface, the illusion broken only when the occasional dancing couple floated right through it. Literally floated, thanks to the buoyancy generators beneath the floor that lifted them on a cushion of air. The party was a gala, which normally would have meant fairy-tale finery but this time, apparently—for those more in the know than I—demanded a more nautical touch. Mermaids drifted by on hovering platforms, their hair architectured to float above their heads. There were org-sized sharks with gnashing teeth and of course the obligatory skanked-up efforts, in this case nude body stockings wired to project shimmering scales across bare abs, chests, and asses.

I wandered, waiting for my orders, wondering what all these people would do if they saw what life underwater was really like, how the ocean had transformed the org world: the pale, swollen flesh, the rusted cars and broken windows, and all the detritus of life interrupted. And then I imagined the transparent dome over our heads cracking, a spiderweb of broken glass spreading across our sky, the water trickling down, like rain, and then breaking through, a hail of glass and a gush of water washing everything away. I imagined the costumed mermaids writhing and flailing, trapped in their tangled hair, their cheeks puffing with one final breath, bubbles streaming out of their mouths and noses until there were none left. I imagined their corpses floating slowly to the surface, leaving me one by one until I was alone with the wreckage. It would be like being the only person left at the end of the world.

I shoved the vision from my mind. That wasn't my fantasy; that was *his*. Jude's. A world purged of orgs. *Purified,* he would have said. I didn't want to think about the things he would have said, or the things he'd dreamed about, but I did, more than I would have liked to admit.

Which is probably why, at first, I thought it was my imagination.

A shock of silver hair bobbing over the crowd. The razor-sharp cheekbones, the unbearable smirk. Slitted golden eyes, resting on mine for an impossible second, flickering away, and then he was gone.

Never there, I told myself, and danced. My mech mind processed music as little more than syncopated noise. There was none of that wild abandon I'd once felt, the loss of body and self in throbbing notes. Only silent commands, from brain to limbs. *Twist. Turn. Jump. Wave. Shuffle. Shimmy.* The motions looked seamless; I knew, because I'd practiced in a mirror. It turned out there was nothing too hard about building a smooth surface for yourself. If you knew the steps, if you knew which muscles to move, if you knew how to smile and how to speak, if you knew your lines and played your part, then it didn't matter what lay behind the pose.

The hands that slipped over my eyes were cold.

The whisper in my ear was familiar.

"Miss me?"

Remember they're watching.

I grabbed his wrists, dug in my nails. Knowing it would make him smile. Then turned around slowly, fake smile fixed on my face. He had one to match.

"Didn't expect to see you anytime soon," I said casually, lightly.

Because he was a fugitive, accused of trying to blow up a laboratory full of orgs. He was guilty; I knew, because I'd helped him—and because I'd stopped him. Not exactly the safe, harmless face I wanted to present to the world.

He nodded, his eyes flickering toward the fly cam hovering above my shoulder, and his full lips curled upward.

"I've been around," he said. "Maybe you haven't been looking."

Riley would be watching this, I realized, keeping my face blank. Riley, who knew only the story I'd told him, a fairy tale in which he'd never betrayed Jude, never seen cold hatred in his best friend's eyes.

You were supposed to stay gone forever, I thought.

The skank fish spotted him and began to swarm. Girls distinguishable only by their hair color rubbed up against him, and he let it stretch on, grinning at the lame flirtations, complimenting one on her scales and another on her elaborate wings, forgoing what I would have thought would be the irresistible urge to point out that fish don't fly. He was weirdly good at it, juggling them with an oozing grace, meeting their eyes with a gaze intense enough to convince them of their special place in his heart, fleeting enough to leave hope beating in the hearts of the rest.

He's what you want tonight, the voice commanded me. Then it gave me my first line.

"Want to dance?"

Before I finished the question, Jude's arms were around me, and we were floating across the dance floor.

"So you've decided the high life isn't so bad after all," I said carefully. Jude twirled me out, our fingers linked tightly so I couldn't escape.

"What's not to love?" We turned and turned. Lights flickered overhead, mimicking the effect of sunlight on water. "I can see how glad you are to have me back."

I couldn't see anything in those cat-orange eyes. I only knew that he wanted something, because Jude always did.

This is all for us, he'd always said. The good of the mechs, not the good of Jude. Just a coincidence, then, that they were so often the same thing.

"We've got a lot to talk about." He dipped me so low that my hair brushed the floor.

"I'm not much for talking these days." I shot a mischievous glance directly into the camera buzzing over our heads.

"And the world sighs in relief."

"Well, you know what they say; talking's overrated."

Which meant *shut up*.

Not an instruction he'd ever been inclined to follow. "When you're feeling chattier, let me know. I'll be a mile past human sorrow, where nature rises again."

"You're an enigma, wrapped in a moron, shrouded in pretension," I said, sweetly as I could muster.

"I aim to please. And, since I gather you do too—" He shot another look at the hovering cameras, and I stiffened, waiting for him to spout some anti-org drivel that would ruin all my work.

He leaned toward me, one hand tight around my waist, the other latched on to my shoulder. His voice was low, but the mics would catch it, as they caught everything, and he knew it. "Let's give the people what they want."

Maybe if I'd known it was coming, I could have ducked out of the way.

Maybe I did know it was coming.

I didn't duck.

Just for the cameras, I told myself.

His lips were as cold as mine, his eyes open, watching me.

No different from any of the others, I told myself.

His lips were so soft.

His chest was silent, an empty cavity pressed against the emptiness of my own. A perfect fit.

This is harmless, I told myself.

It couldn't have lasted more than a few seconds. And then I remembered what fifteen days had almost made me forget: that I could act, that sometimes the puppet could pull her own strings—and that the people liked a fight.

I slapped him.

He saw it coming, like I did; and he let me, like I did. There was a sharp crack, but he didn't flinch. There was no angry red welt left behind on the synthetic flesh. Like nothing had happened.

"When you want me, you'll know where to find me," he whispered. And let go. He melted into the crowd before I could stop him. Not that I would have tried. I told myself I wanted him gone, for good this time.

I almost believed it.

HAPPY TOGETHER

It was proof that we still made sense.

The party raged till sunrise. The glass dome had come equipped with an artificial dawn, orange-yellow light creeping over the dragging dancers and silvery fish—technology that was, for the most part, wasted on the unconscious. I spent the final hours of the vidlife pretending to sleep, my legs slung over one snoring ogre's brawny shoulder, my head in a voluptuous jellyfish's lap. The last holdouts had dropped of exhaustion one by one, bodies tangled where they fell. Once the society olds had slipped off to sleep, the stilted elegance of the early evening had given way to a b-mod-induced ecstasy, bodies floating on Xers, blissed-out orgs bamboozled by the artificial undersea and imagining they were dancing with the fish. I couldn't take behavior modifiers any more than I could drink the putrescent pink Aqua Ambrosia or eat the dolphin-shaped canapés, and I didn't get tired. But I'd learned that orgs don't trust people—or things—that don't sleep. So for the vidlife audience I'd closed my eyes and waited for day.

By the time the cleanup crew woke everyone up, it was nearly mid-afternoon. Fifteen days, twelve hours, forty-two minutes since the game had started. Which meant I was done.

The elevators whooshed us out of the deep; a waiting car sped me back to BioMax headquarters; then security checks and more elevators and I was in the boardroom, the vidlife officially finished, the cameras shut down for good.

"Yes, I think it was productive," I told Kiri, and call-me-Ben, and my father, and the room full of BioMax suits who ambushed me as soon as the mics went dead. Viewer stats and zone feedback danced across the screens lining the conference room, alongside hundreds of network debates raging about my performance. But all eyes were on me.

"No, I didn't encounter more than the usual amount of antidownload sentiment."

"No, it wasn't an undue strain."

"No, I wouldn't recommend a repeat attempt; I'd argue our energies could be better spent elsewhere."

The inane questions went on for more than an hour, but finally, call-me-Ben stood up and extended his hand. I didn't hesitate, or roll my eyes. I'd learned.

"Thank you again for all your help, Lia," Ben said, and I smiled at him, sweetly.

His hand dropped to his side. He'd learned too.

Kiri skipped the handshake. She swept me into a brusque embrace. Normally, she wasn't a hugger, any more than I was, but desperate times, right? It lasted only a second, long enough for a hasty whisper: "It was worth it." And because Kiri had proved she was the only member of the corp who actually understood people, I believed her.

"Are we done here?" I asked.

"The vidlife techs are waiting next door to remove the implant and give you a once-over," call-me-Ben said. "Under my supervision, of course."

"And then—"

"And then, yes, you're free to go."

"I'll wait for you at the car?" my father said.

It was new, this habit of asking instead of telling—or rather, an unconvincing hybrid of the two.

I shook my head. "I'm meeting Riley."

"Oh. Of course." No amateur would pick up on the disapproval behind the curt response, because all of my father's responses were curt. But when it came to deciphering the stormy moods of M. Kahn, I was a pro.

"Don't forget it's Thursday," he added.

"I won't," I said, though I had. "But maybe this once . . ."

Someone else's father might have brushed it off with a smile and given her a free pass out of the weekly family dinner, just this once. *My* father, in the old days, would have shaken his head and forbidden it. Now? The worst of both worlds: "It's entirely up to you whether you choose to keep your word."

Checkmate. "I'll see you tonight."

• • •

One last door between me and freedom, between the bowels of BioMax and the great outdoors. But I stopped before pushing through it, preparing myself.

He won't be there, I thought. *He saw everything I did, and he won't care that it was fake.*

Or he'll believe that it was real. He'll think that was me.

Or Jude got to him first.

If he wasn't out there, I would deal. Riley wouldn't be the first thing I'd lost. If I could survive without my friends, without my sister, without my *body,* I could certainly survive without him. That's what I told myself.

Please, I thought.

And I stepped through the door.

Here's the thing about perfect kisses.

They're worth crap.

Fun, maybe. But it's not like they mean anything. All that melting into another person, lips fusing, souls meeting, romantic garbage? Trust me, your soul is not sitting in your tongue, waiting to take an all-expenses-paid vacation into some loser's mouth.

You want a metric that matters, a way to measure exactly how much of a person belongs to you?

Try the perfect hug.

Riley's arms were around me before my feet hit pavement.

He lifted me off the ground, his arms strong and steady at my waist. I locked mine around his neck and lodged my face in the hollow of his neck and shoulder. For the first time since the vidlife began, I relaxed, went limp in body and brain, and let someone hold me up.

"Miss me?" he whispered, and just like that, Jude's words in Riley's mouth, it was over.

I stiffened; he let go.

I searched his face for some sign that he was playing me, that he'd talked to Jude. But there was nothing lurking in his expression. Which maybe meant he was asking if I'd missed him because he honestly wanted to know.

"You have no idea." It sounded like a lie. So I kissed him. Kissing Riley was rarely electric or breathless or heart-stopping or any of the criteria I'd used to catalog kisses back in my org days. It didn't make me forget myself. But it helped me remember him, and all the ways his body curved to fit against mine. Kissing Riley wasn't just about the mechanics of it, the probing and nibbling and sucking—it was about building a wall between us and the world. It was proof that we still made sense.

But it couldn't last.

"It's Thursday night," I said, flicking my eyes at the ViM temp-tattooed to my left forearm. My newest toy, the razor-thin virtual machine could access the network three times faster than any of my other ViM interfaces, but so far it had mostly proved useful for surreptitiously telling the time. "If I don't go soon, I'll be late."

Riley dropped my hand. "I thought we were going to hang out?"

"I can't skip dinner. You know that's part of the deal."

I could have broken my word, run away. Riley had his new body, and my father couldn't take it away. Riley had—only once—suggested I could come live with him, in the former servants' quarters he was renting. (The owner was hemorrhaging enough credit to be willing to sacrifice the abandoned hovel at the fringe of his property, at least on a month-by-month basis.) He thought I said no because the apartment was beneath me. I couldn't convince him otherwise, because I couldn't tell him the truth. It was too fragile to say out loud.

Truth: My father would only have blackmailed me into coming home if he *wanted* me back.

My mother could barely look at me without crying, and Zo was Zo. But my father wanted me. Even though I was the machine that had replaced his dead daughter, even though he'd once dropped to his knees and begged a god he didn't believe in to give him another chance, to go back in time and let me die.

My father didn't want her, the original Lia. He wanted me, his skinner daughter, under his roof. I couldn't run away.

"Come with me," I said.

"To your *house*? For *dinner*?" He said it like I'd suggested he join me in ritual suicide. "Your father would love that."

"He'll deal."

"You really want me to?"

Actually, I was already starting to regret the idea. But something in his voice made me wonder how long he'd been waiting for the invitation.

"Really."

"And then after . . ."

"Then after, we can talk," I agreed, dreading it.

"I'm not talking about talking."

"Sneak preview?" I suggested, and closed my eyes.

It wasn't a perfect kiss.

But it was close enough.

"Oh," my mother said, when she opened the door for us. She didn't speak again until halfway through the second course. Unfailingly polite, she nodded and smiled and even conceded to shake Riley's hand, paling only slightly at his touch. But she kept her thin lips pressed together and her eyes on the table and clearly longed for the good old days when she could have disappeared into the kitchen for the rest of the night. Not that there had ever been much cooking to be done—the smartstove and the rest of the smartchipped appliances had been taking care of that since long before I was born. But she would have been able to monitor them, offering directives about what to heat and when. Now we had an AI all-in-one to take care of that, which left my mother bereft of distractions.

"I see you brought a friend," my father said flatly, when we stepped into the living room. Riley, who had been holding my hand, let go. My father didn't offer to shake. "Welcome to our home," he said. "Riley, I assume?"

Riley nodded.

"You should have told your mother you were bringing a guest," my father said.

My mother trilled a fake giggle and swept a hand through the air, dismissing the issue. *It's not fine, but I'll say it's fine,* she said, without saying anything.

Suddenly I was tempted to grab Riley and drag him out of there before he had a chance to take in the imported marble, the networked walls, the way the priceless antique breakfront matched the silverware matched the gold-plated wall hangings. I didn't want him to see that the four of us lived in a space large enough for a hundred—at least a hundred people willing to live the way he'd lived in the city—walled off from the likes of him by elaborate alarms, lockdown rooms, and bulletproof glass, waited on hand and foot by a flotilla of mechanical serving machines. Not that Riley had never seen a big house before. Quinn's estate was three or four times the size of ours, a mansion fit for a queen, where ours was barely suitable for a low-ranking duke and duchess. But this was different, because this house—despite the fact that I had no control over anything in it—was mine. It might as well have been an extension of me, and now that he'd seen it, he would see it every time he looked at me.

"At least we won't need any extra food, right?" I said. Mechs don't eat.

My father ignored the lame joke. "Your sister's in her room," he said. Zo was always in her room. Less chance of running into any of us there, I figured. I'd never thanked her for helping me break into the Brotherhood's temple to rescue my friends; she'd never apologized for joining up in the first place. Or for any of the other things she'd done to me since I woke up in this body: treating me like crap, stealing my boyfriend, convincing me that our parents preferred me dead. We'd never once talked about what she'd said the night I ran away. That she missed her sister. That she was trying to protect Lia's life from its usurper, also known as me. It was the last real conversation we'd had. Now, when forced out of her cave, she traded monosyllabic grunts with the rest of us, obviously counting the minutes until she could slink back in.

Small talk taken care of, my father ushered us to the dinner table. Riley trailed me, lingering uncertainly behind an empty chair until everyone else had sat down. Only when Zo appeared did he take the final seat.

"Hey," I said to Zo.

She shrugged in response, eyes widening slightly at the sight of Riley.

My father cleared his throat. "This is your sister's friend—"

"We've met."

Not much surprised my father. But that did.

Family dinners were, as a general rule, unrelieved misery. This one managed to be more miserable than most. My father decided to pretend that Riley was like any other ordinary boy I'd brought home when I was an ordinary girl. Too bad he'd spent all those years of ordinariness scaring the crap out of any guy I'd made the mistake of allowing through the front door. The more questions my father asked, the lower Riley sank in his chair, and the more gruntlike his answers became.

"And what do you *do* with your time?" my father asked.

Riley shrugged.

"He does *Lia*," Zo muttered.

I kicked her under the table. She scooped a forkful of ziti into her mouth, catching my eye as she did, then glancing pointedly down at my empty plate. My mother always laid out a setting for me at these Thursday dinners. As if pretending I still had a stomach let her believe I still had a soul.

"What do your parents do?" my father pressed on.

"Dad!" I said sharply. He knew Riley was from the city. He knew what that meant.

"Dunno," Riley mumbled, and though I couldn't blame him, I also couldn't help wishing he would drop the hulk act and *talk*, even if it meant knocking over the table and shouting at my father to shut the hell up. But this was what he did when he was around people he didn't trust—a group that included almost everyone on the planet: He kept his mouth shut. I knew my father well enough to see the wheels turning, and the giant NOT GOOD ENOUGH sign flashing in his head. Which only made his questions sharper and his frown deeper and guaranteed that Riley would never get why I wanted to be here or why I cared that he wanted me. All Riley saw was the jerk who wanted to know what he intended on doing with his life without a high school diploma and did he even know how to read.

"How do you support yourself?"

"He doesn't need to support himself," Zo said, out loud this time. "He's got Lia to do it for him. With your money."

"Be polite to our guest, Zoie," my mother said quietly.

"I think Dad's got that covered," she said, glaring at him.

Our father silenced her with a look, and she swallowed whatever she was going to say next. I was almost a little sorry. The obnoxious running commentary was oddly comforting, taking me back to all those other dinners when Walker and the boys before him had suffered the same fate, blistering under my father's stare while Zo lobbed her missiles, dancing as close to the line as she could before finally stepping over it. She loved watching the boys squirm, but not as much as she hated it when our parents tried to shut her up.

Zo caught my eye—in the old days this was my cue to join her in battle. I was tempted. But it occurred to me that the last time a boyfriend of mine had been in this house, he'd spent the night in Zo's bed. So I ignored her. She went back to her food, sulking in silence through the rest of the meal.

As soon as the last bite of food disappeared off the last plate, Riley leaped up to start clearing the table. My mother made that half-embarrassed, half-shaming gurgle in the depths of her throat that let you know, in no uncertain terms, you'd made a wrong move. "We have that taken care of," she said. Riley dropped back into his chair as she slid a manicured hand across the AI panel on the table. The servomechs skittered out from the kitchen and began to clear.

"That's right, Mother," Zo said. "What kind of idiot would think that just because we treat people like servants, they should act accordingly?"

"You think I'm too big an *idiot* to know you're talking about me?" Riley snapped, finally speaking up loud and clear—at exactly the wrong moment. I realized he thought she was making fun of *him*—and I couldn't correct him without making him feel even stupider.

"You will not speak to my daughter like that in my house," my father said. He rose to his feet. "And I certainly hope you don't speak to Lia like that, *ever*."

Riley rose to meet him eye to eye. "I give your daughter the respect she deserves," he said, then paused just long enough to give me hope . . . only to make it even worse. "Unlike some people."

When my father got angry, he got quiet. His lips went

pale and thin. You'd think he was retreating. But I knew better. "You had better not be implying—"

"Maybe we should skip dessert tonight," my mother said quickly, in a fluttering voice. She patted an imaginary bulge in her belly. "I'm just back from a binge-purge, and trust me, it's not an experience I want to repeat any time soon." She threw in some obviously fake laughter when it became clear the rest of us wouldn't oblige.

"No one wants to hear about your fat suctioning, Mother," Zo said. "Although I guess that explains why you've got that disgusting vat of fat juice in the fridge. Maybe we should skip dessert if that's what you're planning to—"

"Zo!" My mother's cheeks reddened. "That's tapioca pudding," she assured us. "Not . . . I mean, obviously I wouldn't serve . . ."

"I think the term you're looking for is 'medical waste'," Zo said.

"Your room." My father didn't have to shout—and he didn't have to say it twice. She was already halfway up the stairs by the time he spat out, "Now."

I stood up and took Riley's hand. "I think that's our cue. Thanks for dinner."

"Yeah." Riley gave my mother a quick, awkward nod. "Thanks."

I couldn't believe I'd wasted time worrying about what Riley would think of the house, as opposed to the freaks who lived there.

"A moment, Lia?" my father said, blocking our path to the door. It wasn't a request.

I squeezed Riley's hand. "Wait for me in the car?"

He was out the door before I finished the question. Leaving me and my father alone in the marbled entry hall. Even as the door shut, the tiles were scrubbing themselves clear of any tracked-in mud and dirt, real or imaginary. My mother had trained the house to be even more compulsive than she was.

"This boy . . ." My father let the words dangle between us.

"What about him?"

"How much do you know about him?"

"Enough." *And how much do* you *know about him?* I thought, but didn't ask, because I already knew the answer. My father always did his due diligence.

"Where he comes from . . ." It wasn't like my father to drag things out like this. Usually his proclamations were more like bullets, hitting their target almost before you realized the gun had gone off. "He's not like us."

"Not good enough for us, you mean. I know you're thinking it, so you might as well say it."

At least he still cares, I thought. *At least he still thinks I deserve the best.*

"I say what I mean." He pressed his fingertips together, brushing the base of his chin. A shadow of beard was growing in gray. "And I mean: Be careful."

"Riley would never hurt me." It had been too good to be

true, I thought, this silent truce between us. If he ordered me to stop seeing Riley, I would have to choose. I would have to choose Riley. "If you would give him a chance . . ."

"You mean well," he said, "but you're naive, with limited experience of the world—"

"Limited experience?" I didn't know whether to laugh or throw something. "In the last year I've been kidnapped, blackmailed, and arrested, not to mention *dead.*" He winced, and I averted my eyes. He wouldn't want me to see the moment of weakness. *I* didn't want me to see it. "I think I've got experience covered."

"That's not the kind of experience I mean," he said. I was looking down, so I didn't see him reach for me. But I felt his hand on my shoulder, its steady weight. "You're young. You don't understand that there's such a thing as too much difference. Things can be . . . difficult." Then he sighed. "But I suppose you've earned the right to figure that out for yourself."

I looked up and met his gaze, surprised.

"What were you expecting me to say?" he asked, with a hint of a smile.

"Nothing. I was— Nothing." Suddenly, I wanted to hug him. Not in gratitude or relief, or anything like that. But because I remembered how it used to feel, when I was five years old, when I was ten, to be walled off inside his arms, hidden and safe. "I'll probably be home late."

"As long as you come home."

"You don't need to say that every time I leave."

He hesitated. Also unlike him.

"It's good. Being back home," I said, since he wasn't going to.

"Well, whatever happens, I hope you'll remember that."

I tapped the side of my head. "Computer brain, remember? We never forget." It wasn't true—mech brains were no more reliable than orgs'. But as a lame joke to leaven the mood, I figured it would do.

He didn't laugh.

I wanted to go back to Riley's place, somewhere we could be alone, with walls separating us from the rest of the world. But he didn't want to, and I didn't press. You could fit twenty of his apartments into the Kahn house, and he could do that math as easily as I could.

So we drove into one of the Sanctuaries, a wooded space guaranteed to be empty at this time of night given the late autumn chill, the rain, and the smog so thick you could barely see the trees. The patrols wouldn't even bother hunting for trespassers; this wasn't a night for orgs.

Riley had a blanket in his trunk, and he laid it down in the dirt, as if our mech bodies were too delicate to sit in the damp, rocky soil. But I appreciated the effort, and I appreciated his body curling around mine, his face hidden by smog and night but still *there*. I pressed the back of my hand to his cheek. Solid.

Real. All I wanted was to sit there with him and not talk, not act, for the first time in two weeks. I wanted everything to *stop*.

"Sorry about my father," I said. "He's . . . you know."

"An asshole?"

I couldn't blame him for thinking it. "He doesn't mean it."

Riley laughed.

"Let's just forget about it," I said, sliding my hand down his chest. "I'll never drag you back there. Promise."

He stiffened and pushed my hand away. "That's how you want to play it?"

"What?"

"Like you're doing me some kind of favor?"

"It is a favor," I pointed out. "You hated tonight, didn't you?"

He didn't answer.

"So why would you want to go through that again?"

"That works out pretty good for you," he said.

I'd gotten much better at reading Riley, but I couldn't read this. "What's your problem?"

"Seems like *I* am," he said. "I embarrass you."

"You do not!"

"Took you months to introduce me to your family—"

"Because they're *freaks*."

"—and now you want to make sure it never happens again."

"Because I hate how he treated you." I leaned against him,

hoping the pressure of my body on his would snap him out of this.

"You can't hate it that much," he said. "*You're* going back."

"That's different."

"I don't care what he thinks of me," Riley said. "But he treats you like crap."

"He's trying."

"You keep making excuses. Why are you so scared of him?"

"I'm not!"

"Right. You do whatever he says because you *want* to." Riley looked disgusted. I imagined how much deeper the disgust would run if he realized that it was true. If he knew how much I still cared what my father thought of me, he'd think I was pathetic. Maybe he already did.

"Come on, he's my father."

"So what?"

"*So—*" So what did that mean to Riley, who'd never had one and, according to him, had never noticed the difference? Who couldn't go back home because home was a cement tower with broken windows and puddles of urine and old allies who'd found it to their advantage to ally with someone else? "So can we not talk about this anymore?"

I should have told him what I'd said to my father before we left, that I'd stood up for Riley, that we were on the same team. But I couldn't get the words out. Defending Riley to my father, defending my father to Riley, always the wrong words to the wrong person—always defending someone and still somehow always looking like a traitor.

I wasn't going to let myself get sucked into this fight when I knew what Riley was really angry about. And who. It would be easy to pretend this was about my father, because then we could both pretend he was the problem and I'd done nothing wrong. The easy way out, my favorite exit.

Not anymore.

"Are we going to talk about it?" I said.

"You just said you don't want to anymore."

"Not my father. The vidlife. Jude."

"What does Jude have to do with the vidlife?" Riley said, too eager. "Did he message you?"

He didn't know.

"What did you think of it?" I asked cautiously. "The vidlife."

Riley shrugged. "I didn't watch."

"None of it?"

"You told me I wouldn't like it," he reminded me. "The stuff they'd make you do."

"Oh." I should have been relieved. "So you didn't watch at all? *Any* of it?"

"Did you *want* me to? You said—"

"I know what I said."

"So now you're pissed?" He sounded half bemused, half annoyed. "What, you want me to dig an archive, watch it right now? Because I will." He reached for his ViM, and—even though it was likely a bluff—I grabbed his arm.

"No, you're right. It's not like I'm some kind of famewhore trolling for fans. I just figured you'd be . . . curious."

And maybe a little jealous.

Not that I *wanted* him to be jealous.

I definitely wouldn't have wanted him to see me kissing Caleb or tearing out Pria's hair. And I wouldn't have wanted him to see me with Jude.

But I couldn't believe he hadn't even looked, not once.

"It would've felt like spying on you," he said quietly. "I wasn't going to do that."

I hated myself for questioning him. "I wouldn't have been able to resist," I said. "If it was you."

"I know."

Sometimes I loved that he knew me so well.

Sometimes I didn't.

Something crackled in the bushes. I jerked around, but there was nothing there. No eyes peering out of the darkness. Just the patter of the rain.

"Can we go back to your apartment?" I said, suddenly feeling exposed. If we were going to talk about Jude, we were going to do it where no one could overhear us.

He's not following me, I thought. But that was the thing about Jude—I had no idea what he was doing, or why.

"I told you; it's a mess."

"And I told *you* I don't care."

"I don't know why you'd want to go back to that shit-hole."

"Because I want to go *somewhere*, and you've made it pretty clear we can't go to *my* place."

I shouldn't have said it, scratching the wound before it had a chance to scab over.

"I should go," he said. "You're tired; I get it." I could feel him shifting his weight, getting ready to stand.

"No." I took his hand. We had to get used to each other again. That was all. It had been a long and strange two weeks. We needed to find our rhythm. "Please. Let's . . . talk. Tell me what you did while I was away."

"Same old stuff. You know."

"I don't, actually." Trying to sound playful, not annoyed.

He shrugged. "Doesn't matter."

I felt like we were slipping back to the beginning, before we'd known anything about each other, when there'd been nothing to say. I brushed my fingers along his forearm, then traced them up his arm, along his collarbone, resting them on his chest, over the spot where his heart would have been. "Please," I said again. "I just want to pretend the last two weeks didn't happen, that I was here. With you. So tell me what we would have been doing, so I can picture it."

He choked out a bitter laugh. "You wouldn't have wanted to be here, not for that."

"For what?" I could hear it in his voice: gathering clouds.

"I wasn't going to tell you this—" He stopped himself. "I mean, I wasn't going to *not* tell you. I didn't think it mattered."

It wasn't like Riley to circle the point like this. He was nervous. That couldn't be good.

"Sounds like it matters," I pointed out.

He stood up, crossing his arms over his chest. "I went back to the city."

"What?" Now I was on my feet. "Why would you go back to that place?"

"*That place* is home."

"Not anymore."

"I just wanted to go." He uncrossed his arms and curled one hand into a fist, closing it inside the other. "I knew you wouldn't get it."

Someone had to stop; someone had to give. I drew close to him, though he kept his eyes fixed on the trees. "Riley." I touched his shoulder, but he didn't turn. "That place isn't safe for you anymore. Things are different now."

"Yeah." He didn't sound angry anymore, only tired. "And you're just looking out for me, right?"

"That's my job," I said lightly, as if none of this mattered. I turned him around, forcing him to face me.

He smiled. "Maybe you should ask for a raise."

"I'm pretty satisfied with my current compensation level," I said, touching his lips. "Especially the perks." I leaned forward, I closed my arms around him, *I* kissed *him*.

But he let me. Then we were on the ground again, limbs tangled, bodies sinking into the damp earth, finally in sync. It was how we ended all of our arguments, and so far it was effective. I tried not to think about what we would do when it wasn't.

UNFORGIVEN

Maybe real was a matter of perspective.

I told Riley the next day, on neutral territory. The park was technically called a "free expression zone," but everyone knew it as Anarchy. The brainstorm of some aging trenders and sellout free spirits who'd outfitted their mansions, garages, and shoe closets and still had credit to spare, Anarchy was designed to be a space where no behavior or appearance, no matter how odd, could be punished. The odder the better, in fact—in Anarchy only banality was forbidden, and the only consequence was invisibility. Little wonder it was always full.

Unless you were crammed into a corp-town, *crowds* were mostly the kind of thing you read about in a history book or played at with virtual-reality hordes on the network. Crowds had gone out of fashion right along with pedestrian-packed sidewalks and sardine-can residence buildings and all those empty shells that once warehoused people who wanted to shop, people who wanted to eat, people who wanted to watch. Trap enough people inside a shell like that and the shell becomes a prison; the people become perfect targets. Blow up enough of them and people stop going. For a long time no one wanted to shop, eat, or watch as much as they wanted to stay in one piece. That paranoia had faded with the bad old days of suitcase nukes and bio bombs, but the effects lingered. Why suffer through a crowd when you can have anything you want delivered to your door for free, when you can play with the masses on the network and then, as soon as they get too loud, too sweaty, too smelly, shut them off and be alone again? These days there were clubs and parties, there was high school—there were crowds to be had, real live people clumping together en stinky, sweaty, stuffy masse. But they were always carefully selected, security screened, invitation only. They were always the same. Random swarm of strangers? We left that to the corp-towns, the cities, and the crazies in the Brotherhood. And now, Anarchy.

It was where you went if you wanted to be seen; it was also the perfect place to fade into the background if you didn't. It was a free-for-all that let the luxe class imagine, for a safe, limited time, that they too lived in a lawless city of anything goes. No one was different, because there was no same. It was the kind of engineered, officially sponsored freak zone I was forced to hate on principle—officially endorsed transgression being a contradiction in terms.

That was in principle. In practice I loved it. Anyone could wander through. Anything could happen.

It had become a standard postargument routine for me and Riley. We sat in the same spot each time, a stone bench at the edge of the chaos, and over the course of a slow, quiet morning we eased into each other. Never talking about the argument the night before, staying a safe distance from combustible topics, musing about the weather or the trees or the naked man sprouting a peacock plume. Maybe that was the real reason we kept gravitating back to Anarchy. It was a guaranteed supply of safe, meaningless conversation. And that's what we were doing when I told him—carefully, *safely*—that Jude had resurfaced.

I didn't tell him the truth about what had happened the last time we'd all been together.

And I didn't tell him about the kiss.

"We have to find him," Riley said. He folded his hand around mine. It had been six months, and I was used to the fact that his hand was larger than it had been before, that our palms nestled differently now. His hand no longer felt like it belonged to a stranger. I had known this new Riley, in this body, longer than I had known the last one.

But that was the problem. I couldn't stop thinking in terms of the old Riley and the new one. I knew the different body didn't make him a different person. At least it shouldn't have. But there was something that didn't fit the way it had before. It wasn't the larger hands or the sturdier build or the darker skin.

This body was as handsome as the last, maybe more so, because there was a confidence about him that hadn't been there before, a new comfort with the body and the way it looked and moved. This was the face he'd grown up with. I wondered if, during all those months in a generic mech body, he'd felt like a stranger to himself.

Now he felt like a stranger to me.

The old Riley had been there with me the night of the explosion; the old Riley, my Riley, knew what he'd done to Jude; he knew what it felt like to have the building collapse around him and watch the flames draw closer. This Riley never had those memories, because he'd been backed up on the computer before that night happened. If we were nothing but our memories, then this Riley was . . . different.

Someone, something had died in that fire. But I wasn't allowed to mourn him. I wondered if Riley did. I would never ask. Questions like that hung in the space between us, the silence we pretended wasn't there.

"If he's back, he must want our help," Riley said.

"He didn't look like he wanted help." I hadn't repeated the cryptic words Jude had offered me. *You'll know where to find me,* he'd said, certain I could solve his riddle, and certain I would want to. "He looked like he wanted a party."

"If he's back, why not tell me?" Riley sounded hurt.

"I don't know."

"You don't think he blames me?"

"He can't," I said, because it was too late to tell him the truth: that Jude most certainly blamed Riley, for shooting him, for setting the secops on him, for betraying him, for choosing me.

"If he's been hiding from us, he has a good reason."

"Probably."

It was another gift to him, this pristine version of Jude, who deep down, despite all evidence to the contrary, was a good guy. An imaginary Jude deserving of Riley's imaginary friendship. The fairy tale was real to Riley, and who was I to say that didn't matter? Maybe real was a matter of perspective.

Maybe I would tell myself anything to justify keeping my mouth shut.

"You think we should let this go?" he asked.

It occurred to me that *he* should let this go while *I* did everything I could to track down Jude before he could track down whatever petty revenge scheme he was surely plotting. But all I could say was, "Probably."

It wasn't enough.

"Maybe. But I can't. I've got to know if he's okay."

So we started our hunt.

Searching for him by name proved useless, as expected. But there were cryptic references to a mystery mech popping up at certain elite gatherings, turns of phrase I recognized from my own days as Jude's dummy—"the past is irrelevant," "natural is weak," "natural is hell"—that pointed us in the right direction, underground zones devoted to tracking his sightings. And once we knew where to look, he was everywhere. There he was bobbing in the background of a vidlife; there he was pretending to dose with a pack of zoners; there he was posing with a bunch of skinnerheads, their eyes large with longing. And he'd been noticed. Probably by BioMax, who had apparently decided to ignore the issue as long as he kept his mouth shut and didn't blow up anything else; definitely by a slow-growing cult of net-fans, orgs and mechs alike, who'd established stalker zones that went crazy every time there was a new sighting. Theories flew about who he was, what he wanted, whether he was some kind of messianic figure determined to save us all or the skinner manifestation of original sin, weaseling his way into the org world so he could tear it down from within. The persona and its attendant mysteries were so carefully crafted that I could only assume Jude had cultivated them himself.

Not that Riley could see that, or would have cared if he did. All he saw was confirmation that Jude hadn't disappeared forever. Thus: "We have to find him," again and again, until there was nothing I could do but pretend I agreed. It was like he'd conveniently forgotten the way things had been with the three of us. The arguments. The sniping. The way Jude had held Riley hostage to the mistakes he'd made in the past, and the debt he owed Jude for things he'd done when he was too young to know better. The way Jude had sometimes looked at me like I was nothing, a passing phase, some toy that Riley would eventually get bored with. And then the other times, when he'd looked at me like . . . like he could see straight through me, into the secret at my center, one that I didn't even know myself. Like he and I were the same, and, stuck on the outside, Riley would never understand.

But Riley and I were the only unit that mattered, which was why I went along with him on the search in the first place. We exhausted all the network sources without getting any closer to tracking down our target—Jude's fans were obsessed with him, but their devotion was, without exception, practiced from afar. We needed off-line help, and there was one obvious place to start: the only mech besides Riley who we knew Jude would trust—though he had every reason not to. She was out of commission, so we started with the next best thing.

"You." Quinn Sharpe's face appeared in my ViM, unsmiling. She'd apparently missed me about as much as I'd missed her. "What?"

"I'm fine, thanks," I said sweetly. "Life is good, and yes, I'd love to tell you all about it, thanks *so* much for asking, but I'd hate to interrupt what I'm sure is a busy day."

"Then I guess you shouldn't have voiced," Quinn shot back. "Is that all?"

I could see her reaching for the disconnect. "Wait!"

"What?"

I glared at Riley over the screen. This was exactly why I'd

wanted him to do it. But he'd been under the mistaken impression that, deep down, Quinn liked me.

"I have a favor," I said.

"Then I guess you don't need one from me."

Calm, I instructed myself. *Don't fight back.*

"I'm looking for Jude," I said.

At Jude's name her mask of scorn turned into the real thing. "Why would *I* know where he is?" Quinn snapped. "You think he tells me anything? He hasn't even talked to me since . . ."

"Since you used him to screw over Ani?"

"I didn't *use* him for anything but screwing," Quinn said. "Ani had nothing to do with it."

"I'm sure that would be a huge relief to her."

"Drop the act, Lia. It's not like you care about her any more than I do."

I could hardly care less. There'd been a time when I thought Quinn might actually have loved Ani, or at least whatever the Quinn-world equivalent of that emotion might be. But she'd done an excellent job convincing me otherwise.

"I care," I said.

"Then why are you wasting your time asking me about Jude, when you could be asking her?"

"You know I can't do that."

"Actually, you *can.* Which you would know too, if you gave a shit."

"You're saying she's—"

"Awake," Quinn said. "New body, healed brain, totally compos mentis. Figured you'd know that. Seeing how close the two of you are."

I couldn't believe it. BioMax had been studying her brain, searching for signs of what the Brotherhood had done to it and what they might have learned. They said the research would last "indefinitely," which I'd started to believe meant forever. "I didn't know."

"Obviously."

"Where's she staying?"

"Still in rehab," Quinn said. "The luxurious accommodations where you and I began our own beautiful friendship."

"So have you . . . talked to her?"

There was a pause. Long enough for me to imagine a whole series of unanswered calls and texts, unheard apologies, aborted visits. But maybe I was giving her too much credit.

"Ani's old news," Quinn said. "I've got better things to do. And that goes for this conversation, too."

She hung up.

"Sure you don't want me to come in with you?" Riley asked.

We stared up at the cement monolith.

I shook my head. "I'll be fine." Some lies were necessary, even kind.

The download and rehab facility sat at the heart of a

hundred acres of carefully cultivated wilderness, hidden from prying org eyes and nosy BioMax investors alike. Its location wasn't secret—but it was sixty miles away from the complex that housed BioMax's corporate headquarters. That was a sculpted swirl of glass and steel molded into the corp logo, but its existence was largely symbolic, a concrete manifestation of BioMax's presence in the world, to prove to anyone who saw it—on the network, at least—exactly how much power the corp wielded. *This* building, the faceless stone fortress, was the power itself. All the labs, the devices, the networks, the brains that made BioMax the second largest biotech corp in the world, were here.

Also here: an icy storage room of lifeless, broken bodies awaiting disposal, their grinning skulls hollow as jack-o'-lanterns, their brains scooped out, sliced, scanned, tossed away. Down the hall a new machine, its eyes fluttering behind closed lids, its body rigid, wires feeding in and out of its exposed skull, monitors flashing, a family standing by, worrying, waiting. Or maybe no family, no visitors, just the *thing*, about to wake up and discover what it meant to no longer be human. To be an it.

To be a skinner.

The thirteenth floor would be filled with them—though not as full as it had been a year ago, before public sentiment had turned so sharply against us. Download was now exclusively for the desperate. But I supposed those were in constant supply. Accident victims, sufferers of incurable diseases, they'd all be there, *healed*, defective husk of a body traded for a model in full working condition. Twitchy mechs with spasmodic limbs, their brains learning to control the machine, their tongues learning to maneuver around porcelain teeth, their fake lungs forcing air through a fake larynx, mechs learning to walk and speak and pretend to smile. Every mech needed rehab, although it was a much shorter hell if you'd been there before and your downloaded brain had already formed the pathways needed to control a mechanical body. I hadn't been back for more than a year, since I'd walked out, stiff and new but hopeful—*stupid.* Expecting things to be like they'd been before.

I could understand why Riley wanted to wait outside.

"I shouldn't blame her," he said.

I didn't argue, or agree. I could tell he was working up to something.

"But I guess I do," he continued, after a long pause. "I get that she was mad, but to turn on him like that? After everything?"

Jude and Riley had met Ani in BioMax's experimental facility when the three of them were selected for the first download procedures. The first *successful* procedures, Jude would have reminded me. I could only imagine what he thought of me helping BioMax. Riley claimed to understand—that I was doing what was necessary. That you didn't always get to choose your allies. But I hadn't been there with the three of them; I didn't know what had happened, or what BioMax had done to them. So I knew only what little I'd been told, and what I could guess from the unspoken promises and debts that had bound them together. Until Jude slept with Quinn and blew the whole thing apart.

"It wasn't everything," I reminded him. "It was after one specific thing."

Riley scanned the distant windows, as if he could find Ani through the shaded glass. "One thing," he said. "One time. It shouldn't be the only thing that matters."

I knocked.

There was a muffled sound, something that could have been "Come in," so I did.

It wasn't as bad as I'd expected. Ani was sitting up, wearing normal clothes—which I took as a sign that she was past the days when a perky caretaker would roll her over every morning and dump her into shapeless BioMax sweats, maneuvering rigid limbs through armholes and legholes, resolutely ignoring any and all bare skin. She'd gotten enough control of her body to dress herself. When she saw me, her face didn't move. Which meant either she hadn't remastered her emotional responses—or she was choosing to keep them to herself.

"Who told you I was here?" she said.

"Quinn." I waited for a wince that never came. Her face was empty.

"I didn't want anyone to come," she said. But she nodded at the bed. "You're here. Might as well stay. Sit down."

The room looked exactly like the one I'd had. Featureless white walls, but Ani had posted no pics to remind her of the people waiting for her in the outside world. Before, she'd been one of the most avid zoneheads I knew, taking pics of everything, posting them to all of our zones and guilting us into pretending we cared. But now there wasn't even a ViM screen in sight. It was just the bed, the chair, the desk, and her. She sat so still, she could have been another piece of furniture.

"So, are you . . . doing okay?" I didn't know what to say. But stupid seemed better than silent.

"Would you be?" she asked dully.

"I'm sorry."

"Why?"

"For, you know. All this."

"Why do people do that?"

"What?"

"Apologize for crap they didn't do. I'm the one who should be sorry, right?"

"Are you?

She shrugged.

When I'd found her in the hidden lab, she'd been stretched out on a gurney, naked, her skull peeled back, her eyes staring at nothing, her lips forming a constant stream of nonsense syllables. Sloane and the others had been in the same condition—

because of *Ani*, I reminded myself—but they'd long since been downloaded into new bodies. Only Ani had stayed trapped in the strange digital limbo, a fugue state that call-me-Ben had assured me was painless. Probably.

"So . . . how bad was it?" I asked. "Did it hurt?"

"Which part?" Her face twisted into a scornful un-Ani-like expression she could only have picked up from Quinn. "The Brotherhood experimenting on my brain? Or BioMax experimenting on my brain? Or dying all over again and coming back to life?"

"Any of it," I said lamely. "All of it."

"None of it," Ani said. "Unfortunately."

I didn't ask what that meant.

"Last time I uploaded a backup was at Quinn's estate," she said, and I knew what *that* meant, at least: that when they'd rebooted her in a new body, they'd used Ani's last stored memory. One she'd uploaded before the ambush at the Brotherhood. "But they told me what happened. And I saw some stuff on the network." Stuff like archived vids of Savona preaching while Sloane, Ty, and Brahm hung limply from wooden posts. While the camera flashed to Ani in the audience, Savona's pet skinner.

"It's weird," she said. "Knowing you've done things that you can't remember. It's like, *I'd never do that*—but I did it. Didn't I?"

"Yeah. You did."

"Except it wasn't me," Ani said. "Just a copy of me. And now I'm a copy of a copy."

"Don't," I warned her. If she started spouting Savona's crap about how we were nothing more than computer programs deluded into thinking we were real, I didn't know what I'd do, but it would end with her shutting up.

"It doesn't matter." Then, the ghost of a tentative smile, almost like the old days. A little shy, more than a little playful. "I watched your vidlife. It was . . . different."

"The same, you mean," I said. "As ridiculous as the rest of them."

"I meant, different for you."

"That was the point, I guess. Show the orgs we could be the same as them."

"Acting something out doesn't make it real."

"We're hoping the people who watch vidlifes are too dumb to figure that out."

"I figured it out," Ani said.

"Well . . . you know me."

"Do I?" The last trace of the smile faded away. "I saw you with him."

"Riley? He's waiting outside, but he can come in if you want to see him—"

"Not Riley."

I knew she didn't mean Riley.

"Have you heard from him?" I asked.

Ani shook her head. "What did he whisper to you?"

I shrugged. "Same old Jude. Everything's need-to-know, right? And I guess I didn't need to know anything."

"Didn't look that way," she said.

"He said: 'When you want to find me, I'll be a mile past human sorrow, where nature rises again.' Mean anything to you?"

"No. But then nothing he says means anything to me."

I knew better than to antagonize her when I needed her help, but there was only so long I could keep pretending that Ani was the wronged party. "Look, I know he screwed up, but—"

"If you're going to tell me it doesn't matter, and it was a long time ago, *don't*. Long time for you, maybe. For me it's been a week."

"No. I was going to tell you that if you wanted to get back at him, you should have done it. To *him*. Sloane, the others, they didn't do anything to you."

There was a long silence. I waited to see what would come next, anger or acceptance. I suspected she didn't know either, until she spoke.

"It sounds crazy, doesn't it?" she said, with a weak smile. "That's what I said, when they told me. I thought they were lying. Then they showed me the vids."

"They weren't lying."

"I remember wanting to hurt him," she said. "And I knew

how to do it. He doesn't care about what happens to him. You can't *do* anything to him that someone hasn't already done. I needed something that would . . . I don't know."

Make him feel responsible.

Make him feel deceived. Betrayed. Lost.

Make him give up on trusting anyone, including himself.

She was right; she did know him.

"It was just an idea," Ani said. "I didn't think I would actually do it."

I couldn't imagine how strange it must be to wake up and learn you'd become a different person, somewhere in that dark space between one memory and the next. That you'd done the unthinkable, and you would never remember enough to know why.

Then again, maybe she was lucky: She got to forget.

"I'm not sorry," she said.

I didn't know how I was supposed to respond.

"You can't be sorry for something you didn't do," she added.

"But you—"

"Not me," she said. "Not really."

I wondered whether she actually believed it. I could understand why she wanted to.

"Do you know what you're going to do, when they let you out of here?" I said. Small talk seemed the best defensive maneuver.

"Throw a party?" she said dryly.

"I mean, do you have anywhere to go? Because you could stay with me. . . ." I tried to picture that, Ani bunking in the doily-draped guest room Zo used as a dump site for discarded junk, the three of us gaming, shopping, giggling like it was a fifth-grade sleepover. "Or Riley has some space, and I know he'd—"

"I'm going back to the Brotherhood."

"What?"

She spoke slowly, enunciating for my benefit. "When I leave here, I'm going back to the Brotherhood of Man. Auden has agreed to take me back."

"You've talked to—" I stopped myself. Auden was beside the point. "You can't."

"Actually, I can."

"They *hate* us," I told her. "They're against our very existence. They're trapped in an archaic, delusional, Dark Ages philosophy and can't accept the fact that consciousness is transferable, humanity is fluid, that life isn't defined by flesh and blood, it's defined by our *nature*, and our nature is human. They think—"

"Spare me the speech," Ani said. "I've seen you on the network. I get it. But you don't understand what the Brotherhood is about."

"Oh, really? It's not about ripping your head open and trying to find a way to get rid of us? Because I was there, and I know what I saw. What they did to you."

"That was Savona," Ani said. "Auden's in charge now, and he's different. You, of all people, should know that."

"He *was* different," I agreed. "*You, of all people,* should know that things change."

"And the Brotherhood has," she said, with a serenity I could only assume masked insanity, or at least severe delusion. "So have I."

"Okay, tell me. What does this new and improved Brotherhood have to offer, besides self-hatred?"

"The Brotherhood of Man celebrates humanity in all its forms and services those who have been overlooked or forgotten by—"

"Spare *me* the speech. I've seen the press release. What's it got for *you*?"

"I don't know." Ani wouldn't look at me. "Maybe . . . absolution."

"Ani—"

"Everyone belongs somewhere," she said. "They have to."

I didn't know what to say.

"So when is this joyous reunion taking place?" I asked finally.

"They say I can get out of here in another week." She smiled. "You should go. I don't want to fight. Not with you."

I stood up. "Fine. But I'm coming back."

"I'll believe it when I see it," she said, but she didn't tell me not to, and that was at least a start.

I was almost out the door when she called my name, so softly that I almost thought I'd imagined it.

"I lied," she said, louder. "Jude's been texting. Once a day. I don't write back."

"Oh."

"But I don't delete them."

"Okay."

I waited.

"One of the texts was for you," she said. "If you ever showed up. I don't know what made him think I would even read it."

Maybe because he knows you, as much as you know him.

"It's a zone," she said, then scribbled something on a scrap of paper and gave it to me. It was nothing but a random scramble of letters and digits. "He says when you're ready to see him, drop a text and he'll meet you there."

"Where?"

"'Where the sky meets the sky.' He said you'd understand."

Another riddle. Just as useless. "That's it?"

"That's it," Ani said. "Sorry." She didn't sound it. "If you ask me, you should forget the whole thing. Let him come to you. After what I saw . . ." She was talking about the kiss. I willed her not to make it real by saying it out loud. ". . . he will. Probably at the worst possible time."

It's exactly what I was afraid of.

• • •

Where the sky meets the sky.

A mile past human sorrow.

Where nature rises again.

They meant something; they meant something to *me*. Jude wouldn't have left a clue I didn't know how to follow. I repeated the words, over and over, an unending litany, waiting for something to click. There was an echo of memory, enough to convince me that I had the answer, buried somewhere in my mind. But not enough to dig it up.

Remember, I willed myself, knowing that if I didn't track him down soon, he would come for me again, at the worst possible time—or he would come for Riley, and I needed to get to him first.

Remember.

Remember.

When I finally did, it wasn't Jude's clue—it was that word. *Remember.*

The place itself was a memory. The Windows of Memory, memorial to the fallen, windows that peered out on a sanitized corner of a flood zone, a shadowy city buried beneath the sea. I hadn't been inside the museum since I was a kid—Riley and I always skirted its edge, walking the shore until we found ourselves alone with the water, its algae-slickened surface reflecting the clouds. *Where the sky meets the sky.* And always, on our way back to the car, dripping and content, we passed the sculpted glass antelope, memorial to the city's forgotten victims. I'd paused to read the inscription only once, that first time, but the words must have etched themselves somewhere in my memory, and a network search confirmed my suspicions: "In the midst of our human sorrow, let us never lose sight of the greater tragedy: the death of millions, innocent victims of civilization. As cities fall, may nature rise again."

A mile past human sorrow, where nature rises again; I knew where to find him.

I wanted to be wrong. Because that was *our* place, Riley's and mine. Riley had told me that he'd never brought anyone else there, not even Jude. He wasn't supposed to know how much it meant to Riley, that it was the place he went to be alone—and now, the place he went to be with me.

But that was the thing about Jude, as he so loved reminding us: He had a way of knowing things. Especially things he wasn't supposed to know. Those were his favorites.

I dropped a text at the anonymous zone. *I figured it out.*

The return message came a few seconds later, in the mouth of a cartoonish avatar, its sad puppy eyes and floppy puppy ears a mismatch with the lizardlike torso and dragon tail. It looked like the kind of av you build yourself when you're getting started on the network, designing a zone with all the features of the fantasy world in your head, making up for the increasing drabness of real life. Like this was a game. *Tonight, seven p.m.* The puppy-lizard chirped, in a songbird voice, *"I'll be the strikingly handsome fellow with the charming smile."*

And I'll *be sick,* I thought.

But I knew I would go.

I had never been there at night, and I'd never been there without Riley. Without him, without the sun glinting off the glass spires and shimmering on the water, without the crowds of orgs pretending to mourn, it felt like somewhere else. Somewhere new.

I scaled the fence that separated the tourist area from the wilderness, and padded softly down to the water. There was no reason to think that Jude would meet me at the same spot I always met Riley, but it was about a mile out from the Windows of Memory, a mile from "human suffering." So that's where I would begin. I'd had visions of Jude laying an ambush for me, emerging from the water like some kind of mutant swamp monster, just to hear me scream. If he was hiding, he'd hidden himself well; the coastline was deserted.

It was too dark to see the horizon. The ocean stretched into sky, and standing on the edge of it was like looking over a cliff into nothingness. I imagined what it would be like, wading into the dark water and floating above the silent city of death, with its frozen cars and grinning corpses. Floating away into the vast nothing.

I'd never been one to fear monsters crawling out of the dark—but I couldn't turn my back on the lapping waves. I edged backward up the shore.

And bumped right into him.

So he got to hear me scream after all.

I whirled around. "What the hell are you trying to—*Riley?*"

"Hey." He didn't look surprised to see me. "Did I scare you?"

"What are you doing here?"

"Uh, you told me to meet you here?"

"I did?"

"You didn't?"

"Tell me exactly what 'I' said."

"You told me to pick you up here, and then gave me some coordinates to program into the car for wherever we're going next. You said it was a surprise."

"That didn't seem kind of . . . weird?"

Riley shrugged. "I don't know. I figured it was some kind of romantic . . . something. A girl thing."

"Girl thing?" I gave him a light smack on the shoulder. "Remind me to explain to you why you're never saying that again." I was stalling. Thinking. Waiting for him to see the obvious.

"Wait, if you didn't send that message, then what are you doing here?" he finally asked. "And who were you waiting for?"

"Jude," I admitted. The best lies start with a kernel of truth. "I got an anonymous message to meet here. I figured, who else would want to mess with me like that?"

"Why didn't you tell me?"

Why didn't I? "I didn't want to get your hopes up."

"Too late." He grinned, and I wouldn't have been surprised to spot a wagging tail poking out of his jeans.

"I can see that."

"I knew he'd show up eventually," Riley said.

"Yeah. Can't keep the Three Musketeers apart for long." He was too excited to notice my tone. "Let's go," I added, eager to get out of our place before the specter of Jude spoiled it for good.

The car drove us away from the memorial, away from my house and BioMax and anything even remotely resembling civilization. It navigated over increasingly bumpy roads and unpaved gravel until, finally, we had to override the automatic controls and drive manually. Riley took the wheel while I called out the turns, using my ViM to map the coordinates because the car refused to help. It felt like the Dark Ages. Which was appropriate because, it soon became apparent, that's exactly where we were headed.

In the end, three hours out, there were no more roads. Not official ones, at least. Nothing but weed-ridden stretches of concrete and the occasional barren field, its earth flat and dead enough that we could drive over it with ease. It wasn't until the jagged skyline appeared on the horizon that I understood where we were going, and even then it was hard to believe. But we drew closer and closer, finally coming to the mouth of the tunnel that would lead us inside.

Nothing looked like I expected.

I'd seen images of it on the network, of course, but after a while one dead zone looked pretty much like another. They all featured the frozen parade of abandoned cars choking their escape routes, some doors flung open by long-ago passengers who'd desperately decided to get out by foot, others locking in bloated bodies of the unfortunates who stayed in their cars, trusting the traffic laws, trusting the highway flow, trusting the radio reports of a quiet, orderly evacuation, trusting right up until the moment the toxic cloud or tidal wave or flesh-eating supergerm gave them a final escape.

Not this city.

It was just empty. The bombs had flattened half its buildings and much of its population. The lingering radiation had taken care of the rest. I'd only been in one city before—unless you counted the underwater ruins—and that had been teeming with life. Even the emptiest streets had festered with rats, roaches, gutter rivers of piss. But here nothing moved. There were no bodies in sight, and I wondered if some unfortunate corp crew had moved them out, one by one—how such a thing could be possible when the deaths numbered in millions—or if they had lain fallow all these years, gradually returning to the earth. I wondered how the city would smell, if I could smell.

I couldn't have handled bodies. I'd seen them in the ocean, of course, but that was different. The pale, preserved corpses that floated through the underwater city were dreamlike wraiths—nightmarish, but unreal. Bodies lining the streets, decomposing, swarming with maggots or flies or whatever hardy scavengers could survive nuclear war . . . that was a reality even I wouldn't have been able to deny.

Jude was waiting for us, just beyond the mouth of the tunnel. He lounged on a bench at the center of a small concrete plaza, proud ruler of a broken skyline and a city of ghosts.

We stopped the car.

Opened the doors.

Greeted our long-lost friend.

Jude stood. "Riley." He gave his best friend a once-over, taking in the new body, the new skin, the face that was molded as closely as possible to a face from old photographs. I realized this was a Riley he hadn't seen in almost two years, and wondered if, finally, something had managed to throw Jude off balance. But he stepped forward with a cool half smile. "Didn't think I'd ever see that face again."

"Knew I'd see yours," Riley said, and grabbed Jude, pulling him into a tight embrace. Not one of those guy half hugs, with a loose grip and a slap on the back. This was the real thing, the two of them clinging to each other. Jude's hands were balled into fists. His eyes stayed on me.

He let go first.

"Welcome." Jude spread his arms as if inviting us into his home.

I waited for Riley to ask all the questions I was sure he'd been saving up, about where Jude had been, what he wanted, what he needed, what had happened, what would come next . . . but that wasn't Riley's style.

"You keeping it together?" he asked.

"Always."

And, apparently, with that he was satisfied. My turn.

"What are we doing here, Jude?" I asked.

He laughed. "Still asking the wrong questions, I see. Good to know some things haven't changed."

"So this is it? The top-secret home base? Where are you hiding the groupies?"

"No groupies," Jude said. "Not this time. This time we play it safe. This city has been uninhabitable for decades. They didn't just bomb the place; they infested it with radiation. Viral rad, the gift that keeps on giving. No org's coming within fifty miles, not without protective gear and a significant risk of fatal exposure. It's all ours."

"Ours, as in you're asking us to move in?" I said. "*Here?* Generous as always, Jude. But there's no way in hell."

"And you're the boss, right?"

If he'd been hoping to bruise Riley's masculinity, he was disappointed. Riley just looped an arm around me and grinned. "What else is new?"

So Jude took a different tack. "We don't have to talk about the future now. There's still plenty of ground to cover in the past."

This was it, then. Jude was going to blast us for betraying him. He'd lured us to this heap of ruins so he could toss us into some abandoned bomb shelter, lock us up, throw away the key, move on with what passed for his life. And Riley and I, never aging, never dying, would spend the rest of eternity locked up together—how many days and years of apologizing would it take for him to forgive me, out of sheer boredom if nothing else?

But it was Jude who apologized, to Riley. "I didn't expect you to get caught in the explosion."

Riley shook his head. "Not your fault. I'm the one who wired most of the explosives. My fault I did it wrong."

I watched Jude's face carefully, but of course he was no helpless org, hostage to unconscious emotional responses. No eyebrow lifting, no eyes widening, no dropped jaw. Whatever emotion he did reveal would be intentional, theatrics. For now he stayed blank. "Wrong?" he echoed.

"I'm just glad no one got hurt," Riley said.

"You got hurt," Jude said.

"I mean orgs."

Now Jude did lift an eyebrow. "Wasn't that the point?"

Riley looked uncomfortable. "You wouldn't have done it."

Jude nodded, slowly. "Because you would have stopped me. That was the plan, right?"

"There was no plan," I said quickly.

"I would have stopped you," Riley admitted.

"Lucky that it didn't come to that," Jude said, watching me. "That would be awkward, wouldn't it. If *you'd* set the secops on me. You'd probably be standing here wondering exactly how much I hated you. Whether I'd spent the last six months plotting my revenge, or some such melodramatic scenario."

Riley gripped Jude's arm. "You know I always have your back. Like you've got mine."

"Always," Jude said, and disengaged himself, gently but firmly. "Must be strange, not remembering."

"Yeah."

It was something else I'd never asked him. I'd waited for him to bring it up in his own time; he hadn't.

"Feels like another person, you know?" Riley lifted a hand in front of his face, turned it slowly like he was searching for cracks in the synthetic flesh. "Guess it kind of was."

"Nice model." Jude gave Riley another slow once-over. "Expensive."

"Worth it," I said, curling an arm around Riley's waist. He didn't shrug me off, but he looked like he wanted to.

"Too expensive," Riley said.

We never talked about the fact that his new body had been bought with my father's money. Not since he'd first found out, and freaked. *It doesn't mean he owns you,* I'd told him.

But now he owns you, *doesn't he?* Riley had said. *Was that worth it?*

After that, we put it on the ever-expanding list of Subjects Not to Be Discussed.

"So the last thing you remember . . . ," Jude prompted.

"That night before we went to the temple," Riley said. "We went over the plan one last time, then I uploaded, and then—it's blank. But Lia filled me in on everything else."

Jude's smile had turned predatory. "I bet she did."

"Something you want to say, Jude?" It popped out, though I knew better. That happened around him.

"Nothing I haven't already said. Welcome." He rubbed his hands together, disposing of the unseemly business. "Let me show you around."

He guided us through the dark wonderland of gutted buildings and shattered glass; it made Riley's city look like a paradise. Leave it to Jude to seek refuge in the midst of death and decay, a broken landscape that proved, with every step, exactly how much damage the orgs were willing to do to each other. So many orgs these days liked to claim that organic life was sacred in the eyes of God. But it didn't seem to stop them from killing whomever they liked, whenever they got the urge.

They're no different from you, I reminded myself. *Same mind, same memories. You used to be an org. Whatever they're capable of, you're capable of.*

But nothing in me was capable of this.

"I've only been here for a few weeks, long enough to get the lay of the land and establish that it'll serve our purposes." Jude paused, then added, in a high, squeaky voice, "So where were you before that, Jude?"

"That supposed to be me?" I asked sourly.

"Glad to see you aren't any less of an egomaniac than the last time I saw you."

"Jude—," Riley warned him.

"Kidding," Jude said. He led us up a wide boulevard lined by rubble. There were no weeds poking from beneath the stones, no trees, no bushes, no green of any kind. "But since you asked: I spent most of the time in Chindia, honored guest of the Aikida Corp."

Once a small Japanese pharmaceutical corp, Aikida was now the largest bio- and gen-tech corp in the world, with global headquarters in Chindia and a major presence in every developed country except the United States. BioMax, their primary rival, had made sure it would stay that way. That had been one of the primary conditions when the corps bailed out the government and turned it into their own quaint department of civil engineering—preservation of our inviolable corporate boundaries. Since the Bailout no foreign corporation had done business on American soil unless approved by the corp consortium. "What would they want with you? Unless you got a PhD in gen-tech while I wasn't looking."

"I've got something more valuable than a PhD," Jude

said. When we looked blank, he rapped his knuckles against his forehead. "In here, geniuses. It's worth millions—and trust me, there's not a gen-tech corp in the world that wouldn't pay."

"So they're trying to reverse-engineer the download process and you're their guinea pig?" I asked, surprised Jude would let anyone experiment on him again, no matter the price. "And you're still in one piece?"

"Funny, you sound disappointed."

"Honesty über alles, right?" His stated policy, not mine.

"They didn't touch me," he said. "They've already tried that on other mechs. Stripping them bare—no luck. They wanted something else from me. So we're going to get it for them."

I glanced at Riley, who looked wary. Thankfully. At least I wouldn't have to try to talk him out of whatever insane plan was coming next.

"They need the master code for the brain-scanning program, and the full specs for the neural matrix," Jude said. "We get it from BioMax, sell it to Aikida, and live happily ever after."

"What's with 'we'?" I asked. "You've got your own BioMax connection, as I recall. Get him to give you what you need and leave us out of it."

"After the *incident* at the temple, my connections have dried up," Jude said. "I think I've managed to convince them that I'm harmless enough to drop their ridiculous vendetta against me, but I can't get inside. *You* can."

"But why would I? So you can get rich? What do you need money for when you have all this?" I gestured to the rubble.

"I have what I need," Jude said. "This is bigger."

"This is pathetic. Maybe you haven't noticed, but BioMax isn't out to get us—even you."

"Now who's willing to do anything for money?"

"They don't pay me," I told him. "I work with them because I want to help."

"Right, the party line: mechs and orgs together, one big happy dysfunctional family."

"At least I'm doing something, instead of just whining about how everyone's out to get me."

"And exactly what are *you* doing?" Jude snapped. "Letting them parade you around on the network like a trained monkey? You think playing at being some brainless slut on a vidlife is going to convince anyone of anything?"

"Jude!" Riley's voice held an implied threat—one I was sure he dreaded carrying out.

"You're not exactly the target demographic," I said, evenly as I could.

Jude just laughed.

"Give her a break," Riley said. "She's doing what she thinks she has to."

I didn't need him to defend me. But I couldn't help noticing it wasn't much of a defense.

"Right," Jude said. "Working *with* BioMax." He laughed again.

"You think I'm working *for* them?" I said.

"I think working *for* someone implies payment. And the freedom to *stop* working whenever you want. It implies *choice*. You have none of that. What you have . . . call it indentured servitude. Call it slavery. Call it whatever you want, but the fact is, they *own* you. They gave you that body, and they can take it away."

"I'm not going to argue."

That caught him off guard. "That's a first."

"They own all of us," I said. We were at their mercy; we depended on them to honor their contracts, and our existence. "That's why we *have* to work with them. Because they're all we've got."

"No one owns me," Jude said quietly.

"Sounds pretty. That doesn't make it true."

"As usual, your vision is severely lacking."

"If you mean I lack the vision to see how selling corp secrets to Aikida is going to change anything, then I guess that's another thing we agree on."

"We're not selling them for money," Jude said.

"So what, then?"

"The only way we get free of BioMax is if *we* control the

means to create new bodies and to download ourselves into them. *And* to make sure we store the uploaded memories on a server that no one but us has access to. Aikida is going to help us do that. We get them the specs they need; they supply us with our very own laboratory and production facilities, and a skeleton staff of scientists and engineers that can train us to do everything for ourselves. We sign a noncompete with them, to guarantee that we function only in this country, so we don't interfere with Aikida operations—but beyond that we're free."

"And all of this is going to take place . . ." It was beginning to sink in. Why we were here. Why Jude was so proud of his ghost town.

"Right here," Jude said. "Ground zero of our independence day. A country of our own, inside the one that doesn't want us—let them stay on their side of the border, and we'll stay on ours."

I didn't bother to ask about the benevolent dictator who would inevitably be *leading* this imaginary country of his. Instead: "You're insane."

"You see it, don't you?" Jude appealed to Riley. "We've got everything we need here. Space, privacy, an almost completely intact infrastructure. It could be what we've always wanted. A place to be left alone."

Riley's gaze swept the jagged skyline. He didn't answer.

"Riley, I was thinking you could take a look at the generators?" Jude said. He'd led us to some kind of power plant.

Scorch marks scraped its sides, and one wall had collapsed. "See if I'm wrong about their condition? You know this stuff so much better than I do."

"Not so much better," Riley said, obviously pleased by the compliment.

"So much," Jude insisted. "Take a look?"

"He's not going in there," I said, surprised the building was still standing. "It looks like the roof might cave in."

Riley squeezed my hand. "I'll be back in a minute." And then, like we'd traveled back in time six months and nothing had changed between them, he did exactly as Jude said, and stepped inside.

Which left me and Jude alone.

"So you're lying to him," Jude said. "Again."

"None of your business."

He raised his eyebrows.

"This is better for him," I said. "If you care about that at all anymore, you'll trust me."

"And if I don't?"

"Should I even bother saying please?"

"So you're asking me for a favor," Jude concluded. "I knew you finally grew a spine, but the balls must be new."

"I'm asking for *him*," I said. "He shouldn't have to know what you forced him to do."

"Oh, *I* forced him to shoot me? And set the secops on me?"

"Please," I said again, hating that I had to beg. "You're here, you're fine, so—"

"Stop," he said. "What did you think? That I dragged you here to mess with your pathetic little arrangement? Maybe you think I'm going to blackmail you into helping me with BioMax? I keep my mouth shut to Riley, and you do whatever I say?"

"I'm waiting."

"You really think I'd do that?" he asked. He sounded hurt; he'd always been a good actor. "If you knew anything—" He stopped abruptly and changed course. "I really have been watching you on the network. I see what you're trying to do. You might even have helped a bit, here and there. But you've got to think about the big picture. This is a waste of your time—and your rather ample talents. I'm not going to blackmail you into helping me. I don't have to. Because once you think about it, you'll see that I'm right. Anything else is just postponing the inevitable."

"That's your pitch? I'm going to help you because it's the right thing to do?"

"*This* is my pitch: Korinne Lat. Mara Wells. Portia Bavanti. Tyler—"

"What's your point?" But I knew. I knew those names as well as he did.

"Mechs who've been attacked," he said. "Mechs who've been ambushed or lynched or kidnapped by orgs. And those are just the ones we know about, because why bother to report a crime that's not a crime?" As I'd learned my first month at BioMax, org-on-mech violence increased by 230 percent when mech attacks were officially declared consequence-free. Kicking and punching and strangling a machine were deemed to be property damage, and the mechs had no owners who could sue. (As several corp-controlled courts had ruled; a machine could not own itself.)

"Jude, I know all about—"

"And I could keep going," he said, loudly. "You want more names? How about the names of the mechs who've lost everything because the corps have confiscated their credit and shut down their zones? Because mechs are no longer officially living people under the law; we're *things*. With no standing. No rights."

"Like I don't know that."

"You know, but you still have somewhere to live. You have a father to buy you things. You don't know what it's like to—"

"You think I don't know?" I shouted. "I know exactly how many mechs are getting hurt every damn day. That's why I'm doing this. That's *why* I'm working with BioMax. I'm trying to fix things. *I'm* trying to change them. So what are *you* doing? Hiding out like some kind of end-of-the-world nutcase, waiting for us to get so desperate that we throw ourselves on your mercy? Great plan, Jude. How could I ever have doubted you?"

He didn't look at all surprised, or even disappointed. "Eventually you'll see you're fighting a losing battle."

"Enjoy the wait."

"Frankly, I don't have time for it. So I've got something to speed along your comprehension. Or at least your willingness."

"Finally." Because clearly, everything else had been preamble, priming the pump. *This*, whatever it was, would be why we were really here. "Tell me why I'm going to help you."

"Because it will hurt your father."

"Maybe you should pay closer attention," I said. "My father and I are fine. I have no interest in hurting him."

Jude's hand shot out and grabbed mine before I could pull away. He pressed something sharp into my palm. I assumed it was a dreamer, the tiny cubes that offered mechs a hallucinatory escape from the world. Jude had offered me my very first one in exactly this way. But the object was the wrong size and lacked the dreamer's distinctive etchings along the edge.

Jude was still gripping my hand. "You may not want to hurt him yet," he said. "But trust me, you will."

SACRIFICE

"You'd be a lot more tolerable if you'd just own *your inner bitch."*

It was a flash drive. Nearly archaic, used only for the kind of data you couldn't trust to transmission over the network and so reserved for hand-to-hand exchange. The drive had Chinese ideograms scratched across its length, which I assumed meant that Jude had picked it up during his stint at Aikida. Or at least that he wanted me to think so. I slid it into my pocket before Riley could see, and resolved not to think about it again until I was alone.

Which came sooner than I expected. Nested in Riley's arms, my head safely cradled on his shoulder as the car carried us through the pitch-black night, I didn't watch the nav screen or chart the twisting roads as we swept past. We stopped in an empty lot, the Windows of Memory glowing in the distance, the poisoned sea still a dark hole in the night. My car was waiting.

"You okay to drive home alone, or you want me to follow you?" Riley asked.

I had assumed we would go back to his place. Talk about what had happened.

Or not talk.

"I'm okay," I said.

He'd been quiet the whole way back—uncharacteristically so, even for him. I couldn't tell whether he was disappointed because reuniting with Jude hadn't lived up to his hopes, disappointed in *me* for not sharing his enthusiasm, or just lost in thoughts that he'd decided weren't fit for sharing.

I wasn't expecting to be able read his mind, but I should have at least been able to *guess* at how he was feeling—either that, or I shouldn't have been afraid to ask.

He opened the door for me. I crawled across him, then paused, half in and half out of the car. "Unless you want me to come with you," I offered. "We could go to your place and—"

"It's a mess," he said quickly. Then darted forward and gave me a kiss. It felt perfunctory. "Good night," he said, and then I was out of the car and he closed the door and I was alone.

He waited until I got in the car, which was normal. Then he drove away before I did, which was not. But it meant I didn't have to wait any longer. I pulled out Jude's flash drive, half tempted to toss it out the window. But Jude didn't make empty threats, and he didn't lie. He would hit you with the truth, at least the truth as *he* saw it. Which meant there was something on the drive that I needed to see, even if it aligned with his agenda.

I took out my ViM and uploaded the data to its temp memory storage. Virtual Machines were little more than conduits to the network, not meant for personal storage—under normal circumstances everything got uploaded to my zone and stored on the network—but sometimes you wanted to keep something isolated from the network, to keep it close or erase it for good. Jude's flash drive carried only a single file, an accident report about a crash that had happened a year before. My crash. The process had been standard, under the circumstances: a cursory joint investigation by the car corp and my father's lawyers, to determine liability and assign blame. The report had been compiled while I was still an unconscious lump of wires and synflesh in the BioMax rehab facility, but I'd seen all the details later on, forced myself to read through the series of catastrophic system failures—the shipping truck's chip malfunction, the hole in the sat-nav system, the malfunctioning of my car's backup detection system, a series of minimally unfortunate events culminating in an extraordinary one.

We'd gotten a tidy sum from both the car people and the trucking corp, not that we needed either. The principle of the thing, my father had said. Compensation for pain and suffering. I didn't ask: his, or mine?

I'd studied the report, memorized its key phrases, enjoying the way the legalistic terms sapped the color from what had happened. In the report there had been no pain, no suffering, no imprisonment beneath twisted metal, listening to flames crackle, sirens whine, breathing in the smell of burning flesh. The report was life reduced to its bare essentials, to yes and no, this happened and this did not, life reduced to a schematic of ones and zeros, just like me.

I knew everything about that report.

Which is why I immediately recognized that this wasn't it.

It started off the same, with the description of the circumstances of the accident—and, of course, the results. The itemization of injuries to the org named Lia Kahn and her vehicle. It was the "causes" section that read somewhat differently. No "mechanical failures." No "inescapable misfortune." And no failure of the truck's guidance system.

In this report blame was assigned: to my car. And the anonymous person who'd tampered with it. If this report was correct, the accident hadn't been bad luck or bad machinery or bad karma. It hadn't been an accident at all.

But . . . if this report was correct, then what had happened to it? And where had the other one come from?

Living as a mech, I'd come to understand that some things could be true and not true at the same time; some things could contain their own opposite. But this wasn't one of them. If one of the reports was true, it meant the other was a lie.

I turned on the car and directed it toward home. Watched the night flow past. It was like I could feel him drawing closer, pulling me in. My father, my protector.

I went home because there was nowhere else to go. I went

home to him because I had to know. My father had given me that first report. He had described the circumstances of the accident, filled in the portions that my trauma-scattered brain couldn't remember. He had been my memory.

Kahns don't lie. It had been a family rule for as a long as I could remember. But I was a Kahn, and I lied all the time.

My father's study was forbidden territory. But my father was asleep, along with the rest of the house. And the ViM embedded in his desk would supply direct access to his zone. Whatever he knew would be buried there, somewhere.

I slipped out of my shoes and padded silently into the room, easing the door shut behind me. It creaked softly, and I froze. But there was no noise from the rest of the house.

I hadn't snuck in here since I was twelve, the night my father had confiscated my new pink miniViM—consequence of some petty and long forgotten trespass—and I'd decided to confiscate it back. I'd been caught, of course. Then yanked off the ground, carried up the stairs, tossed into my room, and grounded for a month.

I swept a finger across the screen to switch it on. The screen remained blank, save for a password request and a small white box, exactly the size of a thumbprint.

I'd expected the password protection; that wasn't unusual, especially when it came to someone as paranoid as my father. He had an assortment of passwords he used for various functions, and I'd figured out most of them over the years, so I had been reasonably sure I'd be able to crack this one. But I'd never heard of thumbprint security on a private ViM. And I had no idea how to get past it. Which meant I had to get my answers some other way.

Or just drop this altogether.

"I must still be asleep, because obviously I'm dreaming this."

I flinched, nearly knocking a glass picture frame off the desk. It wasn't a photo of Zo and me—since the accident, all photos of his daughters had been quietly but thoroughly expunged from the house. The face in the glass was our mother's, years younger, her smile shockingly real.

Zo stood in the open doorway, backlit by the hall light, her shadowed face unreadable. "I know Daddy's golden girl would never sneak into his holy sanctum. Invasion of privacy? Violation of the sacred Kahn Family Law?" She shook her head. "Clearly I'm hallucinating."

"Shhh! Please."

"Right." She wasn't whispering. "Wouldn't want to wake him. Wonder what he'd say."

"When I told him I caught *you* sneaking through his stuff? Yeah, I wonder."

"Like he'd automatically believe you over me? Like you're *so* trustworthy and I'm so—"

"That's not what I meant."

"Yes it is."

Yes, it was. But I hadn't meant to mean it.

"And you were right." She laughed. There wasn't much humor in it. "You know, you'd be a lot more tolerable if you'd just *own* your inner bitch." Zo stepped into the office. "Like you used to."

"I was not a bitch!"

Now she laughed like I really had said something funny. "Right. And neither was I."

"Well . . . I wouldn't go that far."

"I blame genetics," she said. "Look where we came from." Zo joined me at the desk, peering down at the blank ViM screen. "So, what are we looking for?"

I didn't answer—I was stuck on that word, "genetics," the one that seemed to imply, in her mind, some common thread linking us together.

"Well?" Zo prodded. "Or should I call our father down to help?"

"No!" She'd said "we." It didn't guarantee I could trust her, but it meant I could try. "There's something on there that I need to find out."

"I'm going to need more details, if you want me to find it for you."

"No point," I said. "He's got a thumbprint lock."

"Of course he does," Zo said. "Which is why I"—she pulled a strip of clear adhesive off the underside of his desk—

"keep the nanotape imprint easily accessible. Sure you don't want to tell me what you're looking for?"

I gaped at my sister, who, last I checked, had slept through every comp-sci class she'd been forced to take. Where had she learned about nanotape? And where had she gotten her hands on some?

"Well?"

"Stuff about the accident," I admitted. "Anything you can find."

"Somehow I don't think Dad's the type to write weepy poetry about his personal tragedies, if that's what you're hoping for," Zo mumbled, but she entered in a password, pressed the nanotape to the thumb pad, and the screen flashed to life. Zo bent over the keyboard and began typing furiously, whipping through files with dizzying speed, not just the obvious news vids and porn, but locked subroutines that unleashed hidden archives and multilayered data dumps.

"I didn't know you were so good at this stuff," I said, because it seemed easier than asking why she was helping me.

"When did you know anything about me?" Zo said, with a flash of anger. She didn't look up until her fingers stopped flying over the keyboard. "There. Done. Everything."

Everything included several files that my father must have thought he'd deleted. Maybe he'd slept through his comp-sci classes as well, or at least the one where they'd taught that most fundamental of rules: Nothing is ever deleted. Not for good, at least. There were dozens of memos, warnings from

BioMax that he was running out of time and better make his choice, references to payouts and consequences, and an ultimate response from our father, with the access code to the car's navigational system and a time his daughter was guaranteed to be in the car: 3:47 p.m. A time I recognized and remembered, because it was the time of the accident.

There had been a day, not long after my download, when my body had frozen. In the middle of a crowd—in the middle of a step—I'd shut down, turned into a statue, unable to walk, unable to move, unable to do anything but think and watch. I could see people staring at me, swirling around me, and I knew I was nothing more than an object to them, easily ignored, easily circumvented. Easily broken.

That was how I felt, watching the words swim across the screen.

I am a machine, I thought, the emotions simmering below the surface, the kind of emotion—the tidal wave kind—that I was always chasing, because it would prove I was still alive. *I can shut this down.*

I couldn't. Not the knowledge, not the understanding, and not what came next.

I couldn't cry, or shake, or collapse.

But I could scream.

My parents were downstairs in seconds. My mother, bleary-eyed and wild-haired, rushed into the room, compelled by some vestigial maternal instinct to throw her arms around me. She stopped herself at the last second, repelled by the force field of reality, of what I was now and who she was and all the space that had swelled between us. Her hand rigid, she patted my shoulder awkwardly, once, twice, her hand barely touching the synthetic skin. "What's wrong, Lee Lee?" She hadn't used the nickname since I'd left rehab.

Even in a bathrobe my father looked imposing, ready for business. He stood ramrod straight, and I could tell he was gauging the moment, trying to decide exactly when and how to ascertain what we'd been doing in the forbidden zone.

"I'm going upstairs," Zo said, her voice as colorless as her face.

"No." I pointed to my parents, then to the small leather couch pushed up against the wall. "You two, *sit*." Then to Zo. "You, stay. We're doing this. All of us. One last perfect Kahn family meeting."

I don't know why they listened. But my mother did, dropping to the couch with a soft *thwap*. Dubious but obedient, my father joined her. He lowered himself gracefully, back straight, feet firmly planted on the floor, leaning slightly forward, as he'd always taught us to do when we wanted to give the impression of paying attention. "It's late; we're all tired," he said. "Whatever this is, perhaps it's better done in the morning." Like he knew what was coming.

I shook my head. "Now."

"Leave it," Zo said quietly. Not an order, a request, which wasn't like her. I was tempted. But I couldn't go to bed in this house, under the same roof as *him*, not after what I'd read. It had to be now, or it would be never, because once this was out, I was never coming back.

"I know what you did," I said, staring at my father. "We know what you did."

Innocent men defend their honor; that's what he'd always taught us. Only a guilty man stays calm in the face of accusation.

But my father stayed calm in the face of everything.

My father.

I saw it all, in his face, in my mind. I remembered the sound of his voice when he was disappointed and when he was pleased, the winks across the table at my mother's expense, his smile on the sidelines of a race, his hands wrapped around mine, lifting a trophy together, placing it on his mantel. His pleading tone as he begged—always dignified, but begging nonetheless—his peers to change their stance on the mechs, to understand his pain, and his miracle. His anguish as he'd begged God for a second chance.

And now I understood why he'd had to invent a God to believe in: so he would have someone to apologize to, when he should have been apologizing to me. All that time, I'd thought he regretted the download—that even though he'd finally accepted his daughter, the machine, he'd never forgiven me for existing.

When it was himself he'd never forgiven, for making me this way.

For killing me.

"I've done many things," he said. "You're going to have to be more specific." A man, innocent or guilty, shows no fear. He'd taught us that, too. *Man or woman,* he was always careful to add. *You'll be as much of a man as I ever was. Maybe more.*

I would show no fear.

I would not stop.

"I saw the files," I said, and because watching him was so useless—and so infuriating—I shifted my attention to my mother. As weak as he was strong, *she* would react. She would see exactly what it was she'd married, what she'd allowed near her children. And wonder why she hadn't stopped him. "Someone tampered with the car's guidance system. Someone *programmed* that accident. Because *you* ordered them to."

My mother's eyes widened, slightly. Slowly, she turned toward my father, waiting for him to deny it. He didn't.

Zo stood exactly where she'd stopped, midway between us and the door, like she was the statue. Unwilling to stay, unable to leave.

"You did this to me." In my head I imagined saying this with cold steel in my voice, showing him how little I cared for what he'd done. How little power he had over me, and how little I regretted losing all he'd taken away. But that's not how it came out.

It came out hysterical, like a child having a temper tantrum, my voice climbing higher, my fists balled. Only my eyes didn't betray me, and only because they had no tears.

"You killed me!"

I could see it in her face: My mother was still waiting for him to deny it.

He didn't.

"It was blackmail," he said. He couldn't even look at me. Instead he turned to Zo, stupid enough to think she would offer a safe harbor. *She won't help you,* I thought, feeling almost sorry for him. And then he kept talking, and the sympathy leaked away. "There was some . . . unsanctioned behavior on my part. Funds were shifted. Temporary . . . aberrations in the balance sheet."

"You were embezzling," I translated, disgusted. "*Stealing.* You, the honorable M. Kahn, who used to punish us for sneaking extra cookies after dinner because it was dishonesty unbefitting a Kahn."

His head bobbed up and down, almost imperceptibly.

"Look at me," I snapped. "Not her; not the floor. *Me. Look at what you did to me.*"

Again he obeyed.

I wondered if someday, looking back, I would at least take pleasure in that. I'd finally beaten him. But it didn't feel that way. It didn't even feel like he was in the room with me. This person, this craven, beaten-down *thing*, seemed like a defective copy, designed to bear judgment in his place.

"They found out about it," he said. "They blackmailed me. I would have gone to prison, lost everything. *You* would have lost everything." It was almost a whine. *Believe me,* it said. *Understand me. Forgive me.*

Never.

"What would you have done without my credit?" he asked, eyes hopping from me to Zo to my mother, searching for refuge. "Any of you? There wouldn't have been anything left. You would have ended up in a corp-town, working off my debt. I couldn't let that happen."

My mother rested a hand on his knee. I wanted to slap her.

"So instead of giving up your money, you gave up your daughter?" I asked. I'd never felt anything like this before, not since the download: an emotion that was so pure, so real. This was different from sex, from fear or pain, different even from the dreamers, with their direct connection to the emotive centers of the brain. Like jumping from a plane, like stabbing myself, this blotted out any awareness of artificial nerves and conduits, stripped away the fake flesh and the mechanical organs, left *me* bare and exposed, nothing left but words and anger.

"They didn't want money," he said. "It wasn't about that. They wanted support for the download from someone like me, someone people would listen to. The whole program was about to go down in flames; they were still waiting on approval for the download as a voluntary procedure and didn't think it was going to come through; they needed someone who would *never give up*." He choked out a noise that sounded almost like laughter. "I suppose they found some poetic justice in it, turning the download's biggest enemy into its biggest supporter. I engineered the legislation that would outlaw the technology, and then . . ."

"And then you got caught."

He nodded.

"That doesn't even make sense. Why not just blackmail you into supporting the download? Why would they need"—I gestured at my body—"this?"

"They needed my support—but they also wanted to punish me," he admitted. "The cruelty was excessive. Unnecessary. But they didn't give me a choice."

"Bullshit. You chose *this*."

"They promised me she wouldn't die," he said, lamely, in that same voice I'd heard him use when he was praying. Choked, miserable, *weak*. "She'd just have a different life, they said. A better one."

The worst part wasn't the things he was saying, or the fact that he actually expected understanding, maybe even forgiveness, even though he hadn't bothered to apologize. It was that he refused to look at me or speak to me. Not just as if I weren't in the room, but as if all his promech preachings had been nothing more than a show, blackmailed out of him. That as far as he was concerned, his precious daughter, the one whose life he'd basically sold off to the highest bidder, was gone.

I exploded. "Stop talking about me like I'm not here!"

"He's not talking about you," Zo said, with eerie calm. "He's talking about me." She gave me a wry, sickened smile. "What am I always telling you?"

"It's not always about me," I said mechanically, not thinking about the words because I was suddenly thinking about the other thing she always told me: that I was our father's favorite. I was thinking about the day of the accident.

I was thinking about the fact that I wasn't supposed to be in the car.

Zo was the one with the shift at the day-care center; *Zo's* key card had started the car, so we could ensure there'd be no record that I had gone instead. In her place.

Seeing me finally get it, Zo nodded.

"No wonder you hate me," she said to our father, her voice steady and toneless, like *she* was the machine. "*She* was supposed to live. But you got stuck with me instead."

He didn't answer her.

Say something, I begged him silently. *Fix this.*

Like he was still my father, who could fix anything.

Instead of a monster who couldn't do anything but destroy. And couldn't even do that right.

The silence stretched on too long. Zo walked out of the room. Seconds later the front door slammed.

"I'm sorry," my father said. Too late.

"Shut up." I wasn't waiting for him anymore. I was waiting

for my mother. To slap him. To beat him. To hug me. To run away from all of us. But she did nothing. "Well?" I glared at her, willing her to fight back. To pick a side.

But she didn't. She didn't even cry.

We were a whole family of machines.

Were, as in past tense, as in we *had been* a family.

Now we were nothing.

Zo was slumped in the driver's seat, cheek pressed against the window, face melting into the thin layer of frost coating the glass.

I pulled open the passenger door and got inside.

"No talking," she said.

"Got it."

I don't know how long we sat there. I don't know what she was thinking. I was trying not to think. Part of me wanted to start the car, get the hell away from the house before our father came out and said something that suckered us into going back inside. But the rational part of me, stronger now as the waves of rage ebbed away, knew that would never happen. He'd surprised me tonight, more than once. But he was still M. Kahn, our father, and he wasn't going to beg.

We were safe in the driveway, for as long as Zo needed to stay there.

Zo needed.

Like Zo needed me to fill in for her that day.

It had been a long time since I'd let myself go there. For everything that had happened between the two of us, I'd kept that locked away somewhere, too deep and dark to dredge up into the light. But now . . . *It was supposed to be her.*

Sisters were supposed to protect each other. Especially big sisters. I should have been glad it was me instead of her. If I believed the things I said on the network every day, believed that mechs and orgs were different but equal, believed that each form offered its own rewards, I shouldn't have cared. So I'd exchanged one life for another. I'd lost nothing but pointless nights zoned out on bliss mods, cackling with Cass and Terra and all the interchangeable orgs who couldn't deal with a mech in their midst. I'd lost a boyfriend who could barely tell the difference between me and my sister, or at least didn't care which of our tongues was in his mouth. I'd lost a family I was better off without.

I'd gained Riley. I'd gained time, *lifetimes*, a brain that could be eternally copied, a body that could be repaired, refreshed, exchanged. I'd trained myself not to think about whether it had been an even trade.

As I'd trained myself not to think about how things would have been different, with Zo in the car, me safe at home.

"I'm not going back inside," Zo said, voice muffled. It was too dark to see if she was crying, and I knew that was the only reason I'd been allowed to stay. "Not ever."

"Okay."

This is not about me, I reminded myself. *Not tonight.*

"So what now?" I asked.

There was a pause. "I don't know." Zo puffed a hot breath against the glass, fogging up the window. Then smeared a finger through the condensation. A lightning bolt Z. For a second she was five years old again, and I was seven, and we were fighting sleep on a long drive, staking our claim on the foggy windows, painting names, flowers, faces—and then watching them disappear. We'd made a competition of it, who faded away first, who lasted. "I don't have anywhere else to go."

Without asking, I reached across her and keyed in a set of coordinates, started the car. "Yes, you do," I said, like a big sister should, fixing things.

What I knew about myself: Given the chance back then, I wouldn't have gotten in the car. I wouldn't have saved her.

At least this time, I could try.

Zo stopped me before I could knock on Riley's door.

"Isn't it kind of rude for us to show up in the middle of the night?" Zo asked.

"It's no big deal."

When she didn't follow it up with the obvious dig about how often I did that kind of thing, I really began to worry.

"Maybe we should go," she said instead.

"He'll understand."

"He doesn't even know me."

I had to laugh. "After that dinner the other night? I'd say he knows you."

Zo laughed too, and it sounded good. But it didn't last long. "Maybe I should wait in the car."

I resisted the urge to take her arm. It was like herding a stray cat. You had to lure it in carefully, let it think the whole thing was its own idea. Or just grab it by the neck and toss it inside.

I knocked.

It took only a moment for Riley to appear. He opened the door just wide enough to slip out, then shut it again behind him. "Hey. What are you . . . everything okay?" He seemed off-kilter, like we'd woken him, but of course mechs didn't sleep; we shut down at night as a matter of convenience and convention, switching ourselves back on with instant alertness. Noise "woke" us, as it did orgs. But there were no dreams to shake off; there were no dreams.

"No," I said. "Not okay. But—" I glanced at Zo. She looked zoned out, and I wondered if she'd swallowed a handful of chillers in the car, or if it was just shock. "Can we talk about it in the morning? We need a place to crash."

Riley paused. "I told you, the place is a mess . . ."

"Riley, this is an emergency."

He didn't move. Like he couldn't see that this mattered more than some unwashed sheets.

I pushed past him. "Whatever you've got in there, it can't be—" I stopped. Stopped talking, stopped moving.

It wasn't a what.

It was a who.

The girl splayed on Riley's bed had spiky red hair, bad skin, and no shirt. Her feet were kicked up on his pillows; her head lolled over the foot of the bed. She tilted her head back, watching me upside down.

"Was wondering when I'd finally see you again," Sari said, with a sly smile like she'd been prepping the line for weeks, waiting for the perfect moment to deploy it. "Welcome to our home."

HOMEWRECKED

For every action there is an equal and opposite reaction.

"What is she doing here?" I hissed.

"She *was* sleeping," Sari drawled. She didn't bother to sit up. Or put a shirt on over the flimsy red bra.

I hooked a finger in Riley's collar and tugged him toward the door. Zo dropped onto a couch in the corner, her face blank, her eyes empty. "Leave her alone," I warned Sari. Then dragged Riley outside and slammed the door behind us. And slammed it again, for good measure.

"Well?"

Riley did his strong, silent thing, trying to stare me down. Not tonight.

"Say something." The apartment had only one real room. Small, flimsy partitions separated the living space from the kitchen from the bed. There was only one bed.

He risked a half smile. "Something?"

"What is that girl doing in your bed?" *Half naked.*

Did every relationship turn into a cliché? I resented the

triteness of it almost as much as I resented the girl on the bed. Half-naked ex-girlfriend—*hot, org* ex-girlfriend—on the bed. Lying, defensive boyfriend. It didn't take a genius to finish the equation. One plus one equaled girlfriend storming out in anger, boyfriend groveling for forgiveness. I'd played the scene plenty of times before. With Walker—given his Pavlovian flirting with anything of the double-X variety—I'd had it memorized, and could deliver my lines in thirty seconds flat.

But Riley wasn't Walker. And storming away wasn't so easy when you had nowhere else to go.

"She needed a place to crash." Riley gave me a pointed look. "You know how that is."

"Don't."

"What?"

"Pretend it's the same."

"You need something. She needed something. That's all I'm saying."

Sure, exactly the same. Except that Zo was my sister, and Sari . . . the last time I'd seen Sari, she'd demonstrated her loyalty to Riley by double-crossing him, kidnapping me, and generally doing everything she could to help out the guy who wanted him dead.

She'd also made it painfully clear that "old friends"—Riley's words—wasn't exactly the most accurate description of their previous relationship. And that while she might not want him back, she had no tolerance for the prospect of someone taking her place.

"So she's staying here," I said.

"Nothing happened. It's not—"

"So she's *staying here.*"

"Yeah."

"How long?"

"Until she can find a—"

"No. How long has she been here?" Sleeping in his bed. Wearing his T-shirts. Or not wearing them.

"A few days," he admitted.

"She just showed up on your doorstep."

He hesitated. "I brought her here."

"You brought her here." I hated how I sounded. Rigid with cold fury, like someone else I knew.

"I told you I went back to the city a few times," Riley said. "During the vidlife."

A few times. He'd told me *once*. But I let it pass.

"I found her in one of those abandoned houses, right on the edge. You remember?"

I remembered. Enough to know that if he'd found her there, it was because he'd been looking. "You told me no one lives there."

"They don't. Not if they have any other choice. But Gray kicked her out. Said he couldn't trust her anymore after what she did."

"He must have pretty high standards." Gray had been her replacement for Riley—at least until it was no longer expedient. Then she'd screwed him over too. If she'd succeeded, I would be lying somewhere in a heap of spare parts; Gray would be dead.

"I found her half starved, hiding in a closet from some assholes who were trying to—" He stopped, shook his head. "She's a friend. I couldn't leave her there."

I remembered a windowless room, ropes digging into my wrists and ankles, chaining me to a chair. Sari's thug looming over me, his ass resting on my knees, his breath puffing against my cheek, his grubby fingers on my skin. "She's not *my* friend."

"You don't get it."

It was the unspoken assumption between us, that his life had been hard where mine was soft, and that made him strong where I was weak. It made me less than. I was tired of the whole thing. No, I'd passed tired a few miles back. I was *done.*

"I get it," I said. "Fine. She's your friend. You had to help her. So why not let me help you do it? Why not *tell* me? I could have found a place for her, found some credit—"

"Your father's credit?" he asked sourly. "I think I've taken enough of that."

The mention of my father brought the whole nightmare to life again. And Riley didn't even know, because we were wasting our time on *this*. But fighting was easier than saying it out loud.

Fighting was the easiest thing of all.

"I'm not my father," I said. "I could have helped."

"So now you know. Help."

I didn't have an answer for that one.

He snorted. "Right."

"Okay, you win. You're awesome. I'm heartless. She's an angel. Does that cover it?"

"I'm not throwing her out."

"I didn't ask you to."

"There's nothing to be jealous about," he said.

"Got it."

"See, this is why I didn't tell you. I knew you'd be like this."

"Like *this*?"

"But I told you," he said. "It's nothing."

"And I told you, *got it*."

"She's just a—"

"Riley. Read my lips. *Not. Jealous.*"

I wasn't. It was a surprise to me too. Yes, Riley was trustworthy, and no, I didn't *really* think anything was going on with Sari—certain as I was she would have preferred it otherwise—but when I was an org, that kind of cold reasoning had traditionally been beside the point. But relationships had been different when I was an org. Even when it was someone who'd barely mattered, there'd been a *need*, a charge beneath the surface when we were together, a vacuum when we were apart. Reasoning was beside the point. The point was the fever, needing the weight of his arms around you, needing flesh, needing to crawl inside him, to lose everything, even yourself—especially yourself—in the joining of body to body, skin to skin.

It was different now, because I was different now. The body was a body, and, for all practical purposes, it was a rental. It didn't come equipped with needs. I *wanted*, but that was different. That was in my head, and that was rational, which was why I could think coolly and calmly through the reality of who Riley was and what he would and wouldn't do. Sari fell into the latter category. I didn't need to worry about his intentions; I worried about hers.

"It didn't occur to you that Wynn sent her?"

"It did. He didn't."

"Because she said so."

"Yeah."

"And she's never lied about Wynn before."

Years ago, when Riley was a kid, he'd stolen something from Wynn, and Wynn's people had struck back, coming after the thief—and settling for the next best thing, Jude. Bashing him into the ground while Riley hid. Which meant, as far as Riley was concerned, it was his fault that Jude had spent most of his life in a wheelchair, dependent on Riley, begging for scraps. But it was also Wynn's, and Riley had held on to that until he couldn't hold on anymore. That's when he went after Wynn with a gun. And shot the wrong guy.

Wynn was never going to forgive the person who murdered

his brother. Which made him a threat—and last time I saw him, Sari was his weapon of choice.

"I'm not letting *him* stay at my place," Riley pointed out.

"*She* might."

"Why, because you can't trust a city girl? But you can trust me?"

"You're not like her."

"I'm *exactly* like her."

I shook my head.

"You don't want to see it," he said.

"You come from the same place," I said. "But you're not the same. Not anymore, at least."

"Right, because now I've got you, and you've got your daddy's credit. Happily ever after."

He didn't know anything.

But whose fault was that? The fight went out of me. "I'm sorry," I said, because that's what you say, even when you're not. "Can we stop?"

He paused. "I should've told you."

I shrugged.

"She's safe," he added.

I hugged him. Stiffly, awkwardly, but it was better in his arms than out of them.

"I need you safe," I said.

"I am."

"I need *you.*"

He laughed and gave me a quick kiss. "You're Lia Kahn, remember? You don't need anyone."

It was a long time before we were ready to talk again. The night was cold, as usual. Riley held me, and waited for me to be ready to explain why I'd come, and why I'd towed my sister along. I could see her through the narrow window, curled up on the couch, head under a pillow. Sari was burrowed into a sleeping bag on the floor. I was tempted to stay outside with Riley, holding his hand in mine, staring up at the dim red glow of the midnight sky.

Riley stroked my hair. "You can tell me," he said. And finally, I did, all of it—everything I'd found on my father's ViM, everything my father had said, everything he hadn't.

"I'm sorry," Riley said.

"That's horrible," he said.

"Tell me what I can do," he said.

And he wrapped his arms around me, and I leaned my head on his chest and imagined he was breathing.

"At least now you know what kind of man he is," he said. Was I supposed to be grateful that he stopped himself from saying the actual *words* "I told you so?" "You don't have to defend him anymore, or listen to him. Now you know he's nothing to you."

He didn't get it. He was right that I would never know what it was like in the city. But it worked both ways. He didn't have a father. And so—I felt horrible for thinking it, spoiled and ungrateful and unfair, but it was true—he didn't know how it felt to lose one.

I stood up. "Let's go to bed."

Riley shut down, and I let him think I would too. But I stayed awake. Listened to the unfamiliar hiss of breathing, in and out, in and out. Held myself still beneath the weight of Riley's arm, as his body molded itself around mine. Tree branches scraped the window, and I watched their shadows play on the wall, seeking animals—monsters—in the flickering dark. A lizard, devouring a snake. A dancing bear with bloody jaws. A ghost.

Zo's eyes fluttered beneath her lids. I hoped she wasn't dreaming about our father. I missed dreaming. But I didn't miss nightmares.

I stayed awake, and I tried to think of what I should have said to my father. The accusations I should have lodged against him, the graphic descriptions of burning and crushing and breaking, the tears of betrayal that, thanks to him, I couldn't shed. But there was nothing. No words. In my head, in the dark, I faced him again and again, and every time there was only silence. There was only me turning away, walking out the door, closing it in his face. I didn't want to yell at him, or listen to more of his explanations, let him find the elusive, magic excuse that would change everything.

I didn't want to talk to him. I wanted to hurt him. And words wouldn't do it.

Another lesson the great M. Kahn had taught us: Words were words, they meant nothing. Facts counted. Deeds counted. Objects counted. Like metal, like concrete. The laws of physics: an object in motion stays in motion until met by an external force. Like a truck.

Laws counted.

For every action there is an equal and opposite reaction.

So I lay awake in the dark, and I reacted. I planned.

And by the time the room lit with the red-orange glow of a rising sun, I knew what to do. Words wouldn't destroy him.

But I could.

The apartment got significantly more crowded when we were all awake. Zo barricaded herself in the bathroom for at least an hour, while Sari stood sentry duty outside it, her back to the living room and her glare locked on the door as if she were practicing her X-ray vision. Every few minutes she would rap loudly; the time in between was spent muttering new and innovative strings of curse words under her breath.

"Wait your turn!" Zo responded every once in a while, the *you impatient bitch* implied. I could only hope she was leaning against the door, scrolling through her zone or playing a quick round of Akira. Partly because it was Zo's style, and I liked watching Sari scowl. Mostly because I was afraid the other option was that my sister was curled up on the bathroom floor, crying.

And if she stayed in there much longer, I was going to have to bust open the door and find out.

But the door swung open, and Zo emerged, dry-eyed. Silent and sullen, which was par for the course. And it's not like I could do anything about it here, in an apartment so small and so crowded that every time Sari crossed the room, she found a new excuse to rest her hands on Riley's waist or his shoulder or the curve of his lower back, gently guiding him in one direction or another, slipping past, her chest brushing his arm or her hair whipping across his face. Not that I was watching.

"Zo and I are going out," I said.

"Good," Sari said, at the same moment Riley said, "Where?"

"Somewhere else."

"Anarchy," Zo suggested.

I looked at her in surprise. There was no way she could know how often Riley and I went there—except, I reminded myself, Zo had always known that kind of thing, back when she'd cared enough to pay attention, listening at walls and peering around doorways like charting every peak and valley of my romantic interludes was mandatory preparation for her own. "Anarchy," I repeated.

"I can meet you there later, if you want," Riley said.

I looked at Zo, who shrugged, beyond caring.

"Just you," I told him.

Sari rolled her eyes.

"Walk us out, Sari," I said. "Let's chat."

Riley looked alarmed. "Lia—"

"My pleasure," Sari said. She followed us out the door.

I stopped just on the other side of it. "I'll be watching you," I warned her, inwardly wincing at how cheesy, clichéd, and—more to the point—useless the words sounded. It was like I was still stuck in the vidlife, acting out the part of jealous girlfriend, reading from a script.

"Whatever."

"He may trust you, but I don't," I warned her.

"And I care?"

This was pointless.

"Come on, Zo," I said. "We're wasting time."

We were halfway to the car when Sari called after me. "Hey! Skinner!"

I turned back. She was playing her fingers with calculated idleness along her collarbone, the hollow of her neck, the bare skin disappearing beneath the low-cut V of her shirt. Reminding me of everything she had to offer. Warm flesh, a beating heart. "He *should* trust me," she said. "But you're right. You shouldn't."

"Huh." Zo raised her eyebrows as we got into the car. "So that's your boy-toy's ex? At least his taste is improving."

I waited for the punch line, but it never came.

• • •

"This place is insane," Zo said, as we settled onto the bench that Riley and I usually claimed. A few feet a way a horde of kids in buffer gear were improvising a game of human bumper cars.

"You get used to it."

"I hope not." She grinned, as three nudists rolled by on retro skates, all of them tethered together by a flowered cord woven through their hair. "I like it."

"Me too."

"Yeah, I can see why. Hard to feel like a freak when you're surrounded by total—" She stopped. Maybe because she saw the look on my face. "Sorry."

"Don't worry about it."

"I meant—"

"I got it," I said. "I'm a freak. You've made that clear."

"I never said that."

"You might as well have."

"All I meant was that I get why you like it here," Zo said softly. "It's like you can disappear. Everyone's putting on a show . . . but it feels like no one is watching."

She did get it.

"I never asked you," she went on. "What it was like."

I didn't have to ask her for an antecedent. "It" was everything. "It" was all the things that would have happened to her, if I hadn't gotten into the car.

Could have been her, could have been her, should have been her.

If it was playing on a nonstop loop in my head, I could probably count on it playing in hers.

"Did it hurt?" she added.

"The accident did," I said. "But I don't really remember that." I lied so easily. "Afterward, after the download? No. Not much hurts. Not physically."

"But you can still . . . things *can* hurt, right?"

I nodded, hoping she wouldn't push further, that I wouldn't have to explain how feeling pain was preferable to feeling nothing.

"And it feels like . . . I mean, you think you're Lia—"

"I *am* Lia." It came out louder than I'd intended.

She didn't argue. She didn't agree, either, but it was a start.

Zo sagged on the bench. "So, what, am I supposed to hate you now? Or are you supposed to hate me?"

"I think we're supposed to hate *him*," I said. It wasn't an answer, but it was easier.

She cleared her throat and looked away. "That Sari's a total bitch, huh?"

Apparently, we were done talking about our father. "Seems that way," I said.

"So . . . what are we going to do?"

"About Sari?" I asked, surprised that she considered it a joint problem. "I'm not sure there's anything *to* do except—"

"No. About *him*."

Tell her; don't tell her.

I looked at her, trying to gauge possible reactions to the plan I'd put together. Figure out whether she could be trusted, and whether this—action, *revenge*—was what she needed rather than something else, something harder. Maybe I should force her to talk.

Or maybe I should just feed her another chiller.

How was I supposed to know?

It had been a long time since I'd known anything about Zo, at least anything that mattered. It wasn't the download—although the whole stealing my friends and sleeping with my boyfriend thing hadn't exactly brought us together. But when was the last time we'd talked, just the two of us, not fighting, not swapping stories about the latest indignity our mother had visited on us in public or sniping about whose turn it was to deal with the dishes, but talked about something that actually mattered?

I couldn't remember.

"We'll figure it out," I told her, and put a hand on her shoulder, feeling awkward. I wondered if this was how my father felt when he tried to comfort me, with those halting, calculated gestures of fatherhood. "You're not alone in this."

She shrugged me off. "I'm always alone." Then, unexpectedly, she laughed. "Get me. Like some kind of twelve-year-old weeper sulking in her room and writing bad poetry. Forget it."

"Zo—"

She stood abruptly. "I'm going for a walk. Check out the freaks."

"I can—"

"No, you can't. You stay; I'll go. I know where to find you," she said.

I didn't follow her.

Zo was still gone when Riley finally showed. Which worked out nicely, because I needed an objective opinion on whether to loop Zo in on the plan.

"I want to break into BioMax's system, find out what else they're hiding, and use it to destroy them," I said.

Riley raised his eyebrows. "Simple as that?"

"I didn't say it would be easy—"

"Try impossible."

"—but we know what they did to me. We know what they did to you. Who knows what else they're hiding? And if Jude's deal with Aikida is legit, and we can get the download tech for ourselves, we won't need BioMax anymore. We won't need anyone."

"Sounds like you've got it all figured out."

I didn't like his tone. But maybe he just needed some time to adjust. Riley was cautious by nature, but he always did the right thing in the end. So I pressed on.

"What do you think—should I tell Zo, or not?"

"Don't do it," he said.

"Really? You don't think she deserves the chance to—"

"I mean you shouldn't *do* it," Riley said. "Forget about BioMax, forget about revenge, don't do *anything* until you've calmed down."

"What are you talking about?" I stood up. It was one thing to be cautious; it was another to suggest that I was being reckless. "I'm *calm*."

He just looked at me.

"This is a good plan," I said.

"This is *Jude's* plan," he pointed out.

"Since when is that not a selling point for you?"

"Since when is it one for you?"

"Which part of 'BioMax blackmailed my father into murdering me' did you not understand?"

Yes, Jude was the one who'd led me to the secret—and yes, I'd reacted exactly as he'd expected, and was now stepping up to do his dirty work, just as he'd planned. Did knowing I was being manipulated make me any less of a sucker? I chose to believe it did. And maybe that was only because I'd been used by one person or another for so long that I could no longer tell the difference. But it didn't matter. The enemy of my enemy was my friend, right? And, even if it was only thanks to Jude's transparent scheming, I now knew the truth. BioMax was my enemy.

"Can't you get what you need off your father's zone?" Riley asked.

"Not enough." Inside that corp there were names, there were dates, there were documents. Incontrovertible proof of what they'd done to me. And, while I was at it, what they'd done to Jude, to Riley, to Ani, the truth about their "volunteers" program, the useful citizens drafted into their experiments, sacrificed to their higher cause. Also: Getting to my father's zone meant going back to my father's house. I wouldn't. "After everything they've done to you? You should *want* this."

"What they did to me," he echoed. "That didn't matter so much, before."

When I was working with them, he meant. Ignoring their crimes for the greater good, because they weren't crimes against me. "I was wrong."

"But you're so sure you're right now?"

"Are you *defending* them?"

"I just think you should slow down," he said. "Think."

"I can't believe this. You're going to tell me that I'm being reckless, given what you've got sleeping on your floor right now?"

"That's different."

"Right. Because it's you," I said. "Because I'm supposed to trust your judgment, but you can't trust mine."

"Lia, come on."

"No! I won't 'come on'!"

"Stop shouting."

"I'm not shouting!"

I was shouting.

"Fine," I said. "So I'm mad. Congratulations, you figured me out."

"You're not mad at me."

"No kidding."

He took my hand and pressed my palm between his. "I love you," he said.

It was the first time.

That wasn't how I wanted it, like blackmail. Words to shut me up.

But I wanted it.

"You believe me?" he added.

I nodded.

I love you, too. I hadn't said it either. And I didn't want to say it now. Not so close to the lie he was about to make me tell.

"I'm worried," he said. "You get that?"

I nodded again, then raised my head and met his gaze. That was how you lied, if you wanted it to work. Head on. Fearless. I knew what was coming.

"Promise me you'll wait," he said. "Think about what you're doing. When you're ready, I'll be there. I'm with you. You believe me?" he asked again. I nodded. "So promise me?"

I didn't cross my fingers. I didn't try to avoid the question or offer a nonanswer that, in retrospect, could technically be considered some flavor of true. No excuses, no escape. I lied.

"I promise." And then, because I hadn't said it and the

silence was hanging there, growing between us, because I needed a truth to cancel out the lie, because it *was* true: "I love you, too."

He kissed my forehead, and then I tipped my face up and he kissed me for real, his eyes tightly shut.

He loved me, and I loved him, but he left when I told him I needed to be alone, and as soon as he was out of sight, I linked into the network.

And then I voiced Jude.

WHAT LIES BENEATH

I didn't ask to be saved.

The coordinates Jude sent took me deeper into Anarchy than I'd ever been before. I texted Zo that I'd meet her back at Riley's, then wove my way through the manicured gardens into a deserted area of densely overgrown brush. Cloudy water from a sewage pipe trickled into a runoff creek, and after staring blankly at it for a moment, I realized it was probably the closest thing the park had to a waterfall. Coincidence, or Jude's twisted sense of humor?

It took him two hours to arrive, which gave me plenty of time to do all that thinking Riley had urged me to do. I finished even more certain than when I'd started. This was the right thing to do. For me, and for all the mechs. Not to mention for my father.

I couldn't go to the authorities, not with what I had. There were no authorities anymore, not objective ones, at least. The secops were all owned by one corp or another—and my father was on half of their boards. The rest of the BioMax execs probably had the other half covered. I needed something splashier than what I had, something that could tear the whole corp apart and take my father down with it. I needed to dredge up the corp's deepest, darkest secrets—and then sell them to the highest bidder. No "authorities" were going to give me justice. That was something I'd get for myself.

"I'm in," I said, as soon as Jude appeared from behind the trees. "But I have some conditions."

Jude laced his hands together behind his head and leaned against a tree. "Let me guess—you'll help me find the download specs if I help you find the dirt on dear old Dad."

"Where did you get the flash drive?"

"Aikida," Jude said. It was rare for him to give up information so lightly, without demanding something—even if it was just abject supplication—in return. "They've been keeping tabs on the BioMax crew for quite a while."

"Is there more?"

He shook his head. "You've got everything I've got."

"Then how did you know about my father?"

"I'm a good guesser. I take it I was right?"

I didn't answer.

"Sure you don't want to take some time and think about it?" he asked. "Wait until you *calm down*?"

His emphasis tipped me off. "You talked to Riley."

"He wanted me to promise that I wouldn't drag you into my—how did he phrase it?—'insane delusions.' Which is a little redundant, if you ask me, but I assume you'll agree that language has never really been his strong suit."

He's only trying to help, I told myself. *He loves me.* But this wasn't the way to do it.

"What did you tell him?"

Jude shrugged. "What he wanted to hear. That I understood. That I would never pressure you into anything. That I'll stay away until you're feeling more like yourself—and if you come to me, I'll walk away."

"You lied?"

"I lied."

My surprise must have shown on my face. Jude had always made one thing clear: His bond with Riley was inviolate.

"I don't see why he should get to make decisions for you when he's doing such a crap job of running his own life," he added.

"He is not."

"Oh, so you *approve* of his sweet little houseguest?"

"I wouldn't say that."

"Right, because you're not brain-dead."

It was a relief to know I wasn't the only one who saw Sari as a threat, but I wasn't about to let him think this meant we'd forged some kind of alliance, the two of us against Riley. There was no line between us; there was no triangle. There was me-and-Riley, and then, outside of that, irrelevant to that, there was Jude. "Riley trusts her."

"Riley has a blind spot when it comes to pretty girls," Jude said. "Maybe you've noticed."

That fell under the category of Not Going to Dignify with a Response.

"What?" he said.

I smiled sweetly. "Trying to remember how I ever found you tolerable."

He shrugged. "Crisis makes for strange bedfellows."

"Never. In a million years—"

"It's an expression!" He held up his arms in surrender. "So much for the education of society's future elite."

"I *know* it's an expression," I snapped. "I'm just beginning to reevaluate whether I even want to be your metaphorical bedfellow."

"Your choice," Jude said. "Unlike some people, I get that."

"So do I." Zo's voice floated from beyond the bushes. She stepped into the clearing. "Or don't I get a vote?"

"What are you doing here?" As if I even had to ask. It was a shame that all spying these days was done by machines, because back in the dark old days of international intelligence agencies and invisible agents slipping through the shadows, Zo would have been a world champion.

"I heard you talking to Riley," Zo admitted.

"That tends to happen when you're hiding under a bench."

"Behind a tree," she corrected me. "The point is, I heard you."

"And then you followed me."

"It's a good plan," she said. "I knew you were lying about not going through with it."

"I guess little sister knows you better than Prince Charming," Jude said. He held out a hand to Zo, then raised hers to his lips with elaborate chivalry. "So this is the famous Kahn Junior. *Enchanté.*"

"And this is the famous Jude. Huh. I thought you'd be taller." She extricated her hand, which flew immediately to her tangle of hair and tucked the unruly strands behind her left ear. I groaned. This was Zo's version of blushing. She probably didn't even notice she was doing it. But—I could see it in his eyes—Jude did.

"And I thought you were a Brotherhood head case," he said. "So I guess our reputations precede us."

She ignored him. "You're taking me with you," she told me.

"I'm not going anywhere."

"When you take him down," she said. "Him and the whole corp. I'm going with you."

"She's spunky," Jude said. "You sure she's related to you?"

"Is he always this big an asshole?" Zo asked.

"Definitely related," Jude said.

This time we both ignored him.

"So?" she prompted me. "Do we have to fight, or do you want to save the energy and give in now?"

"Why would we let *you* in on anything?" Jude asked, replacing his charm offensive with a real one.

"Oh, you two are a *we* now?"

When he didn't crack a smile, much less fire back, Zo realized he wasn't joking. "What's his problem?"

"You," Jude said.

"Yeah, I'm an 'org.'" She made finger quotes around the word. "Deal."

"You're an org who went along with Savona's crap," Jude said. "Who decided we were subhuman, and treated your sister like dogshit you scraped off the bottom of your shoe."

Zo squared her shoulders. "I did what I did. I didn't know—"

"That it could have been *you*?" Jude finished for her. "Changes things, doesn't it?"

"I didn't know what it would mean to join the Brotherhood," Zo said firmly. "And I didn't know . . . Lia. My father's mistakes have nothing to do with that. Neither do you."

"She's right," I said. They looked equally surprised. "We could use her help."

Jude rolled his eyes. "She's twelve."

"She's seventeen," Zo said. "And she's in."

Jude sighed. "Fine. She's in." He smirked at her. "But you owe me one."

She scowled back—Zo's version of batting her eyelashes. "So collect. I dare you." The scowl morphed into a brilliant, triumphant smile when it was clear he was out of ammunition. "In that case, can we get out of here and go plan this thing somewhere civilized?" she added. "I realize you two don't care, but it's about zero degrees out here and I haven't eaten since breakfast."

I let her tromp through the mud ahead of us, which gave me a chance to dig my nails into Jude's arm and, quietly but firmly, make one thing clear. "My sister is *off-limits.*"

"She's an org," he said, as if that settled the issue.

"Like that would stop you."

"Jealous?"

"Screw you."

"Then we don't have a problem."

"Jude . . ." I let it hang there, my tone the best threat I could muster.

"She's a big girl," he said. "Seems like she can protect herself. In fact she seems a lot like you."

"She's nothing like me."

"Really? Huh." Jude put on his *thoughtful* look. "Funny, because she definitely reminds me of someone."

I knew what he was thinking, because I'd been thinking it too, ever since the day I met him.

You, I thought, but I would never say it out loud, especially not to him. *She reminds you of you.*

Waiting was interminable. As was playing along, playing the roles that had been written for me: Riley's dutiful girlfriend, keeping her simmering rage under control; BioMax's willing stooge, putting aside her personal feelings for the sake of a greater cause. This was key, Jude assured me, when I balked at showing my face the next morning for a weekly meeting with Kiri, Ben, and my father. I had to find out what he'd told them, and if they knew that I knew; I had to pretend I was past it, over it, somehow beyond it, or risk losing all access. It seemed like a wasted effort—if they knew, then it was over. Ben might be dense, but surely even he wouldn't believe that I'd forgive the corp for what they'd done, no matter how many "proud to be a mech" soliloquies I may have delivered at their beck and call. But when I arrived for the meeting, Kiri hadn't yet arrived, and Ben seemed neither surprised to see me nor overly solicitous. There was only one small, irrelevant matter to be dispensed with—"Your father says an important matter's come up that he has to deal with, and he'll have to step away from our project for a bit; he said you'd understand"—before we got down to business. I did understand. As far as my father was concerned, this was a family issue, and we would deal with it—or hide it—as a family. My father loved his boundaries, his neat little compartments. This time he'd left all of them vulnerable.

Good.

Ben and I sat there, on our own, waiting for Kiri and doing our best to ignore each other's presence. He buried himself in his ViM screen while I pretended to focus on mine, trying not to leap across the table, wrap my hands around his throat, and force him to tell me what he knew.

But I had to do something.

I started pacing, which seemed like the kind of thing you were supposed to do when you were nervous and frustrated and killing time. But I realized, as soon as I started wearing a track in the rug—seventeen steps to the end of the room, turning on my heel, then back again—that there was a reason people were always talking about pacing but never actually did it. It was boring. And more than a little odd-looking.

"What are you doing?" Ben asked, finally looking up from his screen.

"Nothing." I returned to my seat, taking the long way around so I could catch a glimpse of what he was staring at so intently, just in case it was something I wasn't supposed to see. Which it was, but not in the way I'd expected. "She's a little young for you, isn't she?" I teased.

The girl in the pic couldn't have been more than seventeen. She was pretty, if not in a particularly flashy way. Except for the brown hair, she looked a lot like Zo, though it may have just been her scowl.

"I wouldn't have thought that was really your style," I added. Ben's tastes ran to conspicuously expensive suits that were always fashion-forward, if in the blandest of ways, and I'd never seen him less than impeccably attired. The girl on the screen was wearing some kind of faded flash dress two sizes too small, and *not* in the "oops, my button popped!" kind of way.

Ben slammed the ViM on the table, screen down, and glared at me. "She's my daughter," he said quietly.

"Oh."

That made significantly more sense.

"I didn't know you had a daughter."

"That's right. You didn't."

He didn't lift the screen, nor did he look at me. Not for several long minutes, until Kiri walked in and the meeting began. Then he was all business again, same old Ben, smooth and insincere. Except that he wouldn't meet my eyes. I wondered if the subject of fathers and daughters cut a little too close to home when it came to me—if that meant he knew what BioMax had made my father do.

Or if it was something else. More secrets.

"We have a proposition for you," Ben said, toward the end of the meeting. "And I think once you consider it, you'll see the wisdom in—"

"You're going to hate it," Kiri cut in. *No-bullshit Kiri*, that's how I thought of her, and now I couldn't look at her without thinking, *Did you know?* Who was in the room, when they decided? Who was left that I could trust? Another reason I needed those files—but these offices were just for show; there was no access to anything. Even if I managed to get hold of Kiri's or Ben's ViM and get in remotely, Jude and I were reasonably sure they wouldn't show us much. BioMax, like most corps, kept their dirty little secrets on secure, firewalled servers—likely nothing that could stand up against the full weight of a network invasion, but nothing we'd be able to topple remotely on our own. We had to get in at the source.

"Try me." I offered up a perfect smile. Nothing to hide. What you see is what you get.

"As you know, the Brotherhood of Man has been making overtures in our direction," Ben said. "They claim they'd like to publicly bury the hatchet."

"In our backs?"

Ben cleared his throat. "They have a powerful voice and numerous followers—"

"Hate sells."

"—and if we can tap into that, it could be very helpful to our cause."

"Where is this going?" I asked. Circumlocution was call-me-Ben's specialty; he could talk for hours without saying a thing.

As usual it was Kiri who cut through the crap. "We're staging an event," she said. "A public peacemaking. The Brotherhood will announce their willingness to help incorporate the mechs into society, and BioMax will graciously accept their offer."

Kiri was one of the only BioMax people who actually used the word "mech." It was one of the things I liked best about her. The rest of them all said "download recipient" or "client" or, if they didn't realize I was listening, "skinner." But

Kiri used the name we'd given ourselves. She was smart—too smart to buy into the Brotherhood's line. Maybe Auden was sincere. But that was irrelevant, now that the Honored Rai Savona was back in the picture. "You do realize they've got an agenda?" I said.

"Quite honestly, their agenda doesn't matter to us," Ben said. "Right now they're doing exactly what we need them to be doing. If they take an ill-considered path in the future, we'll take whatever measures we see as necessary."

Translation: Squash them like a bug.

"So what do you want from me?" I was sickened enough being in these offices, facing them, pretending nothing had changed. Throw Savona into the mix—and Auden, who I tried not to think about, *couldn't* think about—and *almost* bearable turned into *not*. "Since it's obviously not my opinion."

Is it ever?

Jude's voice, Jude's disgust. *They want you to dance for them,* I could imagine him sneering, *not talk. Certainly not* think.

"The Brotherhood is extending an olive branch, Lia," Ben said. I hated when he said my name in his oily voice, like he was granting me a gift by acknowledging my identity. *I know what's inside your head,* his expression always seemed to say. *I've seen your flesh peeled away, your brain exposed. I know what you really are.* "We don't want to turn our backs on that."

"Fine. I still don't see—"

"We want you to represent BioMax," Kiri said. "Stand

up at a podium with Savona and Auden, make a little speech, shake their hands, sit down again. Simple as that."

"Simple?" I laughed. "You're a bad liar, Kiri."

"You don't have to marry them," Ben snapped. "You'll speak, you'll shake hands, and then we'll start the music and serve the food and you can go skulk in a corner or visit your friends upstairs or whatever antisocial course suits your fancy."

"What friends upstairs?"

"On the thirteenth floor," Kiri said. "The event's down at our research facility—there's a nice banquet space there, and we think it'll send a good message, get the word out about the limitless technological horizon, all that. We'll be packaging a whole vid segment on the rehabilitating mechs, give the public more insight into the process. Better our turf than theirs, right?"

I nodded, distracted by the possibilities. With all those people it would be easy to slip away from the crowd, into the corners of the building that I'd never been allowed to enter. With an event like this going on downstairs, it seemed likely that the place would be understaffed, maybe even cleared out, which would give us a clear path.

It wouldn't do to give in too quickly. Not when they both knew exactly how I felt about Savona and, I could tell, had come in girding themselves for a fight. So I let them argue and spin and cajole; I let them explain all the ways that this could be a new start for us, that many of the most vicious antiskinners were followers of the Brotherhood and their watching the leaders recant could change everything, that I was the key to forgiveness. Especially given my history with Auden—

That's where I stopped them. "I'll do it."

Kiri beamed. "I promise, if it's a disaster, you're welcome to say I told you so."

"Don't worry," I said. "I will."

I twirled for the mirror, and the nearly weightless silk skirt billowed around me. Under any other circumstances it would have been an optimal opportunity for preening. The sleek ball gown hugged every curve of my perfectly sculpted mech body, and the shimmering blue—which shifted across the spectrum from sky to indigo and back again as I moved—glowed against my smooth, pale skin. Riley brushed his lips against my neck, then traced a finger down my bare back until it reached the sash of silk slung low over my hips. "You sure you have to go out tonight?" he said softly. "You could stay here, and—"

"I'm sure," I said. The ball gown wasn't exactly the pinnacle of delinquent style, and I suspected the idea of breaking into BioMax might have seemed slightly less surreal if I'd been decked out in something more appropriate. But camo gear, even the kind programmed to blend into any background, wouldn't offer much invisibility at the BioMax ceremony. The idea was to blend, and—I shot a final confirming glance at the mirror, taking in the elaborately twisted blond braids, the jeweled designs sparkling along my arms and breastbone, the oceans of silk—I blended.

"Whoa," Riley breathed, eyes widening as Zo stepped out of the bathroom, her shoulders hunched and arms crossed her chest as if she were preparing for attack.

Her hair was clean and shining for the first time in years, pulled up in a loose chignon that highlighted the long arc of her neck. She'd traded in her standard uniform of baggy shirts and sagging retro jeans for an asymmetrical black gown. Satin coated one arm, leaving the other bare, and a latticework of temp tattoos crawled from her wrist to her neck. It looked like her skin was knit from silver lace, and somehow it worked. She looked beautiful, but not in a shocking ugly-duckling-turns-swan kind of way. Zo was still Zo, and crap clothes and greasy hair couldn't hide a genetic bounty for which our parents had paid a fortune. She looked better, but no matter how much she tried to hide it, she'd always looked good. I'd always known Zo was beautiful.

I'd never known how much she looked like me.

Or at least, the me that used to exist, in a different body with a different face. Zo was now almost exactly the age I'd been when the accident happened. And it occurred to me that watching her get older would be like getting a glimpse into the future I didn't get to have.

"You look great," I told her.

She scowled. "Whatever."

"You look like some old lady," Sari commented, from her habitual sulking spot in the corner.

"You look amazing," Riley said. "Both of you."

Zo stopped hunching after that. She kept sneaking glances at herself in the mirror, and I wondered what she saw. If she saw me.

"You sure you don't want me to come with you?" Riley asked. He pressed his hand to the small of my back. As an org I'd found that gesture irresistible—something about a warm hand on cold skin, at exactly the spot where I felt strongest and most vulnerable all at the same time. But I was a mech, and it was just a hand. I smiled at Riley.

"You hate parties," I reminded him. "I realize I look hot enough to make you forget that. But you'd remember as soon as we walked in, and you'd be miserable."

"I don't like the idea of you going alone," he said.

Zo cleared her throat, loudly.

"Both of you, alone," he clarified. "Aren't you afraid your father will be there?"

Zo flinched, but fortunately, his eyes were on me.

"I *hope* he's there," I said. It was only a half lie. We needed him there, if this was going to work. But it didn't mean I was looking forward to the encounter.

"Me too," Zo said, and if you weren't her sister, you wouldn't notice that it was the voice she used when she was lying, and when she was afraid. But there was fury in it, along with the fear. It leaked out exactly the way our father's did, like radiation—stealthy but lethal. "He's the one that should be afraid to see *us*."

I almost believed her. The more time we spent together, the more we fell into our old patterns: me the rule-abiding, cautious good girl, her the wild child who threw herself headfirst into anything, her life a constant dare to the universe to do its worst. While I was playing nice with BioMax, doing my job and pretending nothing had changed, lying to Riley and hating myself for how easy it had become, Zo had spent the last few days with Jude, putting her hacking skills to good use by helping him ferret out blueprints, plot strategies, conspire, spew out one convoluted plan after another until hitting on one that at least had a prayer of working. It all seemed so easy for her, and I'd assumed that was because it *was* easy, because she was fearless. But it suddenly occurred to me that she was fearless because she couldn't conceive of having anything to fear—maybe all this still seemed like something out of a vidlife, a melodrama with an inevitably happy ending. I knew it was possible to delude yourself that way; after the accident, I'd done it myself.

"Zo. You sure you're up for this?"

"I'm sure." She glared at me, daring me to try to talk her out of it or, worse, forbid her.

"Then let's go," I said. That won me a grateful look.

"You don't have to do anything you don't want to," Riley said, as we were leaving. "They can't make you."

I kissed him and wondered when he'd gotten so naive.

There were only a hundred people crammed into the BioMax banquet room, but the walls were net-linked, and thousands of faces stared at us from all over the country. It was easy enough to ignore them; I was used to being watched.

While Zo haunted the room, hovering by the buffet table and avoiding our father, I sat up on the dais with the assembled dignitaries, waiting for my cue. It was usually frustrating the way the mech body created a distance between me and the world, every touch and sound a painful reminder that nothing seemed quite real only because *I* wasn't. But times like this it was an advantage. I could stay locked in my head, watching my body move as if it belonged to someone else, shaking repugnant hands, smiling at the enemy, forming words I would never mean. Standing at a microphone, looking out over an audience of corp directors, BioMax suits, Brotherhood sympathizers, following the script: "I'm so gratified that we can come together in dialogue." "I'm looking forward to our shared future." "Tolerance." "Forgiveness." "Common ground." "This is a new beginning." And other such bullshit.

I was able to tune out as Savona himself took the stage to blather on about his regrets and his reformation. I didn't allow myself to wonder how anyone could overlook the obvious insanity dancing in his eyes, and I didn't allow myself to watch Auden, who was listening from the other side of the central podium. I hadn't seen him since the explosion at the temple, when I'd pulled him out of the burning wreckage. The security-operations guys had dragged him away for questioning while the building still burned, while I was still flailing in a secop's arms and screaming Riley's name.

I'd spent a long time begging Auden's forgiveness and hating myself for what I'd done to him—blaming myself for what he'd become. That was over now. It was his choice to stand by Savona's side, embracing his former mentor with open arms, just as it was his choice to dive into the frigid water and try to rescue me. I didn't ask to be saved.

Auden, who knew better than anyone what Savona had been up to at that temple, and had to know exactly how sincere these pledges of tolerance and shared destiny could be, *chose* to let Savona speak, and let the world believe him. He pretended that he could stay in charge of the Brotherhood, keep Savona in the wings, even though Savona was the pro, the one with the words and the voice, the adult with the gravitas and the credit and the power. All Auden had was the pity vote, and if he thought that would be enough, that was his choice, his mistake. He'd picked his side of the stage. I was done apologizing—to him and for him.

When the speechifying finally wound down, I shook

Auden's hand, and I did it without looking away. Then I shook Savona's, pleased again that the sensations received through my artificial nerves were so thin and colorless. I didn't want the pressure of his palm to feel real; I didn't want to know if it was clammy and sweaty or warm and dry. But I squeezed tight, knowing he was just as repulsed by my touch, and wanting his hell to last as long as it could.

Zo grabbed me as I stepped off the dais, pulling me off to the side. "I can do this part," she said. "If you don't want to."

It was tempting. "You can't. He'd never believe it, coming from you."

"And he'll believe it from *you*?" she asked. "After what he did to you?"

I didn't want to say it. And even more, I didn't want to watch her face as I did. "But he didn't *mean* to do it to me. He meant to do it to you."

Zo didn't flinch.

"When I tell him that makes all the difference, he'll believe me," I said.

"How do you know?"

"Because he wants to believe me. That's how it works."

He was avoiding me. I threaded my way through the crowd, catching glimpses of him over shoulders, through a knot of people, but he was always one step ahead. Maybe I wasn't trying very hard to catch him. The crowd was a bizarre mixture of BioMax execs and the occasional Brother still draped in one of those iridescent robes that had surely been designed for maximal creep factor. There were also a few mechs scattered through the crowd, though none I recognized, probably because no one who'd ever crossed paths with Jude would be naive enough to come within ten miles of this minefield. Even Ani—an obvious invitee—had apparently stayed away, though I suspected that had as much to do with my presence as Savona's. But as I neared the bar, I spotted a vaguely familiar face: Elton Kravis, a mech who'd always been a bit of a moron, so his presence made sense. He was deep in conversation with some blank-faced corp exec, but, fulfilling his moron destiny, abruptly cut it off and veered to his right in pursuit of a gorgeous girl with long black hair and a Brotherhood robe who would have been out of his league even if she didn't believe he had about as much sex appeal as a vacuum cleaner. In his wake he left an empty space in the crowd, affording me a perfect view of my father.

He stood alone in a corner, his face buried in his glass—probably downers mixed with tea, his blend of choice.

I'd thought this part would be easy.

Because what could be easier for me than pretending to be a person I despised? I'd been rehearsing for this moment all year. But once I was standing before him, forcing myself to look up into his unlined face, the eyes that had once been exactly the same shade as mine, I couldn't do it. He would see through it, I was certain. He would know I was more likely to attack than swap small talk. I let myself indulge the fantasy for a moment, imagining a jagged edge of glass raking his skin.

Zo was watching from across the room. She caught my eye and flashed me her cheesiest thumbs-up.

"Hi, Dad." I smiled.

There was a flicker of surprise, then it was gone. He nodded, casually, like he'd expected nothing less than an affable greeting from his beloved daughter. "Lia. Good to see you."

"And you." He couldn't see into my head, I reminded myself. He couldn't see anything unless I let him. "How have you been?"

"Well. Very well. And you?"

We went back and forth, saying nothing, for endless minutes. He was putting on a show for whoever was watching, although almost surely no one was. I waited it out, letting him squirm, because my next move would be less suspicious if he made it for me, thinking it was his own idea. Finally, success: "Would you like to go somewhere more private?" he asked. "Perhaps somewhere we could talk?"

"That would be nice." Formal and proper. I smiled again, letting a dash of pain filter into it, so he would understand I was struggling with the decision, overcoming my own natural inclinations to run. He led me into a private office—our father never attended events like this without lining up a private sanctum to which he could retreat in time of need—and settled at one end of a small couch.

The thought of joining him made my skin crawl. I did it anyway.

"Lia." He stopped, swallowed hard, looked down, then, thinking better of it, forced himself to face me. I stared at the door, watching him out of the corner of my eye. "I didn't expect you'd want to talk to me."

"I don't." It couldn't be too easy, or he'd never believe it, no matter how much he wanted to.

"But . . ."

"But I'm here," I said. "You're my father, whatever happened. So . . . I'm here." I sat flagpole straight, facing forward, hands gripping the edge of the cushion like I was priming myself to run.

"I'm sorry," he said. "I don't know what else to say. I never meant to hurt you."

After all this time, he hadn't managed to come up with anything better than the world's oldest, lamest excuse? *Sorry I had you murdered. Who knew it would hurt?*

"I know," I said.

"You do?"

I closed my eyes for a long moment, let him think I was grappling with a decision, opening a door. I turned and met his gaze. "I know," I said again. "It must have been an impossible situation for you. I can't even imagine, having to pick between two children, but . . ." I reminded myself that Zo would never have to hear what I said next. That they were just words. "You picked me. You wanted *me* to live. And in a twisted way, I guess . . . that proves how much you love me."

This was the tricky part. My father wasn't the touchy-feely type. I let my shoulders slump and tried to make myself look smaller. Weak. "I thought it would be easy to run away. From everything. From you. But now I'm . . . I'm so alone. I don't know who I am, if I'm not your daughter." I lowered my head. Let my voice shake. "I don't know how to forgive you. But I don't know how not to forgive you."

I hugged my arms over my chest and waited, closing my eyes so that I wouldn't have to look at him. A moment later I felt his weight shift on the couch, and then his arms were around me. "I'm here," he said. His hug was as stiff and awkward as ever. "I'm your father, nothing will ever change that. You *are* my daughter. And I've never been so proud of you."

If only he knew.

"I love you," he said.

That's when I stuck him. It was quick and nearly painless, a sharp pinprick on the back of his neck, where it wouldn't leave a mark, and even as he reached to feel for a bump or a bite, his arm dropped to his side, and then, as the toxin worked its way through his system, he slumped back on the couch, unconscious.

I didn't ask Jude where he'd gotten the sleep serum, or the microjector. That was the whole point of Jude: He *got* things. He'd assured me that it was harmless, with no lasting effects. I hadn't asked about that, either.

I stood, staring down at my father, his suit rumpled, spittle dripping from the corner of his mouth. Messy and vulnerable, the two things he'd sworn never to be.

"I could kill you right now," I said.

His eyes fluttered. Could he hear me? "It's better this way," I told him, hoping he could, even if he wouldn't remember. "I'd rather be a machine than have to walk around carrying your disgusting genes." I had looked like him, that's what everyone had always said. "I'd rather be a machine than be any part of you. I'd rather be dead."

It was self-indulgent, wasting time like this.

Not to mention pathetic, giving voice to all the things I was too cowardly to tell him when he was awake. *Someday,* I promised myself. Then I slipped the ViM from his front pocket and pressed his index finger against the nanotape Zo had given me, recording a fresh, clean print. As a final touch, I propped his head on a pillow, leaving the downer glass overturned by his fingertips. He'd think he slipped into the office to get away from it all, dosed more than he'd planned, and zoned out. If all went well, he'd still be out when we returned, and I could slide the ViM back into his pocket. It would be like nothing had happened.

Jude said he wouldn't remember any of this, not the dosing, not the conversation that came before it. He would wake up with a headache, wondering how he'd ended up in the office, wondering why he'd fallen so soundly asleep, never remembering the way I'd humiliated myself before him, accepting his pathetic apology. Or the way he'd humiliated himself by believing me.

I texted Zo to let her know we were ready for the next step. Then it was time for Jude's cue: *Ten minutes,* I texted him. *Then go.*

I slipped back into the thick of the party, swapping facetious small talk with some BioMax functionary whose name I could never remember, trying to follow his boring story of vacationing at some domed golf resort and scoring a hole in one while a lightning storm raged overhead, but all I could think was, *Any second now, come on, now, now.*

Now.

The doors blew open. Jude and his crew of mechs stormed the banquet hall, megaphones blaring the same message as the giant LED boards they carried: SAVONA LIES! The ten mechs elbowed their way into the crowd, hooting and shouting, leaping on tables and chairs and, in one memorable case, the shoulders of a particularly tall and broad corp exec. As they scattered, they released periodic bursts of neon smoke that curled itself into accusatory slogans before puffing into thin air.

The crowd exploded into a mixture of cheers and boos. There were a few high-pitched screams, some laughter, several panicked calls for security—and a hundred slack-jawed, wide-eyed, mind-blown orgs gaping at the wild mechs, backing away whenever one threatened to come near. BioMax reps scuttled back and forth trying to catch the interlopers, but Jude and his cronies zigzagged through the crowd, using orgs as shields and buffers, leaping over furniture and, when necessary, throwing handfuls of cocktail wieners and popcorn shrimp at their pursuers. It was, in the purest sense of the word, anarchy.

And two weeks ago it would have killed me. I stood at the center of the storm, watching Jude tear down everything I'd worked for, knowing it would play on the network for weeks, in constant loops and mashups, the demented mechs bent on sowing destruction through org society.

Exactly as we'd planned.

The crowd was too dense for any kind of effective security protocol—and there were too many witnesses for any kind of violence, especially against the very mechs that BioMax claimed to be so desperate to protect. Which was how Jude managed to weave his way through the orgs all the way to the dais at the front of the room. He clambered up on stage and, as the BioMax reps pushed their way through an increasingly uncooperative crowd, unleashed his j'accuse on Savona: a litany of his crimes, a list of every mech who'd been attacked, lynched, battered, bruised by the hatred stoked by Savona and his Brothers. Name after name after name. It was transfixing.

But I tore myself away. Zo was waiting by the locked door that read AUTHORIZED PERSONNEL ONLY, ready to use the security code on my father's ViM to get us through. Jude had provided as much distraction as we could have hoped for. The room was absorbed by his spectacle; no one would notice two girls disappear behind a wall. But something made me pause in the doorway and turn back. From across the room, an island of calm in the pandemonium, Auden was watching. Savona stood by his side, eyes on the stage. The security team had formed a human barrier between them and the rampaging mechs, and I wondered why they hadn't been dragged off to safety. It occurred to me Savona wouldn't have allowed it. What better way to solidify his martyrdom than to stay publicly calm, stoic even, while the mechs did everything they could to tear him apart?

But I couldn't worry about that now. Any more than I could worry about the fact that Auden was watching us.

"What?" Zo hissed, when she noticed I wasn't moving. "Come on."

"Shh!"

She followed my gaze, and saw him seeing us. Her face went white.

Auden tilted his head, a nearly imperceptible nod. Then turned away.

"Shit." Zo's eyes bugged. "We have to call this off. He's going to—"

"He won't do anything." I yanked her through the door and let it close behind us.

"He *saw* us."

"He won't tell anyone."

"So now you're a mind reader?"

"Trust me," I said, and hoped I was right. "It's fine. He'll keep his mouth shut." Zo didn't ask why I was so sure. A good thing, since I had no answer for her. The truth was, I wasn't sure about anything except that it was probably wishful thinking to imagine Auden would protect us. But I couldn't stop. Not when we were so close. If he sounded the alarm, we would deal. Until then we would keep going.

It was almost too easy. We were well beyond business hours, the halls were nearly deserted, and I could only trust that Jude was keeping the building's secops plenty busy. On the rare occasions that footsteps seemed to pass too close, the maze of corridors left plenty of options for ducking out of sight. We swept past each automated security checkpoint with perfectly legitimate credentials. Our father's security codes flashed from the stolen ViM and, as we ventured into more protected zones, his fingerprint opened one door after another. The blueprints indicated a server room in the basement where classified information—like technical specifications for the download process—would likely be held. These days nearly everything was stored in a data cloud on the network, powered by thousands upon thousands of servers whirring away in top-secret locations. It was why you could make a ViM in any shape and size—the Virtual Machine didn't need to hold any information of its own; it just linked you up to the network and you were off. But nearly every corp had its own small server system tucked away somewhere, a skeleton closet for data it didn't trust to the public storehouse. Walled off from the network, forbidden ViM access, safe from prying eyes. Zo had admitted she'd been studying up on hacking this kind of stuff for years, she and her loser friends whom I'd thought spent all their time loitering in the parking lot burning out on dozers—and she was convinced she could find the data and download it.

But there were no servers in the basement.

"You sure you're reading those right?" Zo asked, snatching the ViM out of my hand so she could see the blueprints for herself. But I hadn't made a mistake: According to the map, we should have been standing in BioMax's main computing center. There were no computers in sight. Instead there was a long stretch of white padded rooms, each with a large window facing the corridor. I felt like I'd stumbled into a mental hospital, except that instead of straitjacketed lunatics, the large cells held machines of various shapes and sizes. Tanks, fighter jets, drones, armored crawlers, none of them much larger than I was—war in miniature. Some were motionless; others wheeled around seemingly at random, bashing into walls and firing blanks at the thick glass. At the end of the corridor we finally found some computers, but instead of massive servers, these were just standard keyboards and screens, some smeared with data, others showing the antics of the imprisoned machines.

"What the hell is this?" I said, gaping at the strange mechanical lab rats.

Zo had already pulled herself up to one of the lab stations. Her fingers flew across the keyboard. I couldn't stop watching the machines. One in particular caught my attention: some kind of armored walker about three feet tall, stumbling around its cell like a toddler learning to walk.

"Lia," Zo said. "You need to see this. Now."

"What is it?"

"It's you," she said in a hushed voice. "Well, not you, but . . . all of you."

"What are you talking about?"

"Will you just look!"

I peered over her shoulder. I read what she'd read. It was a status report, and at first the phrases didn't make much sense. "Rerouted neural pathways." "Reoriented command functions." "Effect of cognitive deficiencies on consciousness." "Subject shows improved learning capabilities with thirty percent of memories intact." But gradually, the meaning became clear, and as I took in the words, the laboratory transformed itself in my imagination. I saw vats of clear fluid lining the walls, and suspended inside of them, gray, pulpy masses with wires snaking in and out. Brains, isolated and nurtured, synapses firing, alive and dead all at once. Imprisoned. I saw a mad scientist's laboratory, death defied, life abominated, nature possessed. I saw myself, and I saw the men who owned me.

I saw the machines. And *they* were real.

The "effect of cognitive deficiencies on consciousness" was, apparently, severe. Strip away a brain's memory, speech, and emotion functions, everything that made a person a person, and you were left with a machine. A machine that, if you programmed it right, would do anything you told it to.

"Tell me I'm understanding this wrong," I said.

She didn't.

"Our uploaded neural patterns can't be accessed by them—by anyone—not while we're still functioning," I said, because that's what I had been told. It was the foundation of the download technology. As long as our brains were active, our functioning neural networks released a signal that prevented the resurrection of any other brain with the same neural pattern. Only one Lia Kahn at a time, that was the hard-and-fast rule. But the neural patterns they were playing with down here were altered, weren't they? *Deficient.* Which made the signal—and their promises—useless.

Zo still didn't say anything.

I couldn't stop watching the machine, the one stumbling on its iron feet.

I couldn't stop wondering whether it remembered its name.

"You can't search for yourself," Zo said quietly. "I tried.

Everything's indexed by some kind of ID number, not name. If I had more time, probably . . . but maybe it's better?"

Maybe it was better I didn't know whether they'd taken a computer program that, under the right circumstances, called itself Lia Kahn, and crammed it into a steel tank? Maybe it was better I not think about what it would mean, what I would be, if my "significant personality markers" were stripped away, along with "superior cognitive function" and "emotive control." If I was lobotomized, with only an animal intelligence left behind.

I'd flown in an AI plane. I'd looked out the window, wondering at the technology that allowed it to decide for itself how fast to fly, where to land. I'd seen the headlines on the news zones: the lives that had been saved by the new AI surrogates, compliant mechanical fighters that shot and crushed and bombed and burned on command, that were smart enough to strategize, pliant enough to follow every command. I'd never given much thought to it, how they'd suddenly, magically, breached the artificial intelligence barrier. Because it had nothing to do with me. I was artificial, I was intelligent, I was a machine, yes. But I was different. I was a remnant of something human; I had started life as something else. They were things; they had always been machines.

That's what I'd thought.

Because, again, that's what I'd been told.

"Why do they need so many?" I asked dully. According to

the records, they'd downloaded more than a hundred of us into various prototypes. Why not lobotomize one brain and download it into everything? More efficient—still evil.

"I think . . ." Zo hesitated, as if understanding it somehow made her complicit. "I think it increases the chances of success. Different neural patterns adjust better to different machines. Some don't work at all."

"So this is their testing ground." I turned back to the video feeds of the padded cells, watching the stumbling machine and remembering what it had been like for me at the beginning, learning to walk. Training my brain to control the artificial body. They'd scared us into cooperating with the tedious rehabilitation process, making it all too clear what would happen if our neural patterns failed to adapt. We'd be frozen, unable to move or speak or see, trapped inside a head with no window to the world, no control. Buried alive inside a mechanical corpse.

"They let them learn," Zo said, "give them commands, see what happens, and when they find a neural pattern that works—"

"Payday." I backed away. "Can you deal with this?" I asked. "Download whatever you can to your zone, get some pics, evidence, whatever—"

"I got it," Zo said. She didn't ask what I'd be doing while she got stuck with all the work.

I returned to the corridor. To the cells. I stood at one of the windows, watching a miniature tank ram itself into a wall, over and over again. I tapped at the glass, but nothing happened. I don't know what I was expecting—it wasn't an animal.

It. I was thinking like them.

But it wasn't an *it*.

It was, had been, a he. Or a she.

Maybe it had been someone I knew, maybe even—

Maybe it didn't matter. It wasn't a person inside that tank. It was electronic data, some of which happened to resemble the data inside our heads. It was bytes of information, flickers of light. Nothing more. It didn't have any effect on us. Its existence was irrelevant.

But if it was nothing, just an imperfect copy, just data, then so was I. And if I was a person, a *someone*, then maybe so was it. Thinking and feeling at some primal level, dumb and mute and trapped, a slave to a stranger's commands.

Zo came up beside me. She didn't speak, and knew better than to touch me. We stood side by side. "I don't know what to do," I said.

"You will."

JUMP

We were supposed to be a fairy tale.

Jude didn't believe it, not at first. We had to show him the files we'd hacked and the vids we'd taken, and even then, I could tell, he wanted to think we'd somehow gotten ourselves turned around, stumbled into an alternate realm with no bearing on the real world. It was the first time I'd ever seen him underestimate the boundaries of org depravity.

On its surface this was less brutal than the antiskinner attacks and lynchings, less bloody than the corp's initial foray into the download technology, its path littered with the corpses of unwilling "volunteers." But I thought I understood Jude's uncertainty and—though he never would have admitted it—his panic. Because *this* was coordinated and systemic. For all we knew, it was the reason BioMax had pursued the download technology to begin with. Certainly, supplying the military industrial complex paid better than a semihumanitarian mission to heal the broken children of the wealthy. Not to mention the domestic-sector applications, which we'd all seen. Which we'd all—the self-revulsion at this thought was overwhelming—used without a second thought.

"How could I be this stupid?" Jude said, as we huddled in his car and told him everything.

"How were you supposed to know?" I asked. "I *worked* there, and I didn't."

"Exactly. Stupid."

I wasn't going to fight with him, even if it would have been easier. "You're right. We were stupid. Now what?"

"You're asking *him*?" Zo said.

"I should be asking you?"

"Since when do you ask anyone?"

I wouldn't have thought I had to remind her that things changed.

"Bossy big sister doesn't exactly translate into fearless leader," Jude said.

"Asshole. I got us this far, didn't I?"

"With my plan," he pointed out.

"My execution."

"Congratulations," Zo said. "You're both equally useless."

"This doesn't have to change anything," I said. "We can still sell the info to Aikida."

Jude frowned. "And let them do the same thing?"

"So we go public," I suggested. "This has to be illegal."

"Not if they don't want it to be," Jude said.

"So what's *your* brilliant idea?"

He didn't answer. That was the worst part. Jude, the one person who shouldn't have been surprised, had somehow failed to question the fundamental truth of our existence. That we were the only copies. That each of us existed as a unique unit, a single person, our identities protected and sacrosanct. It was the lie that allowed us to be human, wasn't it? Because how could I be Lia Kahn if there was a second Lia Kahn wandering the earth, a third, a fourth, a hundredth—how could I be Lia Kahn if there was a battlefield of Lia Kahns, tanks and planes and, for all I knew, vacuum cleaners, all of them somehow, not quite, but mostly *me*? If BioMax could lie about this, they could lie about anything. They could put a copy of my brain into another body, awaken as many Lia Kahns as they liked.

Stripped-down personalities were still personalities; lobotomized brains could still think. Artificial intelligence dictated intelligence. So what made us people and them machines?

Nothing, I thought. *To BioMax, we're all just things.*

There's no sin in lying to a *thing*.

"So we're screwed," Zo said.

"*We're* screwed," I said. "You're . . ."

"Not involved. Right. Somehow I forgot."

I couldn't stop saying the wrong thing. "Let's just go home," I said. Then, because someone had to, even if it was a lie: "We'll figure something out."

The real problem: This wasn't a flaw in the system. This was the system itself. This was the corp that owned us, body and mind. This wasn't something we could fight. But we were going to have to.

I dumped Zo and Jude at Riley's place. Zo lunged for the shower, as if eager to wash off the day. I understood the impulse. Jude was more than happy to ensconce himself on Riley's turf to keep an eye on Sari—the two of them circled each other warily like rival alley cats, and I half expected one to start peeing to mark the territory. True to form, Riley didn't ask questions.

"Let's go somewhere," I told him.

"It's the middle of the night."

"I don't care. Please."

He gave in.

Only one problem: I didn't know where I wanted to go. So we drove aimlessly, watching the muddy browns and grays stream by the window, the river of concrete and mud and smog. The water, that's what I thought of first, the dead city beneath the sea. Our place, with its silent buildings and frozen cars, our city of algae and coral and darkness. It was the first place Riley had taken me, the first place he'd kissed me, back when we'd fit with jigsaw perfection. But we'd gone back too often these last few months, neither of us admitting what we were trying to do. It was a way of going backward. Beyond that fence nothing existed except us. We didn't talk there, not like we used to. We ducked beneath the water and held hands and let the current carry us wherever it wanted to go. We hid.

It was too quiet there; it was too easy. Too still. After everything that had happened, I needed something else—not just the relief of Riley's arms around me, but the relief of adrenaline and fear and forgetting. And then the answer was obvious.

It wasn't our place; it wasn't my place. It had belonged to Jude, once; it had belonged to all of us. I hadn't been back there in nearly a year, because I had been too afraid. It was the place to start over again, because it was the place where things had gone wrong.

I keyed in the coordinates. Recognizing them, Riley tugged me toward him, and we curled up in the front seat as the car veered to the right, taking us west, off the highway, into the country, away.

The waterfall was tamer than I remembered. But it was wild enough.

Riley looked uncertain. "Why here?"

He knew how I felt about the waterfall. "I want us to jump," I said.

"I thought you wanted to talk."

"After."

I led him to the water. We took off our shoes, peeled off our clothes, and waded out to the edge of the precipice, buffeted by wind. The water roared. I could have shouted all my secrets and let the wind carry the words away.

I held out my hand. He grabbed it, squeezed, then let go.

There was no point in counting down. No point in being afraid. I'd leaped from planes. I'd leaped from cliffs. This was no different. If anything went wrong, my brain, my self, was safely copied and stored. Whatever happened to this body, BioMax had Lia Kahn, to do with whatever they wanted. She was their toy. I belonged to them.

I closed my eyes. Lifted my arms to the sky.

Jumped.

It was everything I needed. It was mindless, breathless, timeless, twisting and flailing and falling. The pleasure of the flight met the pain of the rocks. The water carried me down, carried me away. Sucked me under the falls, into a churning storm, the surface lit by a sheet of white water, the river cycloning around me, driving me down, dragging me up, then down and up again, like a bobbing cork, like a doll, like a body.

It was the moment that my brain kicked in, that I thought, *Auden*, and remembered his body sailing over the lower falls, floating at the bottom, facedown, breathless.

I kicked furiously, fought off the storm, and broke free to the surface of the icy river. I floated, ears submerged, eyes to the gray sky.

That's when I saw Riley, his form a shadow against the sun, standing at the edge of the falls, looking down.

• • •

"So, you didn't jump."

"I didn't jump."

We sat cross-legged on the riverbank. Water gushed down from above, its spray misting the air.

"That's okay," I said.

"I *know* it's okay." He was angry. At himself, for freezing? At me, for dragging him here?

At me, for jumping, and leaving him behind?

There was a long pause. "Go ahead," he finally said, sullen. "Ask."

"Fine. Why didn't you?"

He hunched his shoulders, scraping his knuckles against each other. "You know why Jude started this?"

"To remind ourselves of what it means to be a mech," I recited, the familiar words strange in my mouth. It wasn't so long ago that I'd given this speech on a daily basis. "With absolute control must come absolute release. Release from gravity, release from fear."

"Release from death."

Right. I'd left out the most important one, the bright line dividing mech and org. The absence that defined us. No end of the line, no period on our sentence. Endless days and years of downloading from one body to the next. We jumped from the waterfall because we *could*, because we could do anything. The drop wasn't steep enough to permanently damage our bodies—they were too well constructed for that—but we jumped because it didn't matter. If something went wrong, if the body were crushed or drowned or torn apart, we would remain intact. We jumped to defy death, as we defied it every day, by living on, far past our sell-by date.

"I bought it," Riley said. "But since the fire . . ."

I waited him out. With Riley it was the only way.

"It's not the same," he finally said. "Now that I know what it's like."

I understood, or thought I did, but only because I'd become an expert at translating Riley's begrudging admissions of inner life. So, spitting in the face of death was less fun once you'd died yourself.

Not org death—we'd all been through that. But mech death. Waking up yet again in the BioMax lab, with no memory of how you'd ended up there, with a gap in the story of your life. Knowing yourself to be a copy of a copy. It was fear of that moment that prevented me from downloading into a new, custom-made body that would look like the Lia I used to be. It was the fear that gripped me every time I stood on a ledge, the fear I *needed*, if the leap was going to mean anything. It was one thing to know you couldn't die; it was another thing to believe it.

Maybe now Riley didn't.

Since the fire, I'd spent so much time trying to convince myself he wasn't a different person. I hadn't thought to convince him. Even though every time he looked in the mirror, he saw someone different staring back at him. Because of me. Because I'd given him back something I thought he wanted, without bothering to ask.

"I'm sorry," I said. "We shouldn't have come."

He shook his head. "I'm just being stupid."

"You're not."

"Jude's right, you know. They have the power. If something happens, and they don't want to put you into a new body, they don't have to. They can do anything they want. They always do."

I wondered if "they" meant BioMax, or if "they" meant everyone with more power, with more credit, everyone who'd ever used him as a tool or a toy, just because they could. It was nothing new for him; it was status quo.

Maybe that's why, when I put my hands over his and told him what we'd found at BioMax and what the corp was doing to our friends, maybe to us, he wasn't surprised. "Of course" was all he said. "Of course they would."

I'd wanted outrage and shock. Maybe I'd even wanted violence: Riley throwing me off, leaping to his feet, out for blood. But this was more of what I'd gotten when I told him about my father: resigned acknowledgment that he'd been right about the world all along. Surprise that I hadn't seen it coming.

"I know I promised I wouldn't do anything," I said, when he didn't ask any follow-up questions. "But I had to." *And you made me lie to you.*

"I know," Riley said. "I get it. I figured you would."

"That's why you went to Jude behind my back?"

Riley issued a hard laugh. "Not like he listened."

"You should have trusted me."

He raised his eyebrows. "You were lying."

"No, I mean you should have trusted me to decide for myself."

A pause. "Maybe."

But that's what we did: We decided for each other. We lied; I lied. Maybe that was why I'd brought him here, because last time we'd been in this place, we'd been strangers. This was a place for a fresh start. No more lies.

First I kissed him. He closed his eyes, but I kept mine open, sweeping my gaze across his skin, trying to memorize the angle of his cheekbones, the crinkles at the edges of his eye, the way the skin shallowly dimpled below his ear.

"What was that for?" he asked, when I finally pulled back. "Not that I'm complaining."

"I need to tell you some things," I said, before I could think better of it.

"There's more? What's left for them to do?"

"Not them. Me."

The worst part? That didn't surprise him either.

"It's about that night at the temple," I said. "There are some things that . . . you don't know." So easy to phrase it that way, passive and blameless. "Things you don't know" as opposed to "things I didn't tell you."

We still sat cross-legged, facing each other. His hands rested on his ankles, and my hands rested on his. They were my safety line, my barometer. If I could hold on to them, I could hold on to him. If not . . .

I kept going. Eventually, I hoped, gravity would take over, dragging us down to the truth even if I changed my mind mid-fall and tried to pull us up again.

"I lied. About what happened. When I said the sec-ops came before we signaled them—that we had no choice. That's not how it was." *Keep talking*. The faster I talked, the sooner it would end. "Auden found us, and I had to stop him from getting into the building, but then Jude wanted to use him as a hostage, and then—" It hadn't been like this, one simple moment following another, cause and effect. It had been a fractured collage, and now, after so many months trying to forget, it was just a fog.

"Then what?" He spoke for the first time.

"Things got crazy. Jude was going to shoot Auden, so you . . . you had to stop him. Remember? You weren't going to let anyone get hurt. So you . . ." I had told myself, all this time, that I was protecting him from the guilt. I was lying for *him*. But when had I ever been that altruistic?

"I what?"

"You shot him. With one of those pulse guns. And he passed out." I wondered what it must be like to hear your life told to you like a story that had happened to someone else. To hear that you'd done things that you knew, deep down, you would never do. "But Auden had already alerted the Brotherhood, and then it was . . ." I shook my head. "Hell. We hid out inside the lab, and the Brotherhood was outside, and we didn't have any choice."

"So *we* called in the secops," Riley said.

"Yeah. And we told them . . . if they came, if they rescued us and stopped the explosion and the Brotherhood, they could take Jude." That wasn't exactly right; it wasn't how it had been. Saying it like that made it sound like a trade, like we'd given him up. "We didn't have a choice."

"We could have blown the place up," Riley said. "With us inside."

I didn't have an answer for that.

"But you were too scared," Riley said. "Right?"

I'd never admitted it to him. "It doesn't matter now. We didn't do it. We both agreed."

"And then Jude blew the place anyway. With me inside."

We were no longer holding hands.

"This is why I didn't want you to know," I said quickly. "I thought it would be easier—"

"On who?"

I deserved that.

"How do I know this is true?" he asked stiffly.

"It's true."

"How do I know?" he said again.

"You didn't do anything wrong," I said. "We didn't have a choice."

"For all I know, you're lying now, and what you said before was true. Or none of it's true. *Anything* could be true. I'm supposed to *trust* you?"

I reached for him, but he knocked my hand away, hard.

"I'm sorry!"

"It's not that you lied, *again*," he said, frost in his voice. "It's what you lied *about*."

"I didn't think you'd want to know—"

"The truth? Those were *my* memories, my life. Who gave you permission to screw with that? Do you know what it's like, not remembering? Like a big, black nothing. You were supposed to fill it. I trusted you." He screwed up his face, like he would have spit on me, if only he could. "I let you tell me what was real. I *believed* you. I gave you that. And you shit all over it."

I didn't mean to hurt you—my father's lame words, on the tip of my tongue. I swallowed them.

"I made a mistake."

This time he caught my hand in mid-reach, his fingers steel around my wrist. "Don't touch me," he said, and let go. "You could tell me anything," he continued. "And I'd have to believe you, right? Maybe you set up Jude. Or both of us, for all I know. Maybe you were working with BioMax the whole time."

"You don't believe that."

"They're your *partners*, right? Your *allies* in the cause?"

My words; his bullets. He was better at this than I would have expected.

And I wasn't allowed to fight back.

"Jude warned me." He shook his head, furious. "He *warned* me not to trust you."

"We both agreed," I said, getting desperate. I had to make him understand. "*You* wanted to stop Jude from hurting anyone. No matter what we had to do."

He wasn't listening. And part of me understood that the denials didn't matter, because he didn't really believe I was conspiring against him. It was the lying he couldn't forgive. And I couldn't deny I'd done that.

"Funny," he said. "All that time you hated Jude, tried to turn me against him, and now he's your new best friend. Maybe that was the plan? Get *me* out of the way?"

"You know that's ridiculous."

"So explain why you lie to me, and trust him."

"I don't! I mean, I *do*. Trust you. Not him. He's nothing."

Riley laughed. "Or maybe you're lying again. Maybe while you've been screwing with me, you've been fucking him."

It was the ugliest thing he'd ever said to me.

He didn't mean it, I told myself.

He didn't.

"Well? You want to deny it?"

"You really want to have this conversation?" I said, patience fraying. "With *your* ex-girlfriend camping out at the foot of your bed?"

"So we're both liars," he said. "I feel so much better now."

I decided not to think too hard about that one, and trust that he meant he'd lied about her being there, not about why.

"We can start over," I said. "No lies. You know everything now."

He stood up. I was losing him.

"You honestly expect me to believe anything you say?"

Maybe I should have begged. Dropped to my knees. Clung to him. I didn't expect it to work, but maybe I should have tried.

I didn't.

We stood there, side by side, watching the water. I waited for him to walk away from me, and wondered how long it would take me to walk home from here. The thought reminded me that I didn't have a home anymore; I only had Riley's bed, and probably I didn't have that anymore either.

"Riley, I—"

"Don't."

Minutes, hours, I don't know. Mech bodies don't get tired; mech legs don't buckle. We could have stood there forever, as if rusted in place. A monument to something dead.

Finally: "I know you didn't mean it."

For a second I let myself hope. But even the anger was better than what was left in its wake. A vacuum. Every word clear, measured—empty.

"But it doesn't matter," he added.

"It has to."

"It doesn't." He finally turned to me. Riley's eyes were deep brown, not the slate gray they'd been when I first knew him. BioMax had done their best to match the new color to the photo I'd given them, but I couldn't imagine that any org would have eyes like this. And certainly no org had the pinprick of amber at the center of the pupil. Like a keyhole. I watched his eyes and imagined I could see something there that said this wasn't over, no matter what he wanted me to believe.

But I was done seeing what I wanted to see.

"It's too hard," Riley said.

"It" meant "us."

"So that's it? Because it's too much *work*?" I shook my head. No. No. *No.* "That's supposed to be my thing, remember? *I* run away when things get tough. *You* stay. I'm the one who likes it easy, who gets everything handed to me—that's what you think, right? You're hard, you're strong, I'm weak. So now who's weak?"

"I'm not weak," Riley said. "I'm tired."

"Of me?" I asked. My voice sounded small, and I hated it.

"Of this."

"Of us."

"Come here," he said, and opened his arms to me.

I wish I could say I turned my back on him. Not because I hated him or because he was wrong, but because it was my turn to be hard. Pride, dignity—invisible things, imaginary things, like the self, like the soul. They distort reality; they get in the way. But they still matter.

I stepped into his arms. I wished I could breathe in the scent of him, that his skin was warm and his chest rose and fell beneath his shirt.

It wasn't supposed to go like this, I thought. We were supposed to be a fairy tale. A cliché of a love story, the princess and the rogue, the lady and the tramp. We had died and come back to life; we were copies who'd found reality in each other. We were machines who'd found love. The circumstances were extraordinary. How could the end be so damn ordinary?

Just another breakup.

Just another broken heart.

If I really wanted him, I would find a way to fix it, I thought.

If I really wanted him, I wouldn't have driven him away.

But as usual I didn't know what I wanted. Other than his arms around me.

I wanted that, but not enough to hold on when he let go. Imaginary dignity, maybe. But it was real the way we stood there, alone together, nothing left to say. It was real when we walked to the car in step, side by side, not touching, and drove away, mature, grown-up. Separate.

This is really happening, I thought. *This is how it ends*. But I didn't say anything. I didn't do anything.

Mechs don't cry.

And there was nothing else left.

PAYBACK

"He likes to pretend he's strong."

So we were civilized about it. No tantrums. No shouting. No one threw anyone else's clothes out the window. We simply went back to Riley's place, and—because Zo and I didn't really have anywhere else to go, and because I could tell Riley had no stomach for throwing us out—we lived like we'd been living before. Except that I spent nights in the bed and Riley stayed on a chair by the door. Sari and Zo kept a wary eye on both of us. I hadn't told Zo exactly what happened, only that Riley and I were done, and that I was fine, he was fine, everything was fine. I didn't know what he'd told Sari. That wasn't my business anymore.

How mature of us, I thought as we sat silently in the apartment, watching the orgs eat, or brainstorming with Jude to figure out what to do next. *How civilized.*

That was civilization, apparently. Playing the part, wearing the smile, keeping your mouth shut. Centuries built on etiquette and deception. You hurt an animal, it hurt you back—no thought, no hesitation, just a snarling beast, a rabid lunge, a bite. We were better than that. We nursed our wounds, circled each other, waited for something to change.

"No reason we can't be friends," Riley had said before we stepped back into the apartment that first time, so different from when we'd left.

I had nodded; I had agreed. And, granted, it had been a while since I'd had a friend. Maybe this was what it was like.

We were arguing for the fifth day in a row. We, the three of us—Jude, Riley, and me. Three dysfunctional musketeers. The apartment had become our war room. We'd been going round in circles for too long—as Jude pointed out, it seemed only likely that BioMax had recorded our intrusion, that they knew what we knew. The longer we waited, the more time they would have to take care of the problem.

But if they knew, why hadn't they already done something to stop us?

Jude wanted to go to the network. Reveal the truth to the masses—though even he had to admit that the masses seemed unlikely to stand behind us, not when BioMax could promise them AI tech beyond their wildest dreams and, with it, luxury, plenitude, security. "It's not even hurting us," Jude said. "Not really."

I couldn't believe it. "Are you kidding me? You didn't see—"

"That's what *they'll* say," Jude cut in. "And if it's not hurting us, what do they care? What do they care either way?"

"We can't go public," Riley said. "Once we do that, we've got nothing left." He didn't look at Jude. If he was carrying any guilt for what had happened at the temple, he didn't show it. If anything Jude was the one who looked guilty. I wondered what Riley had told him about me—and whether they'd talked about all the things he no longer remembered. But I wasn't allowed to ask Riley, and I wasn't about to ask Jude. "Secrets are power. You don't just give them away." Now he did look at Jude—and at me. "I say we go to BioMax. Tell them what we know, and what we want."

Jude perked up. "Blackmail?"

"Reciprocation," I said. Call-me-Ben's term for it.

"BioMax owns us," Jude said. "We piss them off, that could be it. No more repairs, no more replacement bodies . . ."

"Scared?" Riley sounded scornful. "Since when are you afraid to die?"

"I'm just laying out the facts," Jude said.

"Sure."

"For blackmail to work, you need leverage," Jude said.

"We've got files, pics, what else could we need?" Riley asked.

"If *we* know the public won't care, don't you think *they* know it?"

"Then why keep it a secret in the first place?"

"I'm not saying they *want* it public," Jude said. "I'm just suggesting they have a contingency plan. We don't."

"Exactly." Riley turned to me. "We have no other plan. You

want to go to the secops? To the government?" He laughed at his own joke, like there was anyone who wasn't under the thumb of BioMax or one of its allies. "You want to go to the *Brotherhood*?"

"Lia? What do you think?" That was Jude asking, uncharacteristically. And Riley watching, waiting for me to choose the wrong side.

"I think . . . it could work." Lie. BioMax was too big, we were too small, and walking into the lion's den, showing our hand, seemed insane. But I didn't have a better idea. And I didn't want to argue.

"Two against one," Jude said. "Guess that's the plan."

Unless he'd made a miraculous conversion to the democratic process, Jude going along with this meant he believed it was the best way to go—or else he was giving Riley his way as a gift, because for some inexplicable reason he felt indebted. The last time Jude had let loyalty and guilt guide his instincts, Ani had led us straight into an ambush.

"Guess that's the plan," I repeated.

Because, all other things aside, I wanted it to work.

I voiced Kiri, requesting the meeting. I said I had something important to discuss, that she should bring call-me-Ben, call-me-Ben's boss, anyone who had decision-making power at the corp. Anyone who wasn't my father. Kiri agreed to set it up, and I cut the link, wondering if she knew.

I spent the morning before the meeting at the waterfall. It should have been a toxic zone for me, but somehow that day with Riley had purged it of the past, and it was just a waterfall again. I sat on the edge of a wide, flat rock, dangling my feet in the water and shrouding myself in the thunder of the falls, white noise that drowned my capacity for rational thought. I burrowed into myself—or maybe it was the opposite; maybe I was climbing *out* of my skin. Fusing somehow with the rock and the trees and the open sky. Time ticked by, and I let myself forget what I was waiting for. Until it arrived.

Zo insisted on accompanying me to the corp headquarters—to wait outside, she said, just in case. I let her. When we arrived, I discovered I wasn't the only one who'd brought moral support. Riley was already there—with Sari. I gave him a thin smile and ignored the barnacle. Zo followed suit. But Jude, when he showed up a few minutes later, took a different tack. "What's with the skank?"

She had an arm around Riley but kept her eyes on me, smiling, and I knew the pose was for my benefit. *He's mine now,* that arm said. *He may not know it yet, but I do, and now you do.*

"She'll wait outside," Riley said.

Jude scowled. "She doesn't belong here."

"You want to kick out the orgs, why don't you start with her?" Riley nodded at Zo.

"It's not because she's an org," Jude said. "And you know it."

"I brought her. She stays." Riley leaned in and whispered something in her ear.

Was he doing it to hurt me? The thought was nearly unbearable. But not as bad as the alternative. That he'd brought her because he wanted her here. "Let's go," I said.

Sari gave him a quick hug, and a kiss on the cheek. "For luck," she chirped.

Zo caught my eye and blew me a kiss. "For luck," she said, a drop too sweetly.

At least I wouldn't have to worry about leaving Zo out here alone with Sari. My little sister could fend for herself.

I'd been in the conference room before, the one reserved for very rare face-to-face meetings of the top BioMax executives and their favorite cronies. And I had met M. Poulet before, the chief operating officer, the highest ranking BioMax figure willing to show his face to the public, though it was a poorly kept secret that every corp kept its ultimate rulers hidden. For our purposes Poulet *was* BioMax, and despite the fact that he was built like a walrus, with a mustache to match, I'd never seen anyone face him with anything less than poorly disguised terror. Jude, Riley, and I sat on one side of the long table; Kiri, call-me-Ben, and M. Poulet sat on the other. Three of us—three of them. It didn't feel like an even match.

"Here's what we know," I began. It had been surprisingly easy to convince Jude that I should be the one to speak. No doubt because I'd make a convenient scapegoat when we failed. I doubted any of us had much hope that this was going to work. But I didn't let it show.

I projected the basics onto the ViM embedded in the conference table. Files popped up, and photos of the corridors we'd seen. This was it, I thought. There was no more hiding now, and no more pretending to buy the crap that BioMax was selling. Which meant they wouldn't have to pretend either. If this body broke, they were the only ones who could fix it, or replace it.

But that mattered only if I let myself care.

"You're stealing downloaded neural patterns, lobotomizing them, and turning them into cyber slaves."

I waited for them to deny it.

Call-me-Ben shifted in his seat—that familiar org weakness, the inability to keep his feelings, his guilt, his surprise, to himself. But the other man, M. Poulet, didn't move. His gray, stony face betrayed nothing. It was Kiri who reacted, pivoting between the two of them, obviously waiting for a denial of her own. She didn't get it.

"This is true?" she exclaimed, rising to her feet. "You're actually doing this?"

"*We're* doing this," M. Poulet said calmly. "Or have you forgotten who deposits the credit in your accounts?"

"No," Kiri said, "I didn't sign on for this. Lia, trust me, I didn't know."

I was concentrating on keeping my own reactions under wraps. So I couldn't admit I believed her—and I couldn't reveal my relief.

M. Poulet looked at her like she was exuding a bad smell. "If our discussion is making you uncomfortable, you're perfectly free to go. You can drop off your security credentials on the way out."

I didn't expect her to actually *go*. I appreciated the moral outrage, just not as much as I would have appreciated the moral support. She didn't ask my opinion. Her chair scraped back, the door slammed, and then she was gone. Call-me-Ben looked perturbed; M. Poulet looked bored. "Can we get back on track, please? We're well aware of your hijinks at our recent event, and your intrusion into private property. But we're willing to overlook it. Keep it between us, as it were."

"Private property?" Jude said angrily. I hoped it was for show, because if his *real* emotions were bleeding through, then he'd been thrown more off balance than I thought. "You want to talk about *private property*? How about the theft and destruction of *our* private property? Are we supposed to *overlook* that? *While you kill us off one by one?*"

"We're doing nothing of the sort," M. Poulet said, indignant.

"You're stealing copies of our brains," I said quietly, before Jude could fire back. "And then you're stripping them. There are *people* in those machines. Don't you get that?"

"They're *not* people." It was the first time Ben had spoken. He leaned toward me, elbows on the table, his best earnest expression fixed on his face. "That's what you've got to understand. Without the crucial subroutines that control emotion, memory, all the things that make a personality, these are nothing but arrays of electronic data. There's no consciousness."

"How do you know? What if they can still think? Or feel?"

"They can't. They're machines, computers. Nothing more."

"Did you join the Brotherhood while I wasn't looking?" I snarled. "Because your Savona impression is awesome."

"This technology is a miracle," Ben said, eyes shining. "It's brought you—all of you—back from the dead. And that's only the *beginning*. We're talking about the fusion of man and machine—the possibilities of this technology are limitless."

He didn't have much future as an evangelist. Though even Rai Savona lacked the rhetorical prowess to gloss this over.

"We're not technology. We're people."

"*You're* people, yes—but we're not talking about you. How does it hurt you to donate a copy of your brain to a good cause? How does it change anything to know that a copy of some of your synapses is helping protect the nation or heal the sick? How does that do anything to you, except perhaps make you proud?"

"Funny," Riley said softly. "Almost sounds like we volunteered."

"If this is such a wonderful advance for orgs and mechs alike," I said, "then why keep it a secret?"

"You see how *you've* reacted," Ben pointed out. "We needed to ease the way. Help people understand. Once they do—"

"Enough," M. Poulet cut in. "We don't have to defend ourselves to . . ." He flicked a hand at us. "These." He stood up and pushed in his chair, as if to say, *Meeting's over*. "I would think that with popular opinion of you and your kind at such alarmingly low levels, you'd have better things to worry about than trivia like this. I'd suggest you focus on the bigger picture here."

"Trivia like you turning us into war machines?" I said, disgusted.

"Lia, enough," Jude said. "They obviously didn't come here to reason with us, and we didn't come here to reason with them."

"Ah, finally," M. Poulet said. "We get down to it."

Jude stood up too. A beat later Riley and I joined him on our feet. Only Ben stayed seated, looking bewildered about how the meeting had slipped out of his control. "You're going to stop this," Jude said. "Stop abusing the stored copies. Stop experimenting on us like we're animals. And then you're going to give *us* the means to store our own uploads, and to repair and replace our own bodies. You're going to set us free."

"I assume there's an implied *or*?" M. Poulet asked dryly.

"Or we go public," Jude said. "And it doesn't matter what you try to do to us here—there are people waiting for my signal. If they don't hear from me in the next hour, they're going to release everything we have on the network. You're done."

It was no bluff. Zo was waiting.

"*Do* to you?" M. Poulet sounded like he was holding back laughter. "What exactly would we *do* to you?"

"What wouldn't you do?" Jude said.

Now the peals of laughter burst through, cold and hollow. "I don't know what kind of gangsters you children are used to dealing with, but this is a business. You come in here, wasting our time, making your petty little threats, acting as if we could ever have something to fear from *you*." As he spoke, the joviality drained from his voice, until all that remained was steel. "Let me be perfectly clear: We have *nothing* to fear from you. You're children—not even that: mechanical copies of children. While *we* are a multinational corporation offering the world a new and exciting technology that will improve the lives of millions. You think anyone's going to repudiate that because we're 'inconveniencing' a few skinners?" He smiled coldly. "And you're assuming that releasing information on the network is your right, rather than a privilege you're accorded by the corps who sponsor the zones. You're assuming that BioMax has neither the power, the technology, nor the will to scrub the network—every inch of it—of any inconvenient allegations."

They couldn't. The network was teeming with billions of zones; it was a sprawling kingdom several times more populous than the flesh-and-blood world. It would take a massively sophisticated search-and-destroy algorithm, not to mention ridiculous computational power, to scrub our posts before they leached into the fabric of the network. Not to mention the fact that zones were supposed to be impregnable. Everyone knew there were hackers, and even the best news zones fell prey almost daily to prank posts and attacks, but the whole point of the network was supposed to be the accessibility of information, the impossibility of locking up any truth that wanted to be free. Thousands of potential truths jockeying with one another for supremacy, maybe, but that was supposed to be the democracy of modern life, the freedom to choose our own reality. The freedom to *know.*

Then again, maybe it was time I stopped relying on *supposed-to-be*s.

"What could you possibly be thinking right now?" M. Poulet said, clucking his tongue with fake sympathy. "Perhaps you're wondering where else to turn. Surely *someone* can help you, am I right?" He leaned across the table and skimmed his hand across the screen, bringing it back to life. "Him, perhaps?"

The Japanese man who appeared on the screen was someone I'd never seen before. He looked to be about my father's age and wore a neatly tailored suit with no visible tech, but his red pupils indicated this was no Luddite. I'd seen a prototype of the same lenses at a recent BioMax show-and-tell—they were some kind of artificial cybernetic implant that, among other things, allowed their recipient to process and index visual stimuli as if they were text in a network database. So while I was a stranger to him, his glancing at my face would trigger an automatic network search that would, within seconds, relay to his neural implants anything he wanted to know about Lia Kahn.

But he wasn't looking at me. Neither was M. Poulet. They both had their eyes fixed on Jude. The Japanese man smiled and offered him a shallow bow.

"I think you know M. Sani," M. Poulet said. "Go ahead, congratulate him. Just this morning he and I put the finishing touches on a partnership that will enrich both our companies, not to mention all who benefit from our technological innovation."

Jude just stared.

"I suppose we owe it partially to you," M. Poulet said. "BioMax and Aikida have been rivals for far too long. *You* helped us both see that our interests lay in cooperation, rather than competition."

Finally, I understood why Jude looked like he was about to fall over. We hadn't just been outplayed. We'd been laughed off the field.

"We had a deal," Jude growled.

"And now we've made a better one," M. Poulet said.

"It will be a great endeavor," M. Sani added, enunciating crisply to make up for his slight accent. "We are all looking forward to it."

M. Poulet gave the screen a bow, and it went dark. "Not all of us, I assume," he said to Jude.

Jude didn't say anything. None of us did.

"Surely you didn't think we'd actually let you follow through with your pathetic little plot," M. Poulet added. "You'd do well—all of you—to remember that we're in control here. Surely, Lia, at least you understand how much control we have. And what we can do."

I suddenly understood. *This is the man who sentenced me to death.* He was practically bragging about it. So disgustingly certain that there was nothing we could do to him.

Maybe he was right.

"Will that be all?" M. Poulet concluded. "Because if so, I have some actual business to attend to today."

Call-me-Ben cleared his throat. "Lia, if you and your friends would like to discuss this further—"

"I think they've wasted enough of our time today," Poulet snapped. "We've *both* got busy days ahead of us."

His meaning couldn't have been clearer if he'd fitted Ben with a leash and muzzle.

"My assistant can show you out," Ben said, cowed. Pathetic. Though no more so than we were.

"We can find our own way," Jude said.

"Oh, I think it'll be best for you to have an escort," M. Poulet said. "Don't you? Wouldn't want you wandering off and getting lost on our property again, now, would we?"

So we lost even that battle. We followed Ben's assistant, not speaking, avoiding one another's eyes. We did as we were told.

• • •

We retreated to the outer edge of the parking lot, which was nearly empty but for our two cars. It must have been obvious from our expressions how the meeting went, because neither Zo nor Sari asked. They just watched us warily, waiting for someone to make a move.

"Assholes," I finally said.

Jude snorted. "Can we skip the ritualistic licking of wounds?"

"Right, no point in dwelling on past mistakes," Riley said. "Especially when they're yours."

"Mine? This was your idea."

"My idea to go, yours to talk—and talk, and talk, and talk, and say nothing. As usual. And then there's Aikida." He shook his head. "You're some master strategist."

It took me a second to identify the expression on Jude's face, as I'd never seen it there before: humiliation. And almost as soon as I caught on, it faded away, replaced by pure anger.

Sari draped herself over Riley, her head on his shoulder. "Is anyone going to tell me what happened?"

"What do you care?" Jude spit out. "What the hell are you even doing here?"

"Leave her alone," Riley said.

Jude scowled at Sari. "She's a big girl. Let her defend herself."

"She shouldn't have to."

"And Lia shouldn't have to deal with this crap," Jude said. "But you bring *that* here and rub it in her face. Nice."

"Can we not do this?" I said.

"She's none of your business," Riley warned him.

Jude smirked. "Which *she* are we talking about?"

"Jude, don't." Knowing as I spoke that it wouldn't do any good. "We're all a little tense after—"

"Let him talk," Riley said, loudly.

"Oh, I really don't think you want that," Jude said.

"Try me."

"What should we talk about, Riley? The way you turned me in to the secops? Tried to blame it on *her*?"

"I did not," Riley insisted.

Jude laughed. "Not out loud. But I know how you think, remember? There's always an excuse. She talked you into it; she lied to you. So you throw her away instead of just sucking it up and accepting what you did."

"You don't know what you're talking about," Riley growled.

Jude wouldn't stop. "You ran away when she needed you. Why am I not surprised?"

I didn't need him standing up for me, especially when he was only doing it because he was spoiling for a fight. "Jude, shut up."

"Always on her side these days, aren't you?" Riley said, a nasty edge to his voice.

Sari tugged at his arm. "Forget them. Let's just go."

That was my job—had been my job—the peacemaker, the conciliator, the one who would stand between Riley and the wrong choice, and try to turn him the other way. Now there was nothing I could do but watch as he shrugged her off and finished what he'd started.

"He's the one that should go."

"Where do you get off?" Jude asked. "You should be on your *knees*, begging me for forgiveness."

"Yeah, that's how you like it, right? I crawl around after you, begging. When's it going to be enough?"

"I never blamed you."

"Not out loud." Riley threw his words back at him. "But I know how you think, *remember*? Nothing's ever enough." With every word he took a step closer to Jude, until they were only inches apart. Riley, his body built to its original specifications, was several inches taller, but it wasn't just that. He was *bigger*, his shoulders broad, his muscles straining against his shirt. Jude's lanky, angular form had always seemed like a reflection of his power, all sharp edges and stealthy grace. But next to Riley he suddenly looked small.

"What are they talking about?" Zo asked in a low voice. Not low enough.

"They're talking about the past," Riley said loudly. "They're *always* talking about the past." He poked Jude in the chest, hard enough that Jude stumbled backward. "Right?"

Jude shook his head.

"Everyone else's past is irrelevant," Riley said. "But not mine." He turned to Zo. "Because I hid."

I couldn't believe he was about to say it out loud, here. "When they came for me, I hid, and I let them have Jude. Isn't that right?" He turned back to Jude now, face ugly with anger. "They broke you, while I watched. And you never let me forget it."

Jude shook his head again, harder this time. "We were kids," he said. "I got over it."

"Got over it?" Riley laughed. "Got over being stuck in that chair, letting me wheel you around, letting me feed you, clean up your shit?"

When Jude spoke, we could barely hear him. "Because we were friends."

"Because I felt *sorry* for you. I kept thinking, if I do this one more thing, we'll finally be even. I'll be free."

"You're lying."

"I did everything you said, didn't I? Followed every order. Wasn't for me, you'd have rolled into a gutter and died a long time ago, and it's *still not enough.*"

"Don't do this." Jude said it in a strangled voice. That was the moment I understood what I think he'd understood the whole time. Riley was doing it on purpose. Digging his fingers into the wound. Anything to make Jude lash out.

Because he thinks he deserves it? I wondered. *Or because he wants an excuse to hit back?*

"He likes to pretend he's strong," Riley said, nearly

shouting now, his voice rising as Jude's dropped. "He pretends he's tough, he's in control . . . what a joke. You think a new body changes anything? You think just because you've got your pretty little legs and pretty little face that anything is different? Nothing is different. You're still that sad little boy, all twisted up and useless."

"Riley, please—"

"You're still *weak*."

Jude's fist landed squarely between Riley's cheek and jaw. Riley's head snapped back, but he didn't even sway on his feet.

Jude didn't swing again. Instead, he looked back and forth between his fist and Riley's unmarked face, as if he couldn't believe what he'd done—as if, because there would be no bruise and no blood, nothing to prove it had really happened, maybe it hadn't.

So he didn't see it coming: Riley's arm, Riley's fist, the full force of Riley's rage. Jude stumbled with the impact, and then with the next, and the next—until his own fists rose, as if of their own accord, and he finally began to fight back.

I'd been a target before, experienced sharp knuckles jabbing into my flesh and boots kicking my stomach, had my arms twisted back; I'd tucked into a ball, protected my soft places, soaked in the pain—I'd felt it all but had never *watched* it before, not for real. Never stood on the sidelines as two people tried to tear each other apart—and because in this case the people were mechs, they were having to work all the harder, clawing at flesh so slow to tear, bashing noses that refused to bleed, bones too hard to break. It was different from the fake fights intended to please a vidlife audience; it was wild.

There were no clean punches; there was no delicate dancing around each other like boxers in a ring. They were on each other, arms gripping necks and waists, and then they were rolling on the ground, a cloud of grunts and snarls and thuds—and sometimes a *crack* as a head slammed into the pavement.

All that in seconds, and even as I was watching, I was moving, my legs as autonomous as their fists, no longer in my control. I was moving toward them, I was shouting "Stop! Please! Stop!" and my hands were on someone's shoulders, someone's waist, tugging uselessly, and then someone's elbow caught my jaw and I was flying backward and I was on the ground.

They didn't stop. They didn't notice.

When the ringing stopped and my vision cleared, Zo was by my side. Saying something about sitting down, but I stood up, wondering whose elbow it had been.

Stood up, but stayed where I was. Not because I was afraid, but because I wasn't stupid. I couldn't stop them, and they couldn't hurt each other, not really. None of us could hurt each other anymore.

It lasted longer than it would have if they were orgs, but it couldn't have lasted as long as it felt. And then Jude was on his back, arms splayed, done. Riley knelt over him, fist drawn back.

"Go ahead," Jude urged him. Jagged gashes laced his skin,

and his fingers jutted at angles fingers weren't supposed to. Strange to see so much damage and yet no blood. No repercussions. "Finish it."

And for a moment I thought he was going to. But then Riley dropped his fist. His shoulders slumped, and he stood up.

"Finish it!" Jude shouted. He raised himself a few inches off the concrete, then dropped back again.

Crack.

"I am finished," Riley said. He held out a hand, but not to Jude. For a moment I wondered if he was holding it out for me—wondered if I would take it, if it was offered—but then Sari stepped in and wrapped her fingers in his, and they walked away together.

"Wait," I said.

"Don't go," I said.

Even though he was already gone. I was working on delayed reaction; I was frozen.

Zo was saying something to me, but I couldn't hear it, or didn't want to, not if it would distract me from staring at the space Riley had left behind. I wouldn't listen to Zo, but I let her take my hand and deposit me carefully on the curb. And then I watched her kneel beside Jude, her knees resting where Riley's had been. Her hand brushed the hair from his forehead, with a gentleness I didn't know she had. She spoke his name, once, twice, then—getting no response—bent her head to his chest. Listening.

"No heartbeat," Jude said. She flinched, and jerked backward. "But I appreciate the thought."

Zo helped him to his feet and led him, silent and dazed, to the curb. Then sat him down next to me and joined him on the other side.

"You okay?" I said.

He turned his head to look at me, then turned away. I didn't know if it was disgust for the question, or the closest he was willing to get to shaking his head. *No.*

I rested a hand on his shoulder, lightly, thinking, *This is wrong; he's not the one I should be comforting; this isn't my job.*

But the one I should have been comforting was gone. Still, I took my hand away.

Jude didn't move. He mumbled something.

"What?"

"He said he shouldn't have started it," Zo said.

"You didn't start it."

"I start everything."

"What happened in there?" Zo nodded at BioMax. "Why was he so angry?"

There was a long pause, long enough that I thought Jude wasn't going to answer. "It wasn't about what happened in there."

"Was he right?" I asked. "Have you been holding it over his head all this time?"

"It took about thirty seconds for you to start accusing me of things," Jude snapped. "That's a new record."

"I'm not—" But I was. "Maybe if you'd bothered to talk to him, rather than letting him feel guilty so that you could use him—"

"We talked," Jude said. "Yesterday."

"About what?"

"Things."

"What things?"

He raised his head and turned to me again, golden eyes blazing. "*You*, for one. Want to know what he had to say? What *I* had to say?"

My mouth opened, but nothing came out. I didn't even know what I was afraid of.

Even his smile looked broken. "Didn't think so."

"I'd like to hear," Zo put in.

That got a more authentic smile, but not a response. "It doesn't matter," he told me. "This was going to happen eventually. It had to."

"You're pathetic," I said. "Both of you. This *had* to happen? Like this was some kind of manly rite you both had to go through? A *guy* thing?"

"You wouldn't understand."

"Right. Because I'm *sane*, and I don't go around punching out my best friends."

"Maybe because you don't have any."

"Screw you." I jerked my head at Zo. "Let's go. We're out of here."

Zo didn't move. "I don't think we should leave him like this. . . ."

She may have been right, but I didn't care. "He'll be fine; won't you?"

"I'm always fine," Jude said.

"See?"

Zo didn't respond. She wasn't even looking at me—she was looking past me with an exaggerated expression of horror.

"Nice try. What is it this time, monster behind my back?"

"Worse," Zo muttered.

Of course, I thought. What else could make this perfect day complete? What else could make Zo tremble?

"Girls," our father said. "Is this a bad time?"

GONE

He would be broken, like I was broken.

"Can we go somewhere more private?" my father asked.

Zo and I spoke at the same time. "No."

He lasered a look at Jude. "Then perhaps your friend here would be willing to leave us?"

"No," we said again.

My father sighed. "I don't think it's appropriate to do this in front of strangers."

"Funny how I don't care," I said.

Jude shifted his weight, as if preparing to rise. "I can go."

"No." My hand clamped down on his arm, holding him in place. "You're not leaving. He is."

"Not until you hear what I have to say."

"So say," I told him. "Then go."

"I didn't know you were going to be here, Zoie," he said.

Zo let her hair fall across her face. "Don't talk to me," she said. "If she wants to let you talk to her, fine. But don't talk to me." She retreated to a spot on the curb several feet away, dragging Jude with her. They sat down together, close enough that they could still hear us, far enough to make very clear that she wouldn't be participating in any rituals of apology and forgiveness.

My father sighed again, theatrically, like we were supposed to feel sorry for him and his grand, exhausting efforts. *Why can't I just punch him?* I wondered. It would be so simple, curling my hand into a fist, forcing it into his jaw, wrestling him to the ground. In the end it was nothing but physics, controlling the electronic synapses that would set the limbs in motion, calculating the appropriate speed and angle of impact. *I could hurt him,* as Riley had hurt Jude. It had been easy enough for them to go from words to actions. So why couldn't I?

"Are you wondering how I knew you were here?" he asked.

"You're on the board," I said, glancing at the BioMax building. "You know what they know."

He got the implication. "I didn't know what they were doing," he said. "I never would have allowed it."

"Because you have *so* much power over them."

My father believed sarcasm was the refuge of the weak-minded, those incapable of meeting an argument head-on. He ignored it.

"Now that I do know, I'll—"

"Put up a fight? Careful, Dad. You're running out of daughters."

He cleared his throat. "Your mother is worried about you. Both of you."

"Is she still living with you?" I said.

"Of course."

"Then she can't be too worried."

"Lia . . ."

"Don't say that."

"What?"

"My name." He'd given me that name, after his dead grandmother. It meant "bringer of truth." But when he said it, it meant *I created you. I named you. I own you.*

"I'm not going to beg, Lia. I'm sorry—deeply sorry. You will never know how much. I recognize how difficult it is to forgive, how much strength it takes—"

"So I'm weak?"

"I can see this is useless," he said. "I shouldn't have come."

"Now we agree."

"I don't know what more I can say. I'll do whatever I can to make this up to you, Lia, but I'm not going to beg. I have my limits. I'll always be here, when you change your mind," he said, like it was a foregone conclusion I would. He'd always been this condescending, I realized. I'd just been too oblivious to notice or too desperate for his approval to care.

He walked away.

He had limits, all right. Limits on his capacity to be human, much less a *father*. I believed he was sorry. I believed he truly wanted me to forgive him. He just didn't want it as much as he wanted to preserve his pride. If he actually loved me, he wouldn't hesitate to beg. He wouldn't give up so easily. He wouldn't stand there so stiff and proud. He would be broken, like I was broken.

He wouldn't have walked away.

"He doesn't even want my forgiveness," Zo said, sad and small on the other side of Jude.

"Would he have gotten it?" Jude asked.

But Zo was in her own world; I could hear it in her voice. Jude didn't exist for her right now. Neither did I.

"He didn't want it," she said, sounding distant. "He didn't even ask."

There was nowhere to go. We let the car drive us in circles while we sat quietly, facing away from one another, staring out the window or, in my case, at our reflection. Zo broke the silence. "You know what I like about you being a mech?" she asked, then answered her own question. "It's a lot quieter. You don't do that annoying mouth-breathing thing anymore."

"What?"

"You were a total mouth breather, and it was really heavy sometimes, like—" She sucked in and blew out loud lungfuls of air to demonstrate.

"Did not!"

Jude laughed. It was quiet, and it was over almost as soon as it began, but it was something.

He turned away from the window. "What other charming habits have you been keeping from me?" he asked, a pale imitation of his formerly smug self.

Zo took the opportunity to begin cataloging the many offenses I'd committed against her over the years: the bathroom hogging, the finger tapping, the throat clearing—and what could I do but jump in with a list of my own? Running out of those, we soon found ourselves drifting into a debate over the merits—or lack thereof—of my former friends and, inevitably, Walker, our shared boyfriend, as Jude egged us on. For a moment things seemed almost normal, Zo slipping seamlessly into the annoying tagalong role she'd played back when all she'd wanted was permission to follow me around, and Jude, plainly enjoying the swapping of sisterly grievances, switching his allegiance minute by minute, the better to keep the banter going. But joking about Walker, his stubble, his breath, his brain, which seemed capable of understanding only one rudimentary concept at a time, was a little too much—less because it was weird to be dishing on a guy who'd logged time in both of our beds, more because thinking about Walker made me think about the one who'd followed him, and I wasn't ready to think about Riley yet.

I fell silent. They didn't push it; they changed the subject. It was strange, I thought, barely listening to their debate over some celebrity gossip Zo had seen on a stalker zone, the way three people who'd spent so much time hating one another could function so seamlessly as a unit, understanding the things that weren't said, knowing what to ignore and what to pretend so we could all make it through the ride to nowhere. There was even a moment, Zo teasing Jude about knowing something he shouldn't have unless he'd been secretly perusing the stalker zone himself, when it didn't feel like we were pretending at all. It felt like maybe normal was within reach again, somewhere on the other side of all our disasters.

That was the moment, that first glimmer of inexplicable hope, when Sari's text came in, priority level high:

Come home

Something wrong with Riley

The apartment was cleaned out. Sari's stuff—which had been splayed over the furniture and floor—was gone. Along with mine and Zo's. The small pile of possessions we'd amassed since abandoning Casa Kahn was nowhere in sight.

Sari was gone too.

You notice the strangest things, the most trivial details, when everything's falling apart.

Your eye takes in everything, too much: the fecal brown of the walls, the play of light across the windows, the sounds puncturing the silence, a gasp, a shriek, and an empty hole where your voice should be, but you have no words.

You have no words and you have no volition as your legs

carry you to a body sprawled on the floor, facedown, arms crooked, everything still.

And, finally, you find your scream. "Riley!"

I was on my knees, cradling his head, the day repeating itself with different players. He lay motionless, eyes closed. His uplink jack lay beside him, like he'd been holding it when he fell. Sari had left him like this. Helpless.

"Riley!" I screamed again, thinking, hoping, that maybe, for whatever reason, he'd shut down for the night on the floor instead of the bed; that if I yelled loud enough, if I turned him over and slapped his face and shook him, then he would open his eyes. But if he'd just shut down, the first scream would have woken him. There was no such thing as mech deep sleep. There were just two basic options: On.

Off.

Zo tried to pull me away, but I elbowed her backward. Déjà vu. Like no matter how we started, someone would end up on the ground, someone would get pushed away, someone would be on her knees, desperate.

But Jude was stronger. He took my arm and yanked me to my feet.

I slapped him, harder than I'd hit Riley, harder than I'd hit anyone. "What did you do to him?"

"What? I was with you all day!"

"You must have done something, when you fought—broke something, you must have—"

"Lia. *Stop.*" He grabbed my shoulders, held them steady, so much stronger than me, hung on no matter how hard I thrashed. He waited for me to stop, to face him—and eventually, there was no other choice. The only sound in the apartment was Zo's uneven breathing.

"I'm calm," I said, trying to sound it. "Let go."

He did.

I was calm, and I would force myself to stay that way, until I got Riley whatever help he needed. Then I would figure out who to blame.

It was the last place any of us wanted to go, but there was nowhere else.

We loaded Riley into the car. Gently, although there was no need to be gentle. I tried not to wonder whether he was awake in there, if he knew what was happening. I lifted his eyelid, not sure what I expected to find. All mechs had a glimmer of gold at the center of each pupil. Riley's had gone black.

That means nothing, I thought, as we sped toward BioMax and tried not to worry about what they would do when we arrived. What else could they do after everything that had happened but punish us—punish *him*. I was certain they'd turn us away.

They didn't.

This has happened before, I thought, as we waited in a cramped hallway while the techs worked on him, and I tried to forget what was happening three or four floors below us, machines with our minds and our memories following orders, obeying commands.

What was the last thing I said to him? I thought, and hated myself for not remembering, because the truth was I hadn't said anything; I had watched Riley and Jude break each other, and then I had watched Riley leave. No comment.

I didn't understand why they were helping us, and when the tech emerged from his little room, apology fixed on his face, I waited for him to tell us it had been a mistake, word had come down from on high that Riley was not to be touched.

I couldn't look at the guy's face.

They had tossed three flimsy chairs into the hall for us, and we sat while the tech stood. There was no confusion about who was in charge.

"We've done everything we can think of," the tech said, "but we've had no success waking him up. I've never seen damage like this before. The neural matrix is completely fried."

He said it like he was talking about a damaged exhaust pipe on a used car.

"I was afraid of that," Jude said. "So how long's it going to take to get another body? Or can you reuse this one?"

The tech swallowed hard. "Someone's coming down to talk to you about that."

"Why don't *you* talk to us about it?" Jude said, an edge to his voice.

"I'm not really qualified to—"

"What's wrong?" I said. "Tell us. We can handle it."

Lie.

The guy laid it out in a flat, toneless voice. "This has never happened to us before. The servers are supposed to be incorruptible. But . . ."

"But what?" That was Jude, and I wanted to press a hand over his mouth, because if the tech didn't say it, it couldn't be real.

"But the files have been corrupted. Something must have happened during the uploading process, some kind of bug; we don't know yet. Whatever fried his neural matrix also destroyed his backup copy on the network server. It's been completely deleted."

Deleted.

Not dead.

Not gone.

Delete. Verb, meaning: to eradicate, obliterate, wipe away.

To expunge. To remove.

To erase.

It had been erased.

It, the file, the ones and zeros that had comprised a life.

The world narrowed and slowed, until there was no one but the tech, nothing but his bulbous face, his chapped lips curled up in a sickly smile, like if he pretended it was okay, we would all follow suit, and go happily on our way. I tried.

Tried to focus on the bald patch just above his left ear, the scar slicing through one of his eyebrows, which must have been some kind of vanity mark, as all scars were these days, but it didn't make him look dangerous, just defective. *Bad call*, I thought, and tried to feel sorry for him, but I couldn't feel anything.

Then, suddenly, I understood. This was just another game, more leverage, jostling for position. Corporate make-believe. "You're lying," I said. A deep calm radiated through me. "Riley's fine."

Jude's eyes were open and unseeing. He lowered his head. Zo laid her hand on top of his, and he let it sit there, like he couldn't be bothered to care.

"Don't you get it?" I asked him, almost giddy. "It's a trick. To shut us up." I laughed. "How stupid do we look?"

"Why would I want to shut you up?" the tech asked, confused.

"Not you," I said. "Them."

He was obviously getting nervous—which meant I was onto something.

He cleared his throat. "Maybe you didn't understand—"

"We understood," Jude said dully.

"No, *I* understood," I said. "You're giving up."

"Lia, it's not a trick."

"How do you know?" I asked, hating him. He'd always believed there were no limits to what orgs would do—but he'd chosen now to believe what he was told? Now, when it made no sense? Why couldn't he just believe *me*?

"He's not gone," I said. Mechs lived forever, from one body to another, one copy to another. It was what separated us from the orgs; it was our defining, constitutive quality.

Machines cannot die.

"Let her see him," Jude said.

The tech shook his head. "We don't—"

"Please."

"Fine," the tech muttered, and opened the door for me. "I am sorry."

The door closed, and I was alone in the room. Riley was still, stretched out on a long metal table. Not Riley, not anymore. A body. Its eyes were open. Its face was slack.

I didn't know what I was supposed to do. Cradle his body in my arms. Press my lips to his. Brush his hair off his face. Stand by his side and hold his hand.

But I didn't do any of it. Not because I didn't want to, or because I feared he wouldn't want me to, but because he wasn't there anymore. Maybe I'd known when I had first seen the body lying on the floor. And if he could be erased so easily from the body, it was all too easy to imagine he'd been erased from everything else.

That the body was just a body. Would always be just a body.

That he was gone.

EMPTY

If there were no consequences, it was almost like it hadn't happened.

Of course it was call-me-Ben who came in and found me on the floor, back against the wall, knees pulled up to my chest. It was always Ben, delivering the bad news, delivering the truth, delivering me from evil, Ben, who fashioned himself my savior and all the while, I knew now, was only saving me so I could save him and BioMax, use my face to sell their story, and sell myself out with every word.

I didn't fight him.

I searched myself, tried to find that certainty I'd had, that it was all lies, a game, that Riley was coming back—but it had slipped away. Truth or lie, the end result was the same: He was gone.

Somehow, I left the room and left the body behind. Small things registered: the pressure of Ben's fingers on my arm, Zo's strained grimace, Jude's blank gaze. Nothing mattered.

Then, somehow, we were in a conference room: Jude, me, my sister, call-me-Ben. Again I had to shrug off the strange sensation that the day was repeating itself, rearranging itself with different places and different players. Jude was like a zombie. Zo told him when to walk, when to talk, pushed him into a chair. I couldn't look at him, because Jude was unthinkable without Riley, as—no matter how much I'd tried to deny it—Riley was unthinkable without Jude.

"How does this happen?" I asked Ben. Thinking, *You did this. We stepped out of line, and you punished us.*

Ben held out his hands, encompassing his explanation between them: empty air. "We don't know. I'm so sorry. This has never— We've been caught unawares here, all of us. But I can assure you there's no need for you to worry—if this was a problem with our software, we would have caught it much earlier than this. No, this had to be some kind of external stimulus."

"Someone did this to him," I translated.

"That's our thought, yes."

"Someone like you."

He literally convulsed at the suggestion, his eyebrows flying up as his mouth twisted down and his hands fluttered. Every time I saw him, Ben seemed less and less the preternaturally cool and collected mannequin I'd once known and loathed. His slimy self-assurance had been an almost reassuring constant. I needed it now, something to hate, something steady and immovable to push back against.

"Industrial sabotage," he said.

"No. You did this. To shut us up, to punish us, I don't know. Why don't you just admit it? Why *pretend* you were trying to help him?"

"I'm not pretending. BioMax has an obligation—*I* have an obligation—to honor our contracts with our clients. To help them when they come to us. Doctors don't heal just the people they like."

"You're no doctor."

"Still. What happened in the boardroom has nothing to do with what happens in here. Can you understand that?"

I didn't know who we were pretending that it mattered what I thought. As if I had any power. I had nothing.

"And you know very well that certain factions have been researching this kind of disruption for quite a while now," he continued, when I didn't respond. "If they've succeeded . . ."

I glanced at Jude, certain his eyes were burning through me. But his head was down, his eyes on the table. Maybe he hadn't even heard.

Yes, this could have been BioMax striking back against us after we'd had the asinine temerity to show our hand and try to force theirs. But it didn't make sense—Riley had never been the biggest threat to them; they'd made that very clear in their pursuit of Jude, not to mention their cultivation of me. Shutting him up wouldn't do anything but inflame us, make us more determined to do . . . whatever it was they thought we had the power to do. If they wanted to stop us, there were easier ways.

And, as call-me-Ben said, they weren't the only ones who hated us. I'd seen the lab with my own eyes, the Brotherhood's attempt to find a way to destroy us. To corrupt not just our brains but the brains stored on the servers; to take care of us—to *delete* us—once and for all. It was why Jude had been so determined to blow the place up, with its researchers inside.

But Riley and I had saved the researchers, saved Savona and his scientists, set them free.

I had set them free.

Don't think about it.

"You still aren't telling me how it could have happened," I said. "Or even exactly *what* happened."

"Think of it as a virus. Something must have been done to his uplink jack. He was clearly in the middle of the process when it happened, and it's the best explanation we can come up with for how the stored files would also have been corrupted."

"You're saying this isn't random—someone went after *him*, specifically?"

"Looks like it. The uplinker was most likely sabotaged. The network servers are completely inaccessible, so the damage must have been done on his end. Probably someone close to him, with access to his possessions, someone he trusted. Can you think of any—"

Jude's chair clattered to the floor. He was on his feet, fists clenched, and then he was out of the room, his footsteps echoing down the hall.

"Where's he going?" Ben looked bewildered.

I didn't bother to answer. "Come on," I ordered Zo. She didn't ask questions, just ran after me as I ran after Jude.

Because I knew where he was going. I'd made the same connection. Someone Riley trusted, even if no one else did.

Sari.

We caught him before he had time to drive away, and threw ourselves into the car before he could lock the door.

"Get out," he said.

"I'm coming with you," I told him.

He didn't argue.

I didn't ask where he was taking us. I assumed he knew exactly where to find her. As Jude was so quick to boast, he knew things. The car turned in a familiar direction, and I curled up with my back to Zo and my forehead against the window. Whatever she did, I couldn't see, didn't care. I didn't understand why she was still there, following us from one nightmare to the next, why suddenly every time I turned, Zo was there, the hole I'd finally gotten used to suddenly filled. Like she could wake up one day and decide to be my sister again. Suddenly I hated her, for being able to come back, disappear and resurface and disappear again, whenever she chose, when Riley never would again.

Zo had barely known Riley, and for most of the time she'd known him, she'd hated him, just for being a mech. She'd been part of the Brotherhood, even if she'd helped us in the end. Was that supposed to absolve her? Was I supposed to forget?

The anger came out of nowhere, so strong that I had to wrap my hands around the seat belt to keep them from wrapping around her throat—and then it drained away, as quickly as it arrived. I felt nothing.

The city rose before us, jagged knives stabbing the gray sky. Jude stopped the car long before we got anywhere near the dying towers. Instead he guided us into the dribbling remnants where the city faded into the wilderness, a kingdom of low, crumbling stone buildings, their roofs sagging or caved in.

"She's here," Jude said.

She could have been anywhere. "How do you know?"

"I know." Jude stopped the car in front of a three-story house that looked no different from any of the others, except for the red streaks of graffiti smeared across the stone like it had been marked in blood. "Rats always go back to the nest."

Zo's eyes bugged as she took in the burned-out cars and broken windows, the clumps of orgs with rotting teeth, rotting skin, rotting faces gathered around fires that stank of rubber and dogshit. I realized this was her first time. The stories had haunted our childhood, tales of men like animals, prowling the streets, blood smeared across their faces like warrior tattoos, long nails sharpened like knives, bodies writhing in the gutters, screwing or dying or both at once. For Zo, as it had been for me, the city was a nightmare land, a monster in a bedtime story, the beast that would swallow you whole if you ventured too close. And this decrepit corner of hell was, according to Riley, the worst of the worst: a lawless no-man's-land of the lost and abandoned, the castoffs in a city of castaways, the lowest of human refuse—and the animals who preyed on them. *All the lies they told you about the city,* Riley had said. *That's where they come true.*

"You can stay here," I told Zo.

"By myself?"

I had visions of returning to a car set ablaze, or graffitied and crushed, or returning to find the car gone altogether, and Zo—

I didn't let myself imagine any further.

She drew back her shoulders and opened the door. "I'm not scared," she said. "Let's go."

I should never have brought her here.

Jude didn't wait for us to gather our nerve. He had already started toward the house. I could drag Zo back into the car and drive away, taking her somewhere safe. I could protect her, like I hadn't protected Riley.

Or I could follow Jude.

"Let's go," Zo said again. I let her make the choice for me. She took off after Jude, and I followed, leaving the car and any thoughts of refuge behind.

The house looked worse inside than it did out. There was

no furniture, no light, no visible features but a gaping, splintered hole in the center of the room where the floor had given way. Sari crouched in the far corner, tucked into a blanket, watching the door as if she'd been waiting for us.

She flew to her feet. "I didn't do anything." As she spoke, she backed away, pressing herself against the wall. Jude advanced slowly.

"What did you do to him?"

"You deaf? *Nothing.*"

"Then why run?" His eyes lit on the pile of clothes and electronics she'd snatched from Riley's place.

Sari stepped between us and the treasure hoard. "So?" she spit out. "They don't need it. They've got plenty of credit; let them buy another set of speakers."

"Are we supposed to buy another Riley?" I asked.

She didn't bother to look at me. "What's the bitch talking about?"

"Riley's dead." Jude flattened her to the wall, one hand pinning her wrist, the other at her throat. Zo sucked in a sharp breath, but I didn't move. Couldn't, or wouldn't, it didn't matter. I felt like I was watching them on-screen, with no choice but to wait patiently and see how things turned out.

Sari shook her head. "Fuck you."

"You killed him."

"Shut up."

"Make me."

"You're machines," Sari said. "You can't die."

He grimaced. "Surprised me, too."

She hit at him with her free arm, but Jude grabbed it. Her wrists were narrow, and he was able to hold them both with one hand. His fingers tightened around her throat.

"You're hurting me."

"Good."

Zo leaned into me. "Shouldn't we do something?"

I ignored her, like Jude ignored Sari's struggling. "What did you do to him?" he said, his voice deadened. He was staring past her, into the wall. Like he was the machine she expected, mindlessly pursuing his mission directive.

"Nothing!" Sari shouted. "She said nothing would happen to him."

Jude threw her to the ground. "Who said!"

"Stop it!" Zo screamed.

Jude knelt over Sari, pinning her down. "Shut her up or get her out of here," he said quietly. "Or I will."

I still couldn't move. Zo shut herself up.

Sari wasn't fighting anymore. She lay on the ground, eyes closed. "He's not really dead, is he?"

"Tell me who."

"Just some lady. She gave me something to stick in that thing he used for backing up."

"She walked up to you one day and *gave* it to you?"

"She paid me, okay?" Sari snarled. "She had credit and I

needed credit, and that's it. She told me it wouldn't hurt him. She said you couldn't get hurt."

"She lied."

"How the hell was I supposed to know?"

"What was her name?"

"I don't know."

"What did she look like?"

"I don't remember."

"Tell me *something*!" Jude drove a fist into the rotting floorboards.

"I think she was one of those Brotherhood freaks, okay? She had one of those robes and everything."

Jude slapped her.

"What the hell—?"

"You killed him!" Jude roared.

Absolute control demands absolute release; that's what Jude had always preached. There were no middle grounds, no compromises, only two opposing states, and a lightning trigger between one and the other. He was always in control, every action deliberate, every decision considered. For Jude, even letting go was a willful choice, a verdict delivered after evaluation of all the options; even that was purposeful.

This wasn't.

Zo's nails dug into my arm. It meant *do something*, it meant *stop him*, it meant *fix this*. Or I could stand there and watch Sari die.

"Please," Sari whimpered.

There was no one to stop him, no one to punish him. It was the city: no rules, no consequences. And if there were no consequences, it was almost like it hadn't happened.

No one would miss her, I thought.

Riley had been her only ally—and she'd erased him.

I'm a machine, I thought, as Jude raised a fist, this one not aimed at the innocent floorboards, but at her face, her soft, pliable, breakable org face, the one that was so good at lying and pretending to be someone else, someone good. *I have no soul; that's what they say.*

All I had to do was not act. No one would ever know, except the three of us.

"Stop." I didn't know I was going to say it until the word was out of my mouth. "Jude, don't."

He didn't let her go. But his fist dropped to his side.

"She killed him," Jude said.

I knelt beside him, put a hand on his shoulder, half expecting him to send me flying across the room. But he didn't move. Neither did Sari, still prone beneath him, waiting for me to decide her fate. I hoped she didn't think I was doing this for her.

I hoped she knew I wanted her to die.

"Don't do this," I said.

"I have to."

"This isn't you."

At that he did shrug me off, weakly, and it was unconvincing enough that I tried again, but he grabbed my arm, squeezing tight. "You don't know everything about me."

"He did."

"Shut up."

"Riley told me, that night before the temple, that you couldn't do . . . this."

"He wouldn't have said that."

"He did."

"I can do this," Jude said. "For him."

"This wouldn't be for him."

I felt dirty, invoking him like that. Dirty or not, it worked.

Jude stood up.

Sari didn't wait around for him to change his mind. She streaked past us like a feral cat, disappearing into the shadows. Long, silent seconds passed.

Jude's shoulders slouched. His head lolled on his neck. His arms hung limp at his sides. For the first time it was easy to picture him as he'd been before the download: slumped in a chair, body defeated. Except that in the one pic I'd seen from that time, his eyes had still been alive—something in him had been fighting, *strong*. Unbowed by its prison of atrophied muscles and sagging flesh. Now, when I tipped his head up and forced him to see me, those eyes were dead.

"You shouldn't have come," he whispered.

I didn't say anything.

"I hate you," he said.

I put my arms around him, and he let me, and, dry-eyed and heartless and mechanical, we held each other up.

So what do you do?

What do you do when there's nothing to do next? When it's over, when whatever rage and panic drove you from one moment to the next disappears, and there's no more *must do this*, *must go there*, *must stop him*, *must save him*? When you can't let the day end, because today was the last day you saw him, the last day you heard his voice, the last day he knew? *Today*, when the sun came up, when you opened your eyes, he was still in the world; today is still a world he knew, and so is still a world you understand. *Today* he's still an *is*, his loss something still happening, an unfolding event, a sentence with a question mark; today there's still a *what happens next*.

What do you do when today ends and you know tomorrow will open on a world in which he's dead? Tomorrow and tomorrow and tomorrow, until he's a thing that once happened, a thing you used to know.

People use words like "unthinkable." But what do you do when the unthinkable happens, and refusing to believe it won't bring him back?

How can anything seem unthinkable anymore, when you're a machine, a living impossibility, a stack of memories in a head-shaped box, when you, the real you, died almost two years ago, just like he did?

How could you be stupid enough to forget that the unthinkable happens all the time?

Happens to you.

Which is why you should know exactly what to do: what you always do, what you have to do. Nothing. Because reality doesn't need your permission to exist; tomorrow doesn't need your approval to dawn. You go home, to a place that was never your home, with a sister who by her own choice is no longer your sister and a brother whose shared grief makes him family in a way that shared skin, shared circuitry, shared manufacturer never could. You go home and you lie in a bed that used to be his and you think about uploading the way he uploaded, following his lead, wherever it takes you. You think that if you really loved him, you wouldn't hesitate; you would want his infection burning through your artificial veins.

You would, but you don't, and so you close your eyes and are grateful that you don't have to try to sleep with memories of his face burning the insides of your lids, that you don't have to bury your face in a pillow so the others don't hear you sob and scream, that your hands are still and unshaken. You're grateful, for once, that your body can't feel, that the truth stays lodged in your mind, where it can't hurt, that you can close your eyes and shift your consciousness in that familiar, deeply inhuman way, flicking an internal switch. It's not like falling asleep, fading away. It's like one moment you're awake and in agony and wondering how long it will be before you forget the sound of his voice.

And the next moment—

You're gone.

When I woke up the next morning, Riley was still dead.

Zo was curled up next to me in bed, her eyes slitted and fixed on Jude. I suspected he had been up all night. Maybe watching me, to make sure I followed through on my promise not to upload a backup, just in case Riley's wasn't an isolated case. Or he just hadn't been able to face the end of the day. Riley's last day.

He sat with his back to the wall, eyes open but darting sightlessly back and forth. It was the telltale flicker of his long lashes that gave it away: He was linked into the network, staring at us but seeing his zone or a vidlife or, for all I knew, the president's latest sex vid. Anything to keep the world away.

I poked Zo. "I know you're awake."

For a moment she didn't move, like she could fool me. Then she threw in an admirable pantomime of "waking up." "I am now."

"Uh-huh."

She jerked her head at Jude. "Can he hear us when he's doing that?"

"With perfect clarity," Jude said, gaze still blind.

Zo flinched at his voice. I wondered how long it would be

before she stopped seeing him the way he'd been in the city, like an animal.

"Get up," Jude said abruptly, closing his eyes in the long, slow blink that I knew would disconnect him from the network. "We've got a problem."

I almost laughed.

He smiled weakly. "I mean a new one."

It was the lead story on every news zone. Ben's virus analogy had been more apt than he knew: Riley was patient zero. The infection had spread through the system, and any mech who connected their uplink before word got out had been wiped. Backing up, the process that was supposed to be our ticket to eternal life, now meant death. The permanent, org kind, from which we were meant to be exempt. Jude was already flying across the network, checking in with every mech he knew—and too many of them didn't answer. The rest of us—the "lucky" ones—were dying too, just more slowly. The virus had wiped out our stored backups, and obviously we couldn't make more. These bodies were now all we had.

It was strange, this sudden awareness of vulnerability. It was supposed to be the reason the orgs hated us, the reason there would always be an us and a them. They died; we didn't. And now that we were just like them, it meant . . . nothing? Meant only that now they had the opportunity to get rid of us one by one. Vids popped up of flash mobs surrounding mechs, dismantling them piece by piece, a helpful how-to of the unmaking of a person. Like the virus, or whatever it was, had granted ultimate permission, had turned us from a threat into a target, literally overnight, even though nothing had changed except our mortality, except the fact that erasing us now meant erasing us for good.

"That's what this is," Jude said, still inhabiting some other plane of preternatural calm. "Genocide."

We watched the story unfold on the news zones, scrambled to track down the mechs we knew, and didn't speculate about who was behind it. Partly because we'd already settled on the Brotherhood as the most likely suspect; partly because we were afraid they weren't acting alone. If any of this was BioMax's fault, if this was retribution, then that made it our fault. That made Riley our fault.

The BioMax connection surfaced within the hour, an hour that felt like a week, barricaded in that tiny apartment, poring over the vids, just like old times at Quinn's estate, when we'd locked ourselves behind electrified walls and try to decipher who hated us and what they planned next.

It came in as a joint announcement, simulcast to all the major news zones and dumped into the personal zones of me, Jude, and probably any mech they could track. Rai Savona and our old friend M. Poulet, appearing side by side, faces somber and pale. "When I founded the Brotherhood of Man, I did so to elevate and illuminate, to remind the human race of our unique destiny in God's plan."

Zo snorted. But it was a mark of how serious things were that Jude held back whatever retort must have been on his tongue. I did the same.

"I blame myself for this tragedy," Savona continued. "A tragedy born from the mind of an unstable teenager."

No.

"I felt I had to atone for my own mistakes, and so I allowed myself to overlook the zealot hiding in our midst. I ceded control to a very young, very damaged boy—I gave him a platform and a voice, and I have only myself to blame for his wrongheaded actions."

"The Honored Rai Savona came to us with his suspicions, and our investigation confirmed them," M. Poulet said. "Auden Heller masterminded the release of an insidious virus directed at download recipients, or *mechs*, as they often refer to themselves. We're doing everything we can to apprehend Heller, and our brightest minds are at work on the virus. In the meantime we implore the public to be respectful—"

"Respectful," a pretty word for "not murderous, bloodthirsty, and mad with a furious skinner bloodlust."

"—and we assure all download recipients that the problem will soon be taken care of. But we remind all download recipients that this is a very serious matter. As of now, forty-seven erasures have been confirmed. Several hundred clients remain unaccounted for. The source of infection appears to be the uplink connection, so this is crucial: *Do not upload your backup memories* until we have this problem solved. More information will follow, as soon as we have it."

Forty-seven "erasures." I wondered if they'd all gone by accident. Or if some had been left behind, like me, and just decided it would be easier to let the virus run its course.

It seemed they'd come to the end of the script, when Savona leaned in and grabbed the microphone, eyes burning into the camera lens. "Auden, if you're out there, if you're listening to this, please come to me. I understand, son. You've been hurt, you wanted to lash out and hurt them back, but this is not the way. Come home to the Brotherhood, and help us fix this. Save yourself."

"He's lying," I said.

"Obviously," Jude said. "This has Savona's stink all over it."

"No, I mean, he's lying about Auden."

"Don't you ever get tired of defending him?" Jude asked. "The guy *shot* you. What else does he have to do to convince you he's not on your side? He thinks you're the freaking devil."

"And you think *he* is. So you're not exactly objective on the subject."

"And you are?"

"I'm not defending him," I said.

"Really? Because it sounds like—"

"I'm not defending him for *his sake*. The more we know about what's going on, the better chance we have of stopping it."

"Except we don't *know* that Savona's lying just because you *feel* it. There's a little difference between a fact and a wish."

"So you're saying you think Auden's behind this?" I asked him.

"Honestly?" Jude paused. "I don't think that twonk could plan a picnic, much less a genocide."

"So—"

"So who cares? Either Savona's telling one lie, or he's telling a bunch of them. It's beside the point."

He was right. The point was someone trying to kill us. BioMax, according to the private messages it had sent out to its mech mailing list, was working to "contain" the problem and "strongly suggested" that all download recipients report to a facility they'd designated as Safe Haven, to protect us from org violence and any further attacks while we were in such a "vulnerable state."

A state no more vulnerable than any orgs on any given day, but somehow it felt like walking around with a knife at our throats. Because what if this was just phase one? Org viruses mutated; maybe this one would, too. Maybe in its next variation it would kill us where we stood. We drew power from a wireless grid—if they could hack the servers, no reason to think they couldn't hack the grid, too. Poison us from afar. They'd wiped out our backups—wasn't the obvious next step to eliminate us once and for all? I didn't see how any Safe Haven could keep us safe from that.

HIDDEN

Maybe this would finally make us even.

Two of us had nowhere to go—nowhere safe, at least. But one of us did. So I decided to start with her, the one person I *could* help, or at least protect. The one part of this situation I could control: Zo. I sat her down on Riley's couch, but I stayed on my feet. It was better to say this from above, to loom. Jude sat at the narrow kitchen table on the other side of the room, plainly watching—but without ejecting him from the apartment, this was as much distance from him as I was going to get.

"I think you should go back home," I told Zo.

Then, reconsidering my tone and the presumed response, I said it again, and this time it wasn't a suggestion. "You should go home."

"The hell I should."

"I know you don't want to—"

"Not. Going. To. There's a difference. Never speaking to either of those assholes again. *Never* setting foot in that house."

"Zo, I know that's how you feel now."

"You sound like *him*," she said.

It was a low blow.

"It's safer there," I told her.

"Then *you* should go."

"Zo, come on, I can't just hide out and wait for this to go away."

"Because suddenly you're this brave, conquering hero? Since when do you care about anything but whether your microskirt matches your boots?"

"You don't know me anymore," I said, coldly. "And that was your choice. So you don't get to have an opinion on what I care about."

"I'm sorry," she said. "You want me to say it again? I'm sorry. I'm sorry!" she shouted. "I'm sorry I'm sorry *I'm sorry!*"

"Stop it!"

"Then *you* stop," she shot back. "Stop throwing all that crap in my face every time we disagree about something. So I screwed up. Fine. Like you've never done that. Like you're perfect."

"I never said I was perfect."

"You didn't have to *say* it."

"And you didn't have to say you hated me," I reminded her, "and that I wasn't your sister, and that you wished I was dead. But you did. All of it."

"And I fucked your boyfriend. Don't forget about that one."

Jude couldn't stop himself. "Did she just say—"

"Shut up."

Wonder of wonders, he did.

"That doesn't matter anymore," I told Zo. "I don't care about him. Or any of that."

"Well, maybe there are things I don't care about anymore either. Maybe there are some things I thought that . . . I don't think anymore. Things I said . . ."

"I told you, it doesn't matter."

"You say that, but you still won't trust me."

"It's not about that," I said. "I want you to be safe."

"Since when?"

"Since always."

She snorted. "Like you cared about that when I was helping you sneak into the temple. Or hack Dad's files or crash BioMax. You wanted me along because I was useful, and now suddenly I'm not? This has nothing to do with me being some weak little girl that needs your protecting. You're not that dumb."

Except that I was. Zo was right. Things were no more dangerous—for her, at least—than they'd ever been. And before, I hadn't hesitated to let her help, no matter the risks. Her life, her call. But now . . .

I could have put it on Riley, on the fact that now I understood how things could go wrong and people could disappear. But that was more a reminder than a news flash. It wasn't that I suddenly understood that I could lose Zo; it was that I suddenly couldn't stand the prospect. Somehow she had become my sister again. My little sister. Which meant, somehow, she'd become my responsibility.

Obviously, I couldn't tell her *that*.

"It's because you're a mech and I'm an org, right?" Zo said flatly. "All that bullshit about how we're all the same, all those speeches you gave, it was all crap, right? In the end you draw a line: you on one side, me on the other."

And because it would be easier than convincing her she needed protection—because it would be easier than telling her the truth—I let her believe it. She proved me right by doing what I needed her to do. She left.

"Didn't see that coming," Jude said, once she was gone.

I joined him at the table, slumping down in the second chair. It was missing a leg, and wobbled precariously as I sat down. *Perfect,* I thought, bitter and exhausted. Even the furniture had an opinion on my life. Though for the metaphor to really work, the chair would have to dump me on my ass just when I'd finally let myself relax. I was sure that could be arranged.

"Kind of harsh, don't you think?" Jude added.

"Like you don't believe all that, us and them."

"*You* don't."

"Are we done talking about my sister?"

Jude raised his hands in surrender: *Done.*

Good.

"So what now?" I said. "We obviously can't trust BioMax—we can't let *anyone* trust BioMax. But that's not exactly an action plan."

"They're right about one thing," he said. "It's going to be open season on mechs, and without the backups, dead is dead. We have to get somewhere safe."

"Safe Haven?" I said, incredulous. "You're joking."

"It's not the only option. Let's not forget, while some of us were busy dancing on BioMax's string, others of us were planning ahead." He smiled for the first time since Riley. "'Some of us' equals you, in case you didn't catch that. 'Others of us' would be me."

"As far as I can tell, all you did was hole up in a filthy, irradiated dead zone—" I stopped, suddenly understanding what he was getting at. "You're not serious."

His smile widened.

"It's been the plan all along," I realized. "You're probably glad to finally have an excuse."

The smile vanished. "I didn't want it to happen. I knew it *would* happen. There's a difference."

"So you want us to run and hide."

"You have a better idea?"

"There's got to be something better than holing up like refugees—like animals—in some kind of toxic waste dump."

"Not all of us grew up like you did," he snarled. "For some of us it would practically be luxury."

"Don't give me that city-rat crap," I warned him. "This isn't about me being spoiled. It's about this not being a solution."

"It's a first step," he admitted.

"It's a crappy one."

"And your brilliant plan is . . . ?"

I didn't want to hide. I wanted to stay, to *fight*. I wanted to avenge Riley and destroy BioMax and the Brotherhood and make the world, *this* world, safe for mechs. As Jude would have pointed out, if I'd been foolish enough to say it out loud, it was a pretty speech.

But it wasn't much of a plan.

"BioMax would still be in control," I pointed out. "If anything happened to us and we needed new bodies—"

"New bodies are useless without uploaded memories to download," Jude reminded me. "Which makes BioMax useless too."

"So walk me through this. We collect all the mechs, lead them into their new toxic paradise, and . . . what? Set you up as emperor? Build you a throne?"

Jude slammed his hand against the table. "This isn't a *joke*."

"No, it's a power trip."

"Why do you always have to make everything about me?" Jude asked.

"I thought I always made everything about *me*," I said. "Isn't that what you're always telling me?"

"I never meant—"

"You've made it pretty clear you think I'm spoiled and naive and all-around useless."

"Right." Jude snorted. "That's why I always come to you first. That's why we're figuring this out *together*. That's why I listen to all your bullshit. Because I think you're useless and don't care what you have to say. You really know everything, don't you?"

"I know I'm only here because you don't have anyone else willing to listen to *your* bullshit."

"Maybe you're right!" he shouted. "I don't have anyone else!"

We both stopped.

And I could only assume we both thought of him.

Riley.

"Sorry," he said. "I shouldn't have shouted."

And I shouldn't have picked a fight, just because I was upset about Zo and frightened about the virus and angry about Riley and angry, angry, so unbearably angry that I didn't know what to do except spew it all over anyone unfortunate enough to get close. And all I had left on that front was Jude.

I couldn't apologize. But: "You're right. The dead zone is a good option. For now."

He looked surprised, but he didn't gloat. Like he said, he didn't have anyone else either.

So we sat there calmly and cobbled together some kind of

plan—or at least a first step. We would release what we knew about BioMax, publicly on the network, and privately to all the mechs we could find; we'd do everything we could to persuade them to reject the corp's Safe Haven in favor of our own. Then, somehow, we'd figure out what to do next.

As Jude worried through the logistics of releasing the dead-zone coordinates to the mechs without revealing them to BioMax—though the whole beauty of the location was its inhospitableness to orgs, making secrecy a bonus rather than a necessity—I watched the door, half expecting Zo to burst through with a last word. I was no longer sure I'd done the right thing, sending her away. Even if I had, was it the right thing for her, to keep her safe, or the right thing for me, to give me one less person to worry about, one less person to lose? If things had gone differently, if she'd been the mech and I'd been the org, she never would have sent me home. Though if it had been me, I might have gone without a fight.

I might have gone back to our parents, even after everything that had happened. But not Zo. So where would she go?

And why hadn't I thought about any of this when I was throwing her out?

"She'll be fine," Jude said softly, as if I'd spoken aloud. "She always is."

He reached across the table, like he was going to put his hand over mine, but stopped a few inches short. "Just like her sister."

• • •

For a long time Jude had hoarded his secret that BioMax could track the movement of every mech, just as he'd kept to himself the knowledge of how to disable those trackers. Saving it for a rainy day, he'd promised—the someday when BioMax would be desperate to know where we were, and we'd be equally desperate to hide. Now the monsoon had arrived. He disabled the trackers remotely, and just like that, we were all free. We contacted all the mechs we knew, had them pass the word to everyone they knew, and mech by mech we tried to talk them out of BioMax's Safe Haven and into ours.

Sloane, Brahm, familiar faces from the past agreed without question and headed for the dead zone, bringing handfuls of friends, sometimes mechs they'd picked up along the way, hesitant to trust anyone but desperate to be told what to do. The early arrivals took charge, setting up systems for intake and inventory, helping new mechs feel at home—and helping us figure out how many were left to save. It would have been easier to do in person, and I could tell Jude was tempted, but I insisted on staying at Riley's. He stayed with me.

We broadcast what we knew about BioMax—and, true to their word, BioMax wiped it from the network as soon as we'd posted it. Though it probably wouldn't have mattered—the zones were flooded with unsubstantiated rumors. Suddenly every nutcase with a keyboard had some crucial information about our fates—and much of it came with evidence as persuasive as ours, because what could be easier than creating fake photos, fake documentation to substantiate fake stories? The only authority was the wisdom of the crowd—the more popular the zone, the more appealing its story, the more believable it appeared. There was more than enough noise to drown out the truth. All we could do was keep screaming and hope someone heard.

We persuaded forty or fifty by word of mouth, the mechs we knew convincing the ones they knew. But BioMax, judging from its reports, got at least a hundred, and as reports of anti-mech violence grew, more were coming in every day.

We couldn't save everyone.

Quinn wouldn't take my calls, and as soon as she heard Jude's voice, she cut the link. We heard she went straight to BioMax after that, playing the good girl just to spite us, I supposed, since it certainly wasn't in her nature.

Ani was nowhere to be found; she'd even erased her zone. No one I'd ever known had taken such a drastic move—it was like erasing your own existence. But Ani was used to being invisible. For all we knew, she was sitting by Savona's side again, egging him on—or maybe at Safe Haven, having discovered that the virus didn't discriminate between self-hating mechs and the rest of us.

I tried not to think about the other option, the most obvious excuse for her silence. Every day the news zones added new names to their list of the Erased. Ani's was never on it. But you couldn't make the list unless you'd left someone behind to notice you were gone.

No one at BioMax was taking my calls, not even call-me-Ben. All I got were automated responses offering me coordinates to Safe Haven, urging me to be smart and let them protect me, as if those two options weren't mutually exclusive. Jude was losing patience, as was I, but we were pulling in opposite directions. He wanted to join the mechs in the dead zone—start fresh, he called it. I called it running away.

We argued, a lot. There was too much time, too much anger not to. There was too much shuttling back and forth between one dead end and another, making half-aborted plans, trying and failing and trying again even more uselessly the next time around, too much threatening, too much second-guessing, too much staring aimlessly into space trying to make the pieces fit together, searching for the fault line, the one perfect place to exert pressure that would make our enemies collapse in on themselves, that would right our world. There was too much of everything, except action, except answers. And, of course, except tears. We weren't built for that.

"And what about the mechs at Safe Haven?" I asked, during one of our many arguments. "What happens to them?"

"They get what they get for trusting BioMax."

But he didn't mean it, because one day passed, and another, and he didn't leave. I must not have meant it either, because I stayed too. Even when it became clear that we'd convinced all the mechs we were going to, and that the virus wasn't going anywhere. Safe Haven was bursting at the seams. Even then I stayed and argued with Jude, let him talk me to a stalemate. I knew what we had to do. I was just afraid to do it.

We were still arguing when my ViM buzzed with an incoming vid call from the second-to-last person I'd expected to hear from. The last was my sister, who was ignoring all my messages, including the ones pleading with her to just let me know where she was, and that it was somewhere safe.

The second-to-last was Ani.

When I saw who it was, I relayed it to our wall screen, so Jude could see her too—and she could see Jude. I'd been more worried about her than I'd let myself realize, but now that she'd actually surfaced, I could barely look at her. I had no interest in facing her alone.

"Ani. Hey. You look . . . good," Jude said haltingly. And she did, better at least than she had the last time I'd seen her.

She waved joylessly. "Yeah, I can walk and talk and everything. Just like a real girl."

"Ani—"

"I need to talk to *you*, Lia," she cut in. "Not him."

"Too bad," I said. "He stays."

Even if he looked like he wanted to disappear.

"I'm sorry about Riley," she told me.

They'd reported his name on all the news vids: "the first victim." He was famous.

It had been two weeks, and I still didn't know what to say. "Thank you"? "I'm sorry, too"? "How can you be sorry when you barely knew him?" Or, in Ani's case, "How can you be sorry when you screwed him over and then left him behind?"

"What do you want?" I asked. "Delivering a message on behalf of your pious Brothers and Sisters?"

"If I had known what they were going to do—"

I laughed—a twisted, angry sound, like metal on metal. "You would've stopped them? Have you forgotten that you *helped* them? How do you think they figured out how to do this in the first place? By poking around in *your* brain. Because *you* volunteered. You didn't think we deserved to exist. So congratulations, you must be so proud of Riley. Doing us all proud by getting erased."

Ani looked like I had struck her. "You know what he means to me," she said, in a low, angry voice.

"*Meant* to you. Past tense."

Giving up on me, she turned to Jude. Desperate times. "I never wanted this to happen."

"I know."

"You always said if I needed something from you . . ."

"Anything," Jude said.

I knew what he was thinking. I could hear it in his voice. Ani wasn't Riley, but she was as close as he was going to get.

Ani had been there with the two of them in the hospital, before the download. Ani had known Riley *before*—she was the only person who could share that with Jude, the only person who'd known that part of him, the boy from the city, the boy from the past. Whatever promises they'd made to each other back then, whatever bonds they'd forged, Ani was all he had left. He needed her. Which meant she could use him, and he wouldn't even notice. Or if he did, he wouldn't care.

Since when is it my job to protect him? I thought, surprised by the impulse.

Except that I needed him for the same reason he needed her. We were all fragments; we were the pieces left behind, a shard of Riley in each of us. Losing Jude would mean losing a piece of Riley all over again.

"I can't tell you like this," she said. "We have to talk in person."

So he told her where to find us.

An expensive-looking Stylus pulled up to the apartment a few hours later, its windows too tinted to see inside. Ani slipped out of the driver's door, leaned back in for a moment as if she'd forgotten something, then shut it quickly. She leaned against the passenger side of the car, staring up at the building.

I watched it all from the window.

What was she waiting for?

What was I?

Twenty minutes passed. "Is she here yet?" Jude finally asked. I'd been staring out the window for more than an hour.

I nodded.

"So are you going to let her in?" he said, too eager. I was reminded of Riley's puppy-dog glee when we'd first tracked down Jude.

"Doesn't seem like she wants to come in."

So Jude went out. I watched them greet each other: Jude's awkward half attempt at a hug, Ani's imperceptible step backward, sign enough that he should drop his arms. The silence between the two of them, failed small talk, strained smiles. Then Jude gestured to the house and Ani gestured to the car, and as they seemed to start arguing, I realized why the windows were tinted and what she'd left behind when she got out of the car. She hadn't come alone. And there was only one person she could have brought with her, at least under these cloak-and-dagger terms.

I threw open the door and ran toward the car, because if Jude got there first, someone was going to get hurt. Or killed.

"It wasn't me," Auden said, while I held Jude's arm, tightly, just in case he decided to pounce. "I swear, Lia. I didn't have anything to do with this. Savona needed a scapegoat. I didn't know about any of it until I saw it on the network, and by then—"

"It was too late," I finished with him, fresh out of sympathy.

Ani stood by his side. After everything, she *stood by his side*.

I let go of Jude. It was strange—when Auden's face had been a picture on a screen, being blamed for horrible things he never could have done, I'd wanted to defend him, even protect him. But now, his face in front of me, real and three-dimensional, all I wanted to do was jump in the car and run him over. Ani, too, while I was at it. I couldn't stand the two of them, Ani and Auden, a matched pair of pathetic apologists, half guilty and half self-righteous, secure in the knowledge that *they* could never be held accountable for whatever had happened, they couldn't be blamed, there was nothing they could have done. They were alive and safe, and Riley was dead.

"Tell me you believe me," Auden said.

"What's the difference? What would it change?"

"Please," he said. "I have to know."

"You don't really get to make requests," Jude said. "Not now. Definitely not *here*."

"He needs a safe place to stay," Ani said.

Jude laughed. "So you brought him *here*? Brilliant."

Here to us. Here to Riley's home.

"You said—"

"I said if *you* ever needed anything. That was you singular, not you plus one, especially this one."

"Fine." Ani glared at him. "I should have known. We'll go."

"Go where?" Jude and Auden said it together, disdain in one voice, despair in the other.

"I can help," Auden said. "I have information."

"Try us," Jude said, sounding as bored as Auden did desperate.

"Savona acted like I could take the lead." Auden spoke quickly. "He was going to be a consultant. He said he'd had a change of heart, that he understood what he'd done was wrong—"

"Yeah, we saw the vids," Jude cut in. "What else?"

"He was working behind my back," Auden said. "Gathering loyalists, continuing research into the way skinner brains work—even though the lab was destroyed, his scientists all survived."

And all of us knew why: Because *I'd* insisted on saving them.

"He was setting me up the whole time," Auden continued. "He let me have the spotlight so that I'd be the one to take the blame. And now . . ."

Maybe it was because he had no right to sound so pathetic; maybe it was because the self-pity in his voice sounded too much like my own. But I couldn't take it anymore.

"People are dead!" I shouted. "Not *skinners*, not machines, *people*. Do you get that? Dead and never coming back. And we're supposed to feel sorry for you?"

"I told you, I didn't—"

"Right, you didn't do anything," I spit out. "Savona did it. The Brotherhood did it. But who *made* the Brotherhood? What would it have been without your face and your story? Congratulations, you made all this possible."

"Lia, that's not fair," Ani said.

"You want to talk about fair? How about the fact that Riley's *dead* and you're standing here with *him* like he's your best friend. None of this is your fault, right?" I said, turning back to Auden. "It's Savona's fault for shoving you into the spotlight. It's Savona's fault for somehow making you shoot all those vids and throw all those rallies about how evil the skinners were, how we were monsters, we were threats, how *I* tried to kill you. It's Savona's fault that when he disappeared, you *chose* to take over the Brotherhood instead of disbanding it. I guess you accidentally kept preaching all that crap. A kinder, gentler way of hating people. Brilliant. And it must have been a total accident the way you got hundreds of people to feel sorry for you, and to cheer for you when you told them we needed to die. Oops, right?"

"Lia, keep it together," Jude said. "We should listen—"

"Don't you *dare* defend him. All this time he's been the ultimate evil, and *now* you decide he's on our side? What, you think we should help him? *Now* you think we should feel sorry for him?"

"I think we should listen to him."

"I think we should let the secops catch up with him and blame him for whatever they want. Let him suffer."

I didn't know if I meant it or not. But it was hard to feel sorry, especially with Auden staring at me with those watery, puppy-dog eyes like I'd kicked him in the stomach, like after everything that had happened we were suddenly back where we'd started and I was supposed to be his friend, afraid to hurt his feelings. Like it hadn't hurt mine when he'd told the whole world what I'd done to him, making them believe—making *me* believe—that I'd wanted to destroy him. He hadn't hesitated, because my feelings weren't relevant—they weren't real. A machine programmed to act human couldn't *feel* anything. So what made him think I would feel guilt now, or sympathy? What made him believe I could feel anything?

"We're wasting time," Jude said. "It doesn't matter who's to blame—"

I laughed. "Did you get a personality transplant when I wasn't looking? Maybe a lobotomy? Since when do you think blaming people is a waste of time?"

"Blame him later," Jude said. Then, under his breath, "I will."

"Can we go inside?" Ani asked. "People are looking for him. . . ."

Jude shook his head. "You say you can help," he told Auden. "Help."

Despite his claims, Auden didn't know much, and most of it we'd already figured out on our own. But there was one thing we hadn't expected—and it was big enough for us to invite him into the house.

"I believed it at first," Auden said, settling onto the couch,

Riley's couch, and walking us through it. "Savona hates Bio-Max even more than he hates the skinners; that's what he always said. You can't blame the abomination—you blame its maker."

Jude frowned. "Charming."

"But if they weren't working together from the start, they are now," Auden continued. "There are Brotherhood people working in Safe Haven—people loyal to Savona. And they wouldn't be there unless BioMax wanted them to be."

"How do you know?" I asked. "Have you been there?"

Auden shook his head. "They've got that place locked down. No one gets in without BioMax's permission; no one gets out. Not just skinners—"

"Mechs," Jude corrected him.

"—but staff, too. It's almost impossible to get any information out either."

"But this information somehow made its way to you," Jude said, sounding skeptical.

"There are people still loyal to me. I know I'm right about this. BioMax brought the Brotherhood into Safe Haven. I don't know what it means, but . . ."

If nothing else, it meant Safe Haven was anything but safe. It wasn't news, but it was confirmation. BioMax and the Brotherhood were working together—working to get rid of the mechs. Presumably starting with the ones they had gathered in one convenient location "for their own protection." There was no point in arguing anymore, since it was obvious what we needed to do, and if Jude didn't agree, I'd go alone. I'd see for myself what BioMax was up to, and—whether by persuasion or force—I'd get the mechs out.

"We have to go in," Jude said.

And when he did, much as I hated to admit it, I was relieved.

Auden promised to try to get someone in on the staff side, someone loyal to him who could help us all break out, if it proved as hard as he suspected it would be. I could tell Jude didn't believe he'd follow through. I believed he would try.

We left him in the only safe place we could think of: Riley's apartment.

He's dead, I kept telling myself. *He doesn't need it anymore.* That didn't stop it from feeling like a betrayal. Whether Auden wanted to admit it or not, there'd been a time when he wanted us all dead, or at least was convinced we didn't have the right to live. And now we were using Riley's home to keep him safe.

Maybe this would finally make us even.

"You sure about this?" Auden asked, as we parted ways. He wasn't talking to me.

"I have to," Ani said. "You going to be okay here?"

Jude rolled his eyes. "He'll be fine."

"Yes, he will," Auden agreed. "And if you need me, any of you—"

"Don't hold your breath," Jude said. "Or do, if that's what gets you off. Your call."

"Before you go . . ." Auden hesitated, watching me, as if measuring whether or not he should continue.

Apparently, I didn't pass the test.

"Be safe," he said, but he said it to Ani, and she was the one he put his arms around and hugged tightly. It was the happy ending to a modern parable: Skinner and org bond in the face of adversity, each learning a valuable lesson about the other's humanity. And yet there was a time when Auden had known me better than anyone in the world. So why did he need Ani to teach him that mechs were more than heartless machines?

Why did I still care?

SAFE HAVEN

"It's for your own protection."

Like the machines BioMax designed, the operation was a well-oiled one. The corp had distributed a set of rendezvous coordinates to all mechs. From there we would be taken to the secure resettlement facility, its location and access well protected from the inquiring public. And from there . . . well, from these things got a bit hazy. Without knowing exactly what was going on inside Safe Haven, it was impossible to know how hard it would be to get everyone out, much less figure out exactly what BioMax and the Brotherhood intended to do if we failed. But even if we didn't know what we were walking into, it felt good to be moving again. It felt right.

The coordinates took us to a vast concrete lot lined with rows of trucks and buses, each bearing a freshly painted Bio-Max logo. A thin trickle of cars pulled up to the registration point, disgorging their mech cargo, then driving away. Some were filled with concerned orgs who hesitated on the curb, drawing out the moment with embraces and farewells. But most mechs came alone and sent their cars away on autopilot. As we did, joining the procession of mechs, letting the Bio-Max reps take our names, scan our pupils, check the registration data embedded in our spinal columns. We shuffled down a line of intake staff, finally reaching a man with a white smock and a stiff smile. He had *doctor* written all over him, a game many of the techs liked to play, as if their machinations on our conduits and circuitry made them healers, when in fact they were nothing but plumbers, mechanics, engineers. "Welcome," he said. Cue the mirthless grin. "I'm so pleased you've decided to take the prudent route and join us until this crisis is resolved."

His hand flashed through the air, and then there was a sharp prick at the back of my neck, like something had sunk its fangs into my skin.

I slapped a hand over my neck. There was a rough patch at the tip of my spine, and a hard-edged lump that hadn't been there before. "What the—"

Jude caught the doctor's wrist as it swooped in his direction. "Not unless you tell me what the hell this is," Jude said, glaring at the slim, silver injector that had been aimed at his neck.

"He's nervous," I said quickly. "You can understand that, right?" I tried to sound innocent and unsuspecting, a scared little girl who just wanted to be told what to do. "There are people trying to kill us! Maybe if you just explained . . . ?"

I doubt either of us expected him to. But after a pause he shrugged. "Just a precaution—it helps us keep track of your location," he said. "If you don't get one, we can't let you into Safe Haven."

Jude let go of the man's wrist. "Just a precaution," he repeated, bending his head forward.

"We're not taking any chances," the man said, jabbing the injector into Jude's neck. I flinched, watching the tracking chip slide under his skin. Jude didn't move.

The man slapped him on the back, then patted me on the shoulder. "All set."

I tried to look grateful. Even though I felt like he'd stripped off my clothes and left me bare and helpless on the cement for any and all to see.

Jude looked blank. "I feel better already."

They shoved twelve of us in the back of a truck. BioMax's first step in keeping us safe involved an unpleasantly bumpy ride, the kind of lurching and slamming that in another life would have left me concussed and puking, but in this one just left me with a peculiar ringing in my ears after the sixth or seventh time my head slammed, hard, into the truck's steel wall.

There were no windows.

There was, however, a projector that played a looped vid against the back wall. A familiar face with a soothing voice, telling us all how happy we would be once we arrived at our new home. (*Temporary* home, she was careful to say. Ours until the world was perfectly safe for us again. Like perfect safety was just within reach.) Kiri Napoor—who must have decided her principles weren't worth her job—extolled the virtues of our secluded paradise as images of happy mechs frolicking in a bucolic pasture flickered across the screen.

"Looks better than where I live," one of the other mechs mumbled. He was tall, with brown hair, broad shoulders, and a familiar face that made me suspect his body, like mine, was a generic model. The two girls with him, on the other hand, were strictly custom-made—the elaborate patterns of freckles on one and the deep dimples on the other were a dead give-away, subtle org touches that BioMax never bothered with unless asked.

"Yeah, I'm sure it's a nonstop party," Ani said. Jude shot her a look. Riling up the crowd would be fine—mandatory, even—once we got inside. But first we had to get in. Which meant playing nice.

"I don't care what it is," the dimpled girl said, "as long as it's safe."

The mech next to her, who'd spent most of the ride with her head lowered, long blond hair covering her face, suddenly looked up. "Did you know anyone who . . . ?"

"Couple friends. You?"

"Yeah," the girl said, and dropped her head again. "I knew someone."

She didn't say anything else. I wondered if she was regretting that she'd boarded the truck at all, instead of following in the footsteps of her *someone*, uploading with him, virus or not. Her confession got everyone else going, and soon the truck was buzzing with questions and details, the whos, whats, hows, where-were-you-whens of natural disaster.

"I said, what about *you*?" the guy next to me repeated, poking me like I hadn't heard him the first two times.

Before I could answer, Jude's hand was at his throat. "Don't touch her."

The guy looked alarmingly unintimidated. He grabbed Jude's wrist and jerked it away, then began to rise unsteadily to his feet, lurching toward us.

"Please stop," I said, though part of me wanted to push Jude away and knock this guy out myself.

You're not invincible anymore, I reminded myself. None of us was.

"It's fine," I said, louder. "Please."

"You should teach your boyfriend how to keep his mouth shut," the lurcher grunted, but at least he sat down.

"I don't need you protecting me," Jude hissed.

"And I don't need to watch you get the crap kicked out of you again."

He opened his mouth, then shut it again, and I knew we were both thinking about the last time he'd gotten the crap kicked out of him.

I didn't understand how Riley could be everywhere and nowhere at once.

It was quiet after that, for one hour, then two, the twelve of us scrabbling for purchase as the truck lurched over bumps and veered around corners. There was a long, straight coasting that seemed to go on forever, then a string of mini-quakes as the tires ground over a gravel road. The truck jerked to a stop, flinging me into Jude's lap. We were there.

Safe Haven was a corp-town. It made sense. Parnassus and BioMax were sister corps, subsidiaries of the same bureaucratic overlords, which meant the Parnassus residence facility would be up for grabs. I hadn't been back to a corp-town since the Synapsis attack, and I would have been happy enough to keep it that way.

Not that the two had anything in common. Where Synapsis had been all fake greenery and reflecting ponds, the Parnassus corp-town made no attempt to disguise its primary purpose, which was the mining and making of things that it could transform into piles of credit. The people who lived there were, presumably, secondary. So there were no playing fields, no botanical gardens, no gleaming glass residence cubes with pristine atriums at their hearts. Parnassus workers lived in steel, windowless domes.

There was nothing here to remind me of the Synapsis corp-town and the bloated bodies I'd stepped over in my escape. Nothing except the fact of the corp-town itself, and the claustrophobic feeling that descended as we stepped into steel dome number seven. Residence centers in every corp-town were designed along the same principles: maximum sleeping facilities, minimum means of escape. I'd seen how quickly the Synapsis steel shutters locked down the building at the first triggering of an alarm; this dome was nothing but one huge steel shutter. It locked behind us.

It was obvious we wouldn't to be mingling with the orgs. Those had been cleared out. Way out, judging from the barbed-wire fence we'd passed on our way in. So it was just us. The communal space, an atrium of bare silver paths and sloping steel archways, was mostly empty. A few mechs in identical orange sweats wandered through the metallic park, looking like they had nowhere in particular to go but around and around on the circular walking track. The mechs we'd arrived with seemed equally purposeless, standing around, waiting to be told what to do. So we blended, waiting patiently by the entry checkpoint, neither asking questions of the orgs guarding the gate nor speculating among ourselves what might lie beyond it.

I pulled out my ViM, planning to pretend to check my zone while I snapped a few surreptitious pics for the network. But I couldn't link in.

"I wouldn't bother with that," a woman in a BioMax uniform informed me. "You can't link in from here."

There was a chorus of confused complaints, mine included. I was proving better than I would have expected at blending in. Turned out it was easy to be a sheep.

The org woman cleared her throat. "It's for your own protection. As you know, it's crucial that the location of this resettlement community be known to a limited population, and while none of you would intentionally compromise the safety of your fellow download recipients, we've decided the safest course of action is to jam the network, for the time being."

"But what about our families?" Jude said, sounding laughably alarmed. "It's bad enough having to leave them behind. You're telling me I can't even talk to them?"

I worried he'd gone too far over the top, but the woman looked suitably sympathetic. "We have, of course, made accommodations for communication with friends and family. Those communications will be monitored, and all sanctioned correspondence will go through. A small price to pay for your security and peace of mind, wouldn't you say?"

Disgruntled murmurings, all amounting to: *Sure. I guess.*

I couldn't believe they were accepting it. But then, they'd come here voluntarily, giving themselves up to BioMax's protection. There were mechs here that we knew, that we'd spoken to, that we'd begged to choose us over the corp, showing them the evidence we'd gathered of what BioMax had done, what the corp had stolen from us, because we were nothing but machines, to be pared down for parts. The mechs who'd come here were the ones who didn't care. Someone was trying to kill them; BioMax was trying to save them. It was simple as that.

At this point, trusting anyone was starting to seem impossibly stupid—and now I understood what Jude must have thought of me all those months, watching me on the vids, preaching trust and goodwill as I held hands with the enemy.

Once it had been made clear that the outside world—and its rules and freedoms—no longer existed for us, the intake process could begin in earnest.

They took our clothes.

They made us stand there together, twelve strangers, and strip ourselves bare while they watched. We tried to turn our backs to one another, tried to cover up with hands and crossed legs and awkward contortions, keeping our heads down, our eyes slitted, as the BioMax personnel circulated, searching us for "contraband," for anything that might challenge the safety of the safe haven: knives or ViMs or dreamers or bombs. I closed my eyes as the woman's meaty hands swept my body, and played the game I'd played too many times before, the familiar mantra: *This is just the body; this is not* me. *She can't touch me.*

When her hands fell away and I opened my eyes again, I met Jude's gaze. Alone in the group he stood tall, head up, eyes open. When he saw me watching, his lips moved, and I imagined I could understand the words they formed, a message to me:

For Riley.

• • •

They gave us clothes, freshly laundered, branded with the Bio-Max insignia. Beige and orange, nothing I would ever have voluntarily worn in public, but decisions like that were no longer voluntary. We'd been in BioMax's possession for less than a day, and it was already starting to feel inevitable, the outside world real enough but irrelevant. Every detail of Safe Haven was designed to remind us that this was our life now. *Temporary*, they said, again and again, to the outside world. But in here they hadn't said it once.

I knew we'd made the right decision, not bringing any kind of weapon—there was no way we would have made it through the intake process without getting it confiscated, and probably getting ourselves thrown out along with it. But I would have felt a lot better knowing that when I needed it, I had a way to fight back.

They gave us rooms, narrow steel cylinders with bare walls, four beds, and no storage space, which hardly mattered, since our belongings had been confiscated along with our clothes. (Say it with me now: *For our own protection.*) No light switches, because the lights were all programmed around the corp-town's three-shift working schedule. They would go on when it was deemed time for the workers in this wing to wake up, off again when the curfew hit and they obediently went to sleep. Alarms and strobes marked the beginning and end of each working shift. Small favors: At least they weren't putting us to work.

They weren't requiring anything from us but our obedience—it was quickly becoming clear that there was nothing here to fill the day beyond following orders. It gave us plenty of time to weigh our options and argue about what to do next. . . . Which is why I was lying on the narrow bunk-bed cot, my face inches from the ceiling, trying to catch my reflection in the dull steel, when Quinn Sharpe—exactly as she had when I'd first seen her—poked her head into the doorway and woke us all the hell up.

"This is . . . unexpected," she said, giving each of us a slow, careful once-over, her gaze finally settling on Ani.

I sat up. "We're here to—"

Quinn tapped her lips, then her ear, then pointed to the ceiling. Unmistakable code for *Shut up, they're listening.* And of course they would have cameras in the walls. Corp-town life was predicated on absolute compliance—one slip and, within minutes, you could find yourself shipped out to a city. But all-pervasive fear worked only if you had some way of enforcing 24/7 obedience.

Jude knitted his eyebrows together, frowning. "No VM either," he mumbled. "They must be jamming that, too." Bio-Max wasn't supposed to know about the Voice Mind Integrator that offered Jude and his hand-selected allies a means of silent communication—but apparently they'd figured it out.

"Unexpected or not," Quinn said, "I'm glad to see you."

"Feeling's not mutual," Ani mumbled.

Ignoring her, Quinn came into the room and flung herself down on the empty bed. "I could use some new roommates anyway. Mine snore."

"Somehow I doubt that," I said.

Quinn rolled her eyes. "It's a metaphor."

Jude glanced at the ceiling. "What can you tell us?"

"First you," Quinn said. "What am I missing out there in the real world?"

Jude gave her the rundown of everything that had been happening in the days since she'd turned herself in to BioMax: the useless attempts to eliminate the virus, the increase in anti-skinner attacks. And the whole time, as he struggled for coded ways to paint her a picture of what we were doing here, as if it weren't obvious, she watched Ani. I wondered whether she was using Jude's monologue as a stalling device, to cover for her inch-by-inch examination of her former no-strings-attached whatever, in hopes that the whatever would finally turn to face her, and maybe even forgive and forget.

That hope must have died, because eventually she dropped the act. "You're not even going to talk to me?" she asked Ani, crossing the room to sit down beside her. Ani immediately got up and walked to the opposite wall.

"Very mature." Quinn stood again too.

Ani looked wary, as if expecting Quinn to chase her from one side to the other. Wary but determined, like she was prepared to run.

"So this is it?" Quinn said. "Silent treatment? It's going to get a little awkward around here if we're going to be roommates."

"We're not."

"She speaks!"

Watching them parry, I was again reminded of the day I'd met Quinn and how impossibly difficult it was to get her to shut up and go away when she'd decided you would be her newest plaything. Quinn was a girl accustomed to getting what she wanted.

"Go away, Quinn," said Ani.

"You forgive him, but not me?" Quinn said.

"Who said I forgive anyone?"

"Oh, grow up!" Quinn said. "So I did you, and then I did him. So fucking what?"

"*So what* is you promised you wouldn't."

Quinn laughed. "You're right. I broke my promise. And you got your friends kidnapped and tortured. So I can see why you still feel you have the moral high ground."

It was the thing none of us had dared say. Not Jude, because he was too busy trying to pretend it had never happened. Not me, because I'd spent enough time being a crappy friend.

Which must be why I lied. "Ani, she didn't mean it," I told her. "None of us think—"

"It's fine." Ani dipped her head. The fluorescent lights gave her indigo hair a midnight glow. "She can stay."

I glared at Quinn. "You didn't have to say that."

"It was true," Quinn said.

"So what?"

"Enough," Jude said quietly. "We're wasting time with this crap."

"I said she can stay!" Ani said. "What else do you want from me?"

"Nothing," Jude assured her.

Quinn smiled then, in what could have been triumph or relief, and whatever hardness had been in her voice drained away. "Speak for yourself."

Quinn gave us the grand tour. There wasn't much to see. Corridors of bedrooms, all identical to our own. The central atrium with its sloping steel beams, which looked more like a factory than a "common space for relaxation and socialization." I hadn't been around this many mechs since the time I'd spent at Quinn's estate, but those days had been infused with a determined, sometimes manic joy—not happiness, per se, because certainly there wasn't an overabundance of that to go around. But there was a desperation to confirm we'd made the right choices, and to prove to ourselves that we were living the best of all possible lives. Hence the dancing and the screwing, the cliff-jumping, the sky-diving, the wild parties and the zoned-out dreamers and the couples who lost themselves in the wilds of each other. Call it mandatory fun.

The one mandatory element this resettlement zone was lacking.

Another difference between this and the estate: the presence of orgs, uniformed "volunteers" and "helpers" who wandered through our ranks with glazed expressions and recognizable bulges beneath their jackets: the pulse gun, which discharged an electric pulse that could cut down a mech at twenty feet, frying his neural matrix for at least an hour—and that was assuming the charge was set on low and nothing went wrong. Of course they weren't there to shoot us. They were just there to watch. For our own protection.

According to Quinn, speaking in a low voice and veiled terms, the footage that BioMax had been airing to the viewing public had all been shot in the first few days, a suitable advertisement for idyllic corp living. Once the cameras shut down, so did the dome, locking the mechs indoors. Then came the confiscations of clothing, ViMs, all other belongings, the jammed network and VM signals. Communications to the outside were monitored, so if you wanted to tell your parents what a wonderful time you were having at Camp BioMax, you were free to do so. Anything with more detail or more accuracy was promptly censored. For our own protection.

It obviously wouldn't be necessary to persuade the mechs that they needed to leave. So the real issue was persuading BioMax to let us.

"I get why you came back," Quinn told Jude. "And I'm

not surprised your little lapdog followed along—no offense," she added quickly, before I could bare my teeth. "But I'd have thought you would be smarter," she said to Ani.

"I thought the same about you," Ani said. "Guess I was wrong."

"So you've come to rescue the fair maiden from the tower?"

There was a pause. "And what if I did?"

Another pause, longer this time, like that wasn't the answer Quinn had been expecting. "Then I hope you really like towers. Because you're going to be stuck in this one for a long time."

None of us was ready to admit she was right. There was no denying the fact that we were stuck behind locked doors, without any contact to the world beyond the steel dome, but it's not like we'd expected to walk into paradise. Much less that we'd be able to just walk right out again. We would find a way.

BioMax staff were positioned at strategic points throughout the atrium, but they periodically disappeared through locked doors into some hidden portion of the dome to which we were denied access. It seemed likely that was where we would find our answers, and maybe even unrestricted access to the network that would let us document the conditions here. For whatever reason, BioMax clearly cared about persuading the world that they had our best interests at heart—which indicated that our best interests lay in revealing their lies. We could have used someone on the inside. But if Auden had been true to his word and snuck someone onto the staff, someone inclined to help us, he wasn't making his presence known. We were on our own, and breaking an electronic lock and slipping into a forbidden zone without getting noticed by the cameras or the orgs was going to take more than luck and desperation. When the lights went out at the end of that first day, we'd yet to muster anything.

I'd expected that our best exploring would be done that night, but at ten on the dot we were herded into our dark rooms. The door shut behind us, locking with a loud click.

"Sweet dreams, my heroes," Quinn said. "Can't wait to see who you save tomorrow."

She could pretend she didn't care, but I could tell that even Quinn was allowing herself a little hope. I wasn't the only one who felt motion was better than standing still, even if you weren't sure what you were hurtling toward. I spent the night awake, hoping that the darkness and the quiet would facilitate some kind of brilliant insight about how to sneak into the restricted zone. But my mind strayed—away from what I could do, toward what I should have done. If I'd broadcast what I knew to the network sooner, if I'd found a way to out BioMax or stop the Brotherhood before any of this had ever happened, if all those months ago I'd let Auden kiss me and kissed him back, if I'd never gone to the waterfall and he'd never been hurt.

If Zo had been the one to get in the car that day.

It was getting easier and easier to dream without going to sleep.

Finally the lights flared; the alarm screamed; morning came. And with it a cardboard box of fresh uniforms. How thoughtful of them. I kicked it across the room, and cheap synthetic jumpsuits went flying—along with something else. Something that shouldn't have been there at all. It clattered to the floor, blade gleaming under the fluorescents. Without hesitation, Jude snatched it off the ground and palmed it.

Ani and Quinn watched the door—if the cameras had caught our unexpected windfall and guards came blasting through, at least we'd be ready. Jude perched on his bed, slipped his hand beneath the pillow, and kept it there, drawing strength, I suspected, from the cool blade.

I knelt by the box. There was something taped into one corner: a slim plastic card. I tore off the tape and pulled it out, suspicions confirmed—it was a pass card, an exact replica of the ones the guards flashed as they slipped through their locked steel doors and into the forbidden zone.

I hid it as swiftly as Jude had hidden the knife, tracing my fingers across the smooth plastic.

Auden had come through for us after all.

I drew back my lips, feeling a sudden return to the days when every emotional response was a serious of careful decisions, a memorized series of muscles to be flexed and contracted. *This is a smile. This is happy.*

I couldn't say it out loud, it was too dangerous. But the words played in my head, deliriously certain.

I know what to do with the knife.

TRUST

"You're not going alone."

Don't move," I whispered, holding the blade a few centimeters from his skin.

Jude lay perfectly still beneath me. "Do it already," he hissed.

It was harder than I'd thought it would be. Not the mechanics of it—those were simple. We lay in the bed together. He was on his stomach, and I straddled him, knees tight around his hips. A blanket was draped over my head, blocking the cameras but allowing in enough light that I could see the curve of his neck and the tip of the knife. I pressed my thumb against the spot, a hard, raised ridge at the base of the neck. Easy enough to slide the blade into the skin, peel away the flesh, remove the chip. It had, at least, seemed easy when I came up with the idea.

"You want me to do you first?" Jude whispered, when I hesitated.

"No. I have this."

He'd asked me to do it. Not Ani, not Quinn. He'd wanted the knife in my hands.

It would take no more than the flexing of a single muscle to drive the blade into his back, cut a vital conduit, carve out a life. In the new age of the virus there was only this one body, and Jude was offering his up to me.

I slid the knife across the hard ridge of skin, fast and sure. He gasped, but didn't move. "Almost done," I said. I pressed my thumb against the lump, massaging the chip out through the small incision. It slid into view, coated in a viscous green fluid. "Got it."

He flipped himself over without warning, and suddenly we were face-to-face. His orange eyes glowed in the dim light.

"Your turn."

I lay beside him and bent my head. Exposed my neck. Trusted him.

It only hurt for a minute. Then I was free.

"Screw you!" Ani shouted.

"No, screw *you*!" Quinn leaped at her, fingers curled into claws, and went straight for her eyes. At the last minute Ani hunched her shoulder and shoved it into Quinn's chest. Quinn tumbled backward, and Ani dropped onto her. She seized a handful of hair and gave it a vicious tug. Quinn shrieked.

Jude and I backed away from the gathering crowd, as every guard in the atrium turned his attention to the warring ex-lovers. The fight had been my idea, a lesson learned from the vidlife ordeal. The spectacle of two girls rolling on the ground and squealing exerted a gross but undeniable pull: instant diversion.

Two of Quinn's friends had taken temporary custody of our tracking chips. Which meant that if we timed our escape correctly, no one in front of the cameras or behind them would witness us inching backward, sliding along the wall until we reached a nearly hidden door, swiping a pass card across the ID panel, and slipping out of our world and into theirs.

I didn't know what I'd been expecting, but it wasn't this bare limbo, like a holding cell: metal walls and floor that made it feel like we were in a giant tin can.

"What's the plan, idiots? You going to stand there until you get caught?"

"*Zo?*" I whirled around. "What the hell are you doing here?"

"Um, saving you?" My sister dragged us a few feet down the corridor, then through an open door. She slammed it behind us, leaving us in total darkness. The space was large enough to fit the three of us, but only just. And something that felt suspiciously like a broom handle was poking into my lower back.

"Zo, did you just stuff us in a janitor's closet?" I asked.

She snorted. "You really want to go with that as question number one?"

I cursed Auden. Of all the saviors to recruit, he chose my *sister*?

"You know what I'm still waiting for?" Zo asked.

"I'm guessing a thank-you." Jude's voice floated through the darkness. The closet was cramped enough that Zo's arm was squashed against my side and Jude's leg was pressed against my own.

"You shouldn't be here," I said.

"Neither should you," Zo said. "So I hope you figured out what you were supposed to do with the knife. Or we're all screwed."

"Auden sent you?" I was going to kill him.

"He didn't have enough Brotherhood connections to get anyone in on that end," she explained. "Fortunately, he had me."

"Let me guess, you charmed your way in," Jude said.

"You're not the only one with BioMax friends in high places," Zo said. "You know that guy Dad used to invite over for dinner, until he hit on Mom?"

"Tyson somebody?"

"Tyson Renzler. Let's just say, apparently I take after Mom more than we thought."

"Tell me you didn't—"

"Ew! No!" She shoved me, hard. "But he's had some creepy thing for me since I was fourteen. Always told me I should come to him if there was anything I needed—and made it *very* clear that he was perfectly okay keeping Dad in the dark. So here I am, folding towels, washing linens, and breaking you guys out. You mad?"

"Sort of mad."

Sort of grateful.

"You knew I wouldn't go back home," Zo said.

"Told-you-sos later," Jude said. "What do you know? What do we need to know?"

"Something's happening on Sunday." Zo affected a businesslike tone that I suspected she thought would make her sound older. "They're all whining about not wanting to wait."

"Wait for what?" I asked.

She shook her head. "I don't know. Something needs to happen on Sunday, and if it works, they can start phase three, but if it doesn't happen, they'll have to wait another month."

"And phase three is . . . ?"

"I don't know that either," she admitted. "I poked around all I could without getting caught, but there's nothing on file. And no one will tell me anything. That's all I got."

"Okay," Jude said. "So we work backward. What's phase two?"

"Getting us all in one place," I guessed. "For whatever reason."

"So we're here. Now what?" Jude asked. "What else is back here? What are they all doing while they're waiting around for phase three?"

"I don't know . . . offices, security monitoring, that kind of thing." Zo sighed, but at Jude's urging she kept going, describing in detail everything that lay on the BioMax side of the wall. He stopped her when she got to the generator room that had been deemed off-limits to all personnel.

"Why would they need their own power generator?" Jude asked. "And why would it be off-limits?"

"Not to everyone," Zo clarified. "I hung around for a while one afternoon, just to see what was going on. Some of the Brotherhood people definitely go in and out. They're not wearing robes or anything, but I recognized them. From before, I mean."

Jude leaned forward. "Does that mean you've seen inside? Even a glimpse?"

"Maybe. I guess. Just a bunch of equipment."

"Was there a compression generator?"

"A what?"

They went back and forth, Jude spewing out technical terms, Zo trying to remember whether she'd seen a giant cylinder or a massive cube, and what kind of equipment had been carried in and out, and eventually I zoned out, trying to imagine why a spare portable power plant could be of any interest to anyone, much less any danger. Arguably, extra power indicated that they were looking out for us, ensuring that if anyone tampered with the main power supply, our bodies would continue to function. Without electricity we were nothing; we were little more than mute and lifeless dolls. Power was everything. The pulse guns had proved that. Too much power could be as dangerous as too little, shorting out our networks, leaving us temporarily useless.

I froze.

What would happen if they found a bigger gun, one that turned temporary to permanent? One that could target several mechs at once.

"It sounds like it could be an EMP bomb," Jude said. "Set off a big enough electromagnetic pulse and—"

"Get rid of us all in one shot." I hadn't known such a thing existed.

"A big enough EMP blast wouldn't just short-circuit us," Jude said. "It would wipe us. Completely."

"And the virus wiped the backups," Zo said, sounding horrified.

"They're not this stupid," Jude murmured, thinking out loud. "I get wanting us out of the way so we can't claim proprietary ownership over the AI tech; I get that they don't want us making noise—but what's the strategy? What's the spin on pretending to save us, then turning around and wiping us out?"

"The Brotherhood!" I saw it all laid out now, the inevitable path, starting with the day we'd strolled into BioMax and set it in motion, so arrogant, so stupid, thinking we could talk a multibillion-dollar corp out of their multibillion-dollar profit. "Why do you think they're here? BioMax lets them in, under the radar, then turns them into a scapegoat. They did it to Auden, and now . . ."

"They're doing it to Savona?"

I could already see the press conferences Kiri would arrange, the note of sorrow in M. Poulet's voice as he explained the tragedy, bemoaned how foolish he'd been to trust Savona, to close his eyes to the danger of the Brotherhood and their infiltrators. What a tragedy: a safe haven transformed into a mass grave.

We'd known we were going to have to get the mechs out; now we knew we had less than a week in which to do it. And now we knew exactly how determined BioMax would be to stop us if we tried to leave. They wouldn't care who got hurt. Probably the more the better, as far as they were concerned. For all we knew, an escape attempt could offer them the perfect pretense to unleash their doomsday plan early. Which meant we had to move fast—but carefully.

Jude and Zo started throwing out ideas, bad ones, apocalyptic scenarios cribbed from video games, with the mech hordes storming their guards, scaling the walls, breaking free, leaving bodies strewn in their wake.

"It's easier than that," I said, seeing what they couldn't, because they hadn't been there, in the last corp-town, when the sirens blared and the orgs toppled like dominos, leaving me and Riley on our feet, utterly alone. Jude had once argued that the orgs would be willing to let a thousand mechs die if it would save a single human life. What was I willing to do to save a thousand mechs?

"It's like you always say, Jude. They're orgs. They're weak. We use that." I waited for him to get there before I could say it, so it could be his idea, and his responsibility. But he didn't. "We knock them out," I added. "If we could get access to the ventilation system . . ."

"We walk out of here, no questions asked," Jude said.

"Uh, except for the part where you have no way of doing it," Zo pointed out. "Unless you happen to walk around with some kind of magic sleeping potion in case of emergencies."

"No," Jude said. "But I know a guy who does."

"Great. You 'know a guy.'" I said. "So we just sneak out of here, meet up with your 'guy,' somehow sneak back in, or hope they're moronic enough let us walk through the door again, without searching us this time. Easy?"

"We could slip it to Zo," Jude said. "She could get it into the vents."

"He's right, I could—"

"You could *not*. What happens when they find you passed out by the vent access port and realize what you did?"

"So, better idea. *He* slips the stuff into the vents, *you* get everyone out—and I make it all possible by meeting up with this 'guy' in the first place. Tell me how to find him."

But I knew where she'd have to go to find him. The same place all Jude's 'guys' were. The place you lived when you were the kind of 'guy' who dealt in illegal bioweapons and various other diversions of the delinquent class.

"Are you forgetting what Auden said? No one leaves here without permission, not mechs, not staff."

"I'm not exactly staff so much as Tyson Renzler's pet project," Zo said. "If I want to leave, trust me, I can make it happen."

"Which means this will work," Jude said. "I can tell her exactly how to find this guy and what she needs to say to him, no problem."

"You want her to go into the city, *by herself,* and trust that your 'guy' won't take advantage of that?"

"He's a friend," Jude said.

"Yeah. I've met your *friends*."

"I can do this," Zo said. "I'm not scared."

"Then you're an idiot. So now you're really not doing it."

"Lia," she said. "Trust me. Just, for once, *trust me*."

I peered at her in the dark, trying to decode the shadowy outline, piece together the expression on her face.

"I am scared, okay?" she admitted. "But I can do this. Let me."

I didn't care how many mechs it would save; I wasn't willing to risk my sister. But maybe I didn't get to decide that for her. "One condition," I said.

"Anything."

"You're not going alone."

She already knew where to find Auden.

• • •

Ani and Quinn helped spread the word to the rest of the mechs. It was a whisper campaign, notes scrawled in dust and wiped away, murmured in willing ears, even razored into flesh as our blade made the rounds. Word spread that it was time to get out, that staying here was death, that there would soon be a signal.

But there'd be no signal and no escape unless Zo came back with what we needed—and all the plotting and whispering and strategizing in the world wasn't enough to distract me from what would happen if she never came back at all. What had I done, sending her into the city? I could picture her stepping over steaming piles of garbage, pressing herself against peeling building fronts as packs of rats (both the rodent and human variety) skulked past. I could even picture her following Jude's directions to the towers themselves, decaying strongholds protected by legless and armless children who thought they were sentries, who hoisted machine guns nearly as tall as they were.

That's where my picture faded. Because I couldn't picture her getting in, and I couldn't picture her getting out again, and I didn't care how high the stakes were or how many of us would die if this didn't work—none of it was worth what I'd done, letting her believe she could do it on her own.

But two days later it appeared, buried beneath our morning

supply of linens, two slim aerosol tubes of Amperin, and a note bearing only two words:

Your turn.

She was safe.

It was a matter of waiting. Zo still had the hard part—disabling the ventilation system security. She'd give us the signal if and when it worked. When it came, Jude and I would head for the vents while Ani and Quinn coordinated the rest of the mechs, alerting them that the time had come. She'd warned us it might take five minutes to get a clear shot at the computer system, or it might take hours. There was no way of knowing. And so we waited, keeping one eye on the giant screens overhanging the atrium. They broadcast messages to keep us calm, sanitized news of the outside world and assurances of how quickly our prison term would end. Soon, hopefully, they would go dark, just for a blink-and-you'd-miss-it moment, and that would be Zo. It felt strange to be sitting on a bench side by side with Jude, as if we were just two friends out for a day in the steel-encased park. *We're allies,* I thought. *Not friends. There's a difference.* Though it was becoming increasingly unclear exactly what it was.

"Can you believe your sister?" Jude said, lounging back on the bench, legs stretched wide.

"What?"

"Everything." Jude shook his head. "She's impressive."

"For an org, you mean."

"For anyone."

I'd never known Jude to admit respect for an org, much less this kind of naked admiration. "Don't."

"What?" Voice oh so innocent.

"You know what."

"No . . . apparently only one of us is a mind reader."

"Forget about Zo."

"Ah, sibling rivalry. Ugly, Lia. Doesn't become you."

"You're hilarious."

"And you're a joke. You really think I'd go after your sister?"

"It wasn't a suggestion."

He raised an eyebrow. "Jealous?"

"What? No!"

The self-satisfied smile appeared. "Jealous."

"You're disgusting."

"There's no shame in it—who wouldn't want this?" His hands did a little *eat your heart out* flourish over his body.

I grabbed his hand and bent it backward, several inches farther than it was supposed to go.

"Hey!"

"Ready to shut up?"

"Ready to let go?" He yanked his hand away before I could. Still stronger; always stronger. "I was teasing, psycho."

"I'm not joking about this, asshole."

"You really want to do this? Now?"

"Got nothing better to do."

"Fine. No Zo. I swear."

"Whatever that's worth."

"Psycho *and* paranoid. Great."

"I'm not saying it again—"

"Listen to me," he said, suddenly serious. "I will never pursue your sister. With or without your permission. You know that. You know why."

"Actually, I don't." But I was starting to get a very bad feeling. There was only one reason he would stay away from someone temptingly off-limits, just because I'd asked him to, just because she was my sister. Either he was lying, or . . .

"This is not going to happen," I said, suddenly aware of every inch of my body and its too-close proximity to his. "You. Me. *Never.*"

"I didn't say anything."

"Riley was your best friend!"

"You think I don't know that?"

"Never," I said again. "Even if I wanted it to. Which, to be clear, I don't."

"You think *I* do?" Jude said quietly. "It's the last thing I want."

"I hate you," I said, and in that moment, with a wave of revulsion and rage stronger than I'd felt for anyone, even Savona, it was true.

"You are so angry," he said.

"Your observational skills never cease to amaze me."

"No," he said. "I mean you're *always* angry."

"Of course I am."

"So just tell me *why*."

I couldn't believe it. All this time I'd thought we understood each other. That there was one common bond tying us together, one empty space that both of us were trying desperately to fill, one white-hot fire of purpose and revenge driving us both. And now he was *confused*? "Why aren't *you* angry?" I said, only barely resisting the urge to shout. "He's dead! And no matter what we do, even if we fix everything and save everyone, he's still *dead*. And you just . . ."

"What?"

"You accept it." I wanted to slap him.

Jude flinched like I had. The bright golden point flickered at the center of his pupils. "I'm angry."

"Not like I am."

"You want me to throw a tantrum? Will that convince you?"

"Joke about it," I said. "Pretend it's nothing. Whatever."

"Lia, look at me."

"I am looking at you." But I wasn't. I was looking at his forehead, and the silver lock of hair that kept slipping over his eyes. I was looking at his hands, slim fingers resting on the bench, unclenched and untroubled. I was looking at the door just over his shoulder, wondering what would happen when we broke through, if changing what came next would matter even though it couldn't change what had come before. I was looking anywhere but at him.

"I didn't get to say anything to him, before it happened." It was the first time I'd said it out loud. "I didn't get to tell him . . . He thought I didn't care." I could still see myself in that parking lot, would always see myself, frozen, looking up at Riley, cartoon shock painted across my face. Looking at him and judging him and saying nothing. Letting him walk away.

"You're wrong."

"I should have gone with him," I said.

"Great idea," Jude said. "You could have both uploaded, and then you'd both be dead. Is that what you want?"

"It's what I should want."

Now it was Jude who looked away.

"Why did you?" he asked finally. "Let him leave."

"What do you mean?" But I knew what he meant.

"That day. If you wanted to stop him, why didn't you?"

He asked like he already knew the answer. That made one of us. But before I could come up with something, two BioMax goons appeared before us, jackets strategically swept back to reveal their holsters, refuting an argument we hadn't thought to make.

"I'm going to need you to come with us," one of them said.

"Kind of busy here," Jude said, looping an arm around me. His other hand crawled across my knee and up my thigh. "If you know what I mean . . ."

I forced a smile. "What he said," I told the guard. "Maybe you could come back later?"

"Now," said the talky one, while the other one rested a hand on the butt of his pulse gun.

Jude and I exchanged a look: Whatever this was, we were going to have to postpone the strike. Ani and Quinn had their eyes on us from across the room, and hopefully Zo was catching this on one of the monitors and would figure out she needed to wait. Assuming, of course, they hadn't caught Zo, too.

We followed the guards along the same path we'd mapped out for ourselves—through the locked door, down the corridor, coming nearer and nearer to the central vents.

I wondered if there was some way we could turn this to our advantage. I had the toxin on me—if we could distract the guards for a minute and slip away . . . "Maybe if you told us exactly what the problem is?"

"No problem," the chatty one said. "Not anymore." He grabbed me, snatched my thrashing arms behind my back, looping them together with plastic twine. I screamed, and he shoved something thick and scratchy into my open mouth, then pulled a bag over my head. I was blind, mute, and bound, all in under ten seconds. And from the sound of things—an angry *oof* from the other guard, a scuffle, a muffled scream, then silence—things had gone about the same for Jude.

Meaty hands folded my knees to my chest, and I felt myself lifted off the ground for a moment, then gently placed back down. *Into* something, it turned out, because soon the ground lifted beneath me, like I'd been loaded into a giant sling, and, cradled in the darkness, we began to move. Going somewhere—wherever this guy wanted me to go.

So much for saving the day. But I wasn't thinking about the mechs we were leaving behind—I was thinking about myself.

I was afraid.

He can't hurt me, I told myself, the familiar mantra kicking in, except now it was a lie, because now this body was all I had, and if he broke it, that was it. No more second chances. No more extra lives.

No more Lia.

FOR YOUR PROTECTION

You don't try to understand the Grim Reaper; you don't forgive.

S*o this is how garbage feels,* I thought, *right before it gets dumped.*

Scared. Hopeless. And very alone.

Would they leave me in a landfill? Toss me in a lake? Bury me so deep no one would hear me scream, which I would only be able to do once decades passed and the gag in my mouth decayed to dust? Or maybe they'd decided to get rid of me for good. A trash compactor would do the trick, though why grind up the body when it would be so easy to wipe the mind?

I wondered what it would be like to not exist. Maybe some part of me still would, deep in the bowels of BioMax, where for all I knew they'd lobotomized my stored neural patterns the way they had so many others, and some other, obediently simple-minded version of me was piloting war planes and enjoying target practice on guerrilla warriors.

This is what human garbage thinks about, on its way to

the dump. Until the bag drops to the ground and hands reach in and pull it out.

Then all thinking stops, replaced with blind, animal panic.

Even when the garbage is a machine. Simulated emotion seems real enough when that emotion is stark terror, when every inch of you is singing out an alarm of *I don't want to die.*

They pulled out the gag, and the scream began again as if it had never stopped.

"Enough drama, we get it," a deeply familiar but somehow alien voice informed me. Alien because I'd never heard it sound like this: authoritative, impatient, absolutely certain.

Familiar because it belonged to my mother.

I was in a van, windowless and in motion, filled with people I would have preferred never to see again. Jude and I sat in the back, sandwiched between the two BioMax guards, who, as it turned out, didn't work for BioMax at all. They worked for my mother. Who sat in the front seat, shoulder to shoulder with call-me-Ben.

At least it looked like my mother, but my mother wasn't the type to hire armed guards, or to kidnap her own daughter, or to bark commands like "Shut him up"—when Jude's gag came out and then promptly went back in again until he'd promised to behave—and "Stop acting like a child." She'd always been the one who acted like a child, so easily persuaded by my father that whatever she'd done was wrong.

My mother didn't have steel in her voice.

"What's *he* doing here?" I asked, glaring at call-me-Ben, because starting with him was easier than figuring out what this new mother had done with the old one.

"Ben's doing me a favor," she said.

"If that's what you want to call it," Ben said, then mumbled something that sounded suspiciously like "blackmail."

She favored him with an icy smile. "I simply explained to your friend what I knew about the inner workings of his corp and how reluctant he might be for certain information to emerge."

"We've already gone public with everything," I said. "No one cares about what BioMax does to mechs."

"Your version of 'everything' is somewhat narrow, dear. And the 'public' isn't exactly anyone's greatest concern. Ben knows that when I talk, the right people listen. So he decided on a different course."

"Kidnapping me?"

"Extricating you from a dangerous situation," my mother said. "One I would never have guessed you were foolish enough to put yourself into. I wasn't about to leave you there."

"So you trusted *him*?" Jude asked.

"You're here, aren't you?" she said coolly. "*Both* of you. Though I can't say that was my intent."

The guards dropped their heads. "I told you, taking him seemed like the best way not to make a scene," one of them mumbled. "Didn't think you'd care—"

"And I told you, I'm not paying you to *think*."

"Did your mother learn her gangster talk from watching the vids?" Jude whispered.

She cleared her throat, pointedly.

"What the hell is going on, Mom?"

"There's something *wrong* about this whole situation, and that corp-town wasn't safe for you," she said.

"I've tried to assure your mother that her fears are misplaced," Ben said. "But she won't believe me."

"The question isn't whether I believe him," my mother said, as if he weren't there. So at least one thing hadn't changed: She was still treating the help like dirt. "Living with your father, I've become quite skilled at knowing when people are lying. Your friend Ben here isn't—he's just ignorant. M. Poulet, on the other hand, is like your father. Nothing but lies, all the way down. And whatever's going on there, I don't want you to be a part of it."

What about Zo? I almost said, but stopped myself. Because either she didn't know Zo was there—in which case I wasn't about to enlighten her—or she *did* know, and didn't care. In which case she'd learned more from my father than the ability to spot a liar.

"Who *are* you?" I asked instead. "And what have you done with my mother?"

"I know what you think of me," she said. "I played the part I had to play. I did my job. But think about it: Your father may treat me like a fool, but does he really seem the type to marry one?"

"Nobody's saying you're a . . . fool." Not out loud, at least. Had I been imagining it? Had she been like *this* the whole time, and I hadn't noticed? Or had she, for whatever perverse reason, spent the last seventeen years in hiding? "If you're so good at seeing through bullshit, then I guess that means you knew all along? What he did? What BioMax 'made' him do?"

All the air went out of her. "No."

"And when you found out, you didn't see the need to do anything."

"I stayed," she said.

"Fucking right. You stayed."

"Watch your language," she said. "Yes, I stayed. *That's* what I did. If he was capable of . . . what he did—"

"Murder his daughter," I said loudly. "That's what he did."

"If he's capable of that, he's capable of anything."

"You were watching him," Jude guessed. "*Guarding* him."

"Someone had to. Make sure he stayed in line. Make sure he stayed miserable."

"Even if it meant you were miserable too," Jude said.

"No more than she—" I stopped myself.

"Deserves?" my mother suggested.

Ben cleared his throat. "Give your mother a break."

"Shut up, Ben." The response came in chorus, my mother and me in sync.

"It doesn't matter why I stayed," my mother said. "I did. Which is how I knew it was time to help you."

"I've tried to explain to your mother that she's over-reacting," Ben said.

"Nothing unusual about that," I agreed, fingering the vial of Amperin adhered to my upper arm. "Now that you've done your motherly duty, any chance you could drop us back where you found us?"

"You see, M. Kahn," Ben said, "they're perfectly happy to—"

"They're *children*," my mother snapped. "What makes them happy isn't really my concern."

"With all due respect, M. Kahn, *I'm* not your kid," Jude said. "If you want me to contact my parents, I'm sure they'd be happy to take me off your hands."

She laughed. "So I see you've told all your friends about your idiot mother, Lia." She twisted around in her seat to get a better look at him. "You think I don't know about you? That you came from *nothing*? That you have no parents? You think I didn't learn everything I could about the person who stole my daughter right out from under me?"

"Jude didn't *steal* me. I'm not some *thing* that belongs to you, like your stupid Chindian tea set."

"You'll be safe at home," my mother said. "Both of you."

"It won't be for long," Ben said. "I'm taking a tech crew out to one of the server ships on Sunday. They're pretty sure they can cut off the virus at the root, restore the server integrity, and then all this will be behind us."

"Always the optimist. You must—" I stopped, mouth open, the rest of the thought vanishing as his words registered, and everything clicked into place.

Sunday. As in the day that phase three would be put into action.

Because if it doesn't happen now, we'll have to wait another month.

For security reasons they sent launches to the server farms only once a month. It was the best way to minimize and control access. Everyone knew that.

"I must what?" Ben prodded, when I didn't continue.

But I shook my head, gears turning. *Sunday.* So we had three days. Three days to figure out what they were planning to do at that server farm—and stop them.

"Forget it," I said. "You're in charge, right? We're just children. Do whatever you have to do."

"I will," my mother said.

So would I.

The van pulled up to the estate. Jude had never seen it before. But I could tell, from the way he looked at me, that he'd just had all his suspicions confirmed. I was exactly the person he'd always thought I was: the poor little rich girl, doing what Mommy told her to do because it was easier than fighting back. He didn't say a word to me, or to any of us, as the guard escorted him into the house. Ben caught hold of me before my guard and I could follow.

"I know you hate me," he said quietly, keeping his eyes on my mother and his voice low enough to ensure she wouldn't hear.

"I don't have any feelings toward you one way or another. You're irrelevant."

"I wasn't part of what the corp did to you," Ben said. "I didn't even know about it at first."

"Even if I believed you, it doesn't matter. And I don't believe you."

"We've done good things." Ben sounded desperate. "This technology is a miracle. It can change everything. Artificial intelligence. Space exploration. Medical miracles. We've only just begun to imagine the possibilities. It can save us all, like it saved you."

I almost bought it. Could he actually be this naive? Maybe. Did it matter?

Not at all.

"Let me prove it to you," he said.

"Prove what?"

"That I'm trying to help. Some of us—*most* of us—mean well, Lia. We've always been on your side." He handed me a folded-up printout. "When the time is right, this is where you'll find him."

"What the hell is that supposed to mean?"

"You'll see."

Curiosity overpowering judgment, I started to unfold the paper, but he stopped my hands. "Wait until you're inside," he said, glancing again at my mother. "You might want to keep this one to yourself."

"Lia." My mother pointed to the front door. The guard stood at the ready.

"Maybe don't be so hard on her," Ben said.

"Seriously? You want to give me advice on being a good daughter now?"

"You don't have kids," he said. "If you did . . ."

There was nothing I hated more than the familiar *you haven't been there, so you can't really understand* crap. Which I was about to point out to him, when I noticed how distant he looked, and wondered if he was thinking of his own kid, the girl about Zo's age, who, I gathered, hated him about as much as I did.

I decided to let it pass.

"Can I go now?"

"Right. Of course." Ben put out his hand for me to shake, then dropped it after a few seconds when I didn't move. "I'm sorry," he said.

"Why? According to you, you didn't do anything."

"That doesn't mean I'm not sorry," he said. "I hope someday you'll understand that."

Here's what Ben would never understand: When I woke up in the hospital that wasn't a hospital, facing the doctor that wasn't a doctor, unable to speak, unable to move, the mirror reflecting a fright show with dead eyes and exposed skull, he'd been the one to tell me the truth of what I was, and he'd been the one to roll me into that silvery morgue to see my hollow, ruined body, the body he'd taken away. Whatever happened next, whatever role he had or hadn't played in setting up the car accident, in lobotomizing our stored neural patterns, in manipulating and lying and plotting a mechanical genocide, it would never matter. He was the face of what I had become, the face of BioMax, the face of death. You don't try to understand the Grim Reaper; you don't forgive.

You turn your back on him—knowing there's nothing left he can do to you—and go inside.

It was strange to be back in the house, my second home-coming in six months, and like last time, much as I wanted the house to feel like a prison, it felt like home. The same overwrought antiques, the same stiff chairs and couches that screamed *Don't sit on me!* lest some disastrous spillage occur. The same virgin-white rug that had never felt the touch of a shoe. The only difference: my father, slumped on the gray love seat, his head down but eyes unmistakably fixed on the door, my father, who was always in motion, consumed with impossibly important business, planted there like a piece of furniture, posture sagging and defeated. My father, around whom the world turned, sitting on the sidelines, making no move to interfere or even react to my arrival; my mother barely acknowledging his presence. I was almost sorry I hadn't been around to watch him adjust to his new domestic reality. I suspected he was wondering if, back when he'd had a choice, he should have just opted for prison. Losing a daughter was one thing. Being bossed around by my mother? For him that would surely be intolerable.

My mother and the guard flanked me on either side as we trooped up the stairs.

"Lia." I thought I heard my father's voice trailing behind me, but it could have been my imagination, and I didn't look back.

"This is for your own good," my mother said. "You'll thank me some day."

"Been reading from the parental-cliché handbook again?"

"Put her in there," she told the guard, gesturing to my room. Jude was already inside.

"You can't *make* me want to be your daughter," I told her. "You know that. You can keep me prisoner here as long as you want. It isn't going to change anything."

"You *are* my daughter," she said, cold and calm. "Whether you want to be or not. So consider yourself grounded."

She brushed her lips against my cheek, lightly enough that I barely felt them, quickly enough that by the time I thought to push her away, she was gone. The guard shoved me into my bedroom, then switched the room into lockdown mode, sealing us in. The setting had come standard with our security system—drop-down bulletproof shutters over the windows, network jammers, electronic locks, all designed to turn your average everyday bedroom into a prison. Designed for keeping burglars out—used most often, in our house at least, for keeping unruly daughters in. Zo had lived half her life in lockdown mode, but it was a new one for me. Still, I'd heard Zo complain enough to know that throwing my weight against the door or clumsily trying to pick the lock with a paper clip wasn't exactly going to cut it.

Predictably, Jude had his head buried in one of my drawers, but at least he wasn't pawing through my underwear. "Find anything you like?" I asked.

"Nothing that's going to get us out of here," he said, rapping a fist against the window shutter.

I unfolded the paper Ben had given me, scanning the dense chunk of file names and techno jargon for something that would make sense. *This is where you'll find him.*

I'd seen this kind of thing before, when Zo had hacked our father's ViM to try to get us some answers. It seemed like a million years ago, but I recognized the way the file names were diagrammed into decision trees, branching across the page.

It was a map, I realized—and then realized I'd seen many of these file names before. It was a fragment of the network hierarchy of the internal BioMax servers. The secret, isolated ones that stored brains ready for stripping and dehumanizing, for loading into BioMax's "intelligent machines." And one of the file names was circled, a meaningless string of numbers. I knew, from our BioMax break-in, that the lobotomized brain patterns were stored by ID number rather than name. This one was 248713, and there was a second file marked 248713b. But it was the original that was circled in red, with Ben's handwriting beneath it: *intact.*

I handed the page to Jude. After all this time, it still seemed strange that my hands weren't trembling. Because my brain felt like it was vibrating inside my head, bouncing off the inner walls of my skull in sync with the seconds ticking by, time running out. "Tell me if that means what I think it means," I said, and watched him run his eyes down the page, tried to mark the exact moment he saw what I'd seen, and understood.

He saw it. Then he said what I couldn't, because I was afraid to believe it.

"Ben gave you this?" he asked.

"He said . . . he said, 'This is where you'll find him.'"

"Riley," Jude said. "They stored a copy of him."

The paper floated to the floor, and Jude looked down at his hands, as if his fingers had acted on their own accord. He didn't move to pick it up; he didn't move at all. "He's still out there, somewhere."

I nodded.

Somewhere a circuit board, an electronic file, bits and bytes, somewhere ones and zeros, flipped in a precise order, the billions and trillions of quantum qubits that made a life, trapped inside a computer, trapped underground, trapped.

But alive.

RIGHTEOUS

It wasn't the most promising of revolutionary cabals.

We couldn't save him.

Not yet.

Riley was the one variable in all of this that wasn't teetering on the edge of catastrophe. Safe—or relatively so, in a database, free-floating in the ether—Riley could wait. I didn't want to let myself believe it was true, because if Ben was lying, if I let myself hope and then had to lose him all over again . . .

But once the idea was in my head, I couldn't get rid of it. The idea of Riley being gone forever had been the impossibility; this last-minute reprieve felt inevitable. His death had never been real.

This had to be.

"You think he's aware?" I said. "His mind's all there. How do we know he's not trapped in there, afraid and alone? How do we know it doesn't hurt?"

"It doesn't," Jude said. "He's not."

"But how do we *know*?"

"We have to believe it," Jude said, sounding like a deranged Faither. "Because if we don't . . ."

Then we wouldn't be able to leave him there. *For just a little longer,* I promised him. *Until we fix everything.*

Like there was much chance of that happening while we were locked up in my bedroom behind bulletproof windows and network jammers. If my mother didn't want us out, we weren't getting out. My father had spent years turning the Kahn house into a fortress. I'd always taken his word for our security and its necessity, never worrying that the barbarians would break down the gates, never chafing against his boundaries from my side of the wall. I'd been the good girl, and good girls didn't know how to break out of bedroom prisons.

They left that to bratty little sisters.

I pounded my fists against the door, again and again, harder each time, knowing that my mother would lose any game of wills she tried to play, because she was only human, and I was not. I could bang on that door for the rest of eternity.

It took less than an hour to wear her down.

"I'm not letting you out," she said, from the other side of the steel door. "This is for your own good."

"I know. I was just thinking, maybe if you let me get in touch with—"

"We don't need any more of your helpful little mech friends

swarming around here," she said. "I think one is enough, don't you?"

Jude, who was trying to break through the window despite my assurances it was virtually impossible, stopped his useless tinkering long enough to give the door a dirty look.

"It's not that." I rested my weight against the door, letting my forehead kiss the cool steel. When was the last time my mother had come up to my bedroom? When I was seven? Eight, maybe? However old I was before I'd gotten "too old" for bedtime stories and tucking in. *Stop babying her,* my father had said, and then I'd jumped on board with *I'm no baby,* and my mother had blushed, and that had been it: no more nightlights, no more stories, no more sweet-dreams kisses. My bedroom became my property, and I got my bedtime stories off the network; my mother retreated to the estate's other wing. "I'm thinking about Zo."

"What about her?" came the slow, careful response from the other side of the door.

"I'm worried about her."

"Have you talked to her?" she asked.

"No. Have you?"

No answer.

"If she knew that I was here, maybe she would . . . you know."

"*Forgive* me?" My mother's voice twisted on the word. Proving again, she was no fool.

"She doesn't have to forgive you," I said. "She just has to come home. And maybe she will, if she thinks I was willing to."

"Why would you want her to think that?"

Good question. "It's not safe for her out there on her own," I said.

"What are you doing?" Jude whispered. I waved him off. My house, my mother, my sister: my game.

"But it's safe for *you*?" my mother said.

"I'm different," I said. "Zo's still a kid. And besides, I'm stuck here, right? So maybe something good can come out of it. Maybe if Zo knew the truth about you, if you gave her a chance to know what was actually going on—"

"I stayed with your father," she said. "That's what's going on. I let him do whatever he wanted. No one's wrong about that. It's just the truth."

"It's not the whole truth. She deserves to know that."

There was a long pause. "I'll think about it," she said.

I wasn't ready for her to leave. "Mom."

She didn't say anything. For all I knew, she was already gone. I didn't know her anymore; I didn't know what to expect.

"Thanks," I said finally. I meant it to help the lie.

Or maybe I just meant it.

There was another eternal pause. Then, "For what?"

"For trying."

• • •

It was past midnight when the door eased open. "Shut up and let's go," Zo hissed, before Jude could open his big mouth and wake the house.

She brandished a slim silver cylinder that I assumed she'd used to pick the electronic lock. "You are *so* lucky you're not an only child," she whispered, as we crept out of the bedroom and down the hall toward Zo's old room.

"And *you* are so lucky that Mom still knocks herself out on chillers every night, or your big, clomping feet would get us both thrown back into Kahn jail."

She grinned. "You're welcome."

Zo's bedroom was better equipped for a breakout than mine. "Nothing I haven't done before," she whispered, grabbing a compressible wire ladder from under her mattress and hooking it to the window frame. She swept out a gallant hand. "Ladies first."

It had been a strange year. But there'd been nothing stranger than scaling the side of my own house, dim moonglow lighting the ladder rungs as I climbed, hand over hand, three stories down. Feeling like a criminal, stealing into the night with the Kahn family valuables, and our father might have pointed out that was exactly what I was doing—*my most valuable possessions,* he called us when we were little, and I'd taken it as a compliment, proud to be valued more highly than the new car. His to protect; his to destroy. Mine to creep through the darkness, following Zo as she darted in and out of the motion detectors' sweep, avoided the cameras, deactivated the electronic gate, led us to freedom—freedom in the form of a beat-up two-door Chevrelle, Auden at the wheel.

"How'd you know?" Jude asked, as we piled into the car.

"Got the call from Mommy dearest." Zo snorted. "Like I was supposed to believe Lia came crawling home, and wanted me for one big family reunion? Big sis is stupid—"

I jabbed her in the side.

"—but not that stupid," Zo allowed, grinning at me. "And clearly, you're lucky to have such a proficient juvenile delinquent for a sister."

"Yeah. I guess I am."

We holed up in Riley's place, memories of him everywhere, looking for a way to fix what we'd all helped to break. Zo wanted to sneak back into the corp-town, bust everyone out. Auden wanted to go public, turn himself in to the authorities—turn himself into a martyr, if it would help, or a devil, if that would help more. And Jude was characteristically silent about what he actually wanted, uncharacteristically silent about everything.

But Zo couldn't risk showing her face at the corp-town again, not with our mother on a rampage and Zo's presumably suspicious disappearance timed with our own. Quinn and Ani had their own share of the toxin. We had to trust them to figure out something to do with it. Auden's plan was just as craptastic, relying as it did on mythical *authorities* of an objective nature unaffiliated with any of the corps, unswayed by power and credit we didn't have. Given that all of the secops were owned by one corp or another, that BioMax was in business with all of them, and that the Justice Department—the only arm of the government not officially licensed out to private enterprise—was also the one that hated mechs the most, we had a better chance of tracking down a unicorn. Turn himself in and he'd promptly disappear, only to resurface once BioMax and the Brotherhood had done whatever they planned to do and were ready to parade their scapegoat for public shaming.

We'd dropped what we knew and what we suspected about Safe Haven onto the network, posting it to every zone we could—knowing that most would get purged by BioMax and the rest would likely be lost in the noise, seeming no more or less credible than any of the other rumors flying about the skinner plague, as it was being called. Some probably even believed us—not just the crackpots who matched our claims with conspiracies of their own, but the occasional sane, sober observers who were inclined to suspect the corps were up to no good. Some wished us well, some even raised a little online ruckus, but none was in a position to help.

We were on our own. Two machines. Two orgs. Four teenagers with no power and no plan. At least Auden was on the run from nefarious cult leaders and corporate overlords. As opposed to me, hiding out from my mother.

It wasn't the most promising of revolutionary cabals.

"We can't do anything about what's going to happen inside Safe Haven," I said. "But we can stop phase three. Or at least we can try."

"We can't stop it if we don't even know what it is," Jude said, sounding defeated.

"Whatever it is, it's happening on that server ship on Sunday," I said.

"You *think*," Jude said.

Zo and Auden agreed that it was the only thing that made sense with what little else we knew. The once-a-month window had given it away. "If we can get on board with Ben's team, we can figure out what they're doing," I said. "We can stop them."

"Great," Jude said sourly. "So all we need to do—assuming your *blind hunch* is right—is sneak on board a high-security facility floating in a secret location in the middle of the Atlantic and stop a team of determined and presumably armed genocidal maniacs from completing their nebulous mission. Brilliant plan."

"Glad you agree."

Jude was, of course, right. The plan—or, rather, ambiguous idea completely lacking in practical execution—wasn't brilliant so much as insane. Especially the part that involved us getting ourselves onto a server ship without anyone noticing and, more to the point, without getting tossed overboard. The network servers were overseen by a private consortium of tech and security corps, its operations designed for maximal transparency (for those whose job it was to watch) and maximal secrecy (for the rest of us unwashed masses). They floated on massive ocean freighters, each the length of several football fields, shadowing the coastline, their endless rows of whirring machines processing the data of millions while armed guards—or armed machines, or, for all any of us knew, armed armadillos, or some deadly combination of all three—patrolled the corridors, sworn to protect the network with their lives. Ships set out once a month with reinforcements, repairs, representatives from any corp who needed to address problems with their dedicated servers—ships that plotted a top-secret course radioed to the captain on a special frequency only once the boat had X-rayed and analyzed every single thing, animate or in-, to come aboard.

The server farms were governed by no law but the law of expediency. Its servants followed a prime directive, to the exclusion of all else: Protect the servers. Protect the mindless hordes who trusted every piece of their lives to the security of the floating machines. Trusted not just their zones, their relationships and memories, but their jobs, their life savings, their lives—whenever they trusted their automated cars or their high-speed elevators or the biofilters that kept their air breathable and the wireless energy that kept everything humming, including me. The guardians of those ships protected all of us who acted as if the data cloud floated in an impermeable bubble through some alternate, inaccessible realm, as if we weren't living in a virtual world built almost entirely on the switches and circuits and routers floating through poisonous waters and roughing stormy seas.

That, at least, was what we'd heard.

That was the only thing anyone knew about the server farms: rumors. Everyone knew a guy, who knew a guy, who used to work for someone who staffed one of the ships. Everyone had heard something, but no one knew anything. I'd once overheard my father arguing with one of his board members about whether or not the servers operated as independent international entities or were wholly owned American enterprises, and much as he'd tried to disguise it, the truth had been clear: Even he had no idea. Everyone knew—or at least "knew"—that once a month an elite group got access to the servers to upgrade them on behalf of their own corps, but either they were shielded from penetrating any of the ships' secrets, or the ghostly overseers had a way to make them keep their mouths shut. Access to the servers meant access to everything. We were a world of connectivity; a linked-in globe. It was our pride as a human race. And apparently, it worked only if none of us knew how.

"We're thinking too far ahead," I said suddenly.

Auden laughed quietly. "I wouldn't say that's exactly your problem, Lia."

"No, I mean it. You're right, Jude—"

He held up a hand to stop me. "Moment of silence, please, while I enjoy this history-making moment."

I smacked his arm. Lightly, but not too lightly. "You're right that we have no way of getting on that ship or figuring out what's going on—not by ourselves. And maybe you're right that I'm just guessing. We need more answers. We need help, from someone who knows *exactly* what BioMax is up to—or at least knows how to find out."

That woke him up. "Ben?"

"He's leading the team, right? Whether he knows about phase three or he doesn't, he's going to be there when it happens. So either he gives us the information we need, or he makes sure that *we're* there when it happens, too."

"And why would he do that?" Jude asked.

There was a time when I would have hesitated to ask the next question. This time I didn't. "Do you have a gun stashed here somewhere?"

Surprised, Jude shook his head. That was problematic. I'd counted on him having easy access to a weapon, as he always seemed to. We could get in touch with another of his city contacts, but that meant complications, and time . . .

Auden cleared his throat. "I do."

• • •

"But it's my gun," Auden said, as we were packing up to leave.

"It's safer to leave someone behind," I said. "If anything happens and we need reinforcements—"

"Bullshit."

"Auden . . ."

"You don't want me along; just say it."

I didn't want to.

"You don't trust me," he said.

"No, I don't."

"But that's not it," he said.

"No. It's not."

He scowled. "It's not your job to worry about me."

There wasn't time to protect his feelings—and after everything that had happened, maybe that was no longer a huge priority. "You're weak," I said. "The limp, the lung issues, what happens when your body gets too stressed . . . You could be a liability."

He didn't flinch. "See? It wasn't so hard to just say it."

"Fine. I said it. So now you'll stay here?"

"Not a chance."

"You're not—"

"I can do this," he said. "I'm not as weak as you think."

"Or you're weaker than *you* think. And we find out at the worst possible time."

"Let him come," Jude said.

"What?"

"If he says he can do it, he can do it."

"You're kidding me," I said. "What, are you hoping he'll do something stupid and get himself killed?"

"He looks weak," Jude said. "It doesn't mean he is. And you don't get to decide what he's strong enough to do."

"Thanks," Auden said, sounding surprised.

"I'm just saying what's true," Jude said. "I still hate you."

"Back at you."

"It's wonderful that you two are bonding, but this isn't some kind of self-actualization field trip," I snapped. "We can't afford—"

"We can't afford not to use everything we've got," Jude said over me. "Besides, he owes us."

"I can do this, Lia," Auden said.

I shrugged, and waved him out the door. At least he hadn't asked me to trust him.

Jude followed, but Zo hung behind, watching me carefully.

"What?" I said finally.

She paused, looking unsure whether or not to risk it. "So you're not going to try to talk *me* out of coming along?"

"Would there be any point?"

She shook her head.

"Then what are you waiting for?"

For a second I was afraid she was going to hug me. But instead she just smiled and ran past me out the door, practically skipping, as if she were seven again and I'd given her the secret password to the big-kids' clubhouse. I told myself that she knew exactly how serious this was and how big a risk she was taking, and that—as she'd proved to me over and over again—she was old enough and tough enough to decide she wanted to take it.

After the accident it had quickly—though maybe not quickly enough—become obvious that I wasn't the same person I used to be. It had taken another year to figure out that Zo wasn't either. But I finally got it. She was, after everything, still my little sister. But she was also Zo Kahn, someone I'd never bothered to know, not really—and now that I did, it was clear that protecting her from herself was neither an option nor a necessity. It was also clear that, as far as she was concerned, this wasn't just my fight. It was ours. So she was going to risk everything for it. And I was going to let her.

It had been easy enough for Zo to hack through the privwalls on Ben's zone to discover he lived on a modest estate less than twenty miles away. The zone offered a cornucopia of Ben trivia: He lived alone, on the opposite coast from his ex-wife and teenage daughter, who, judging from the number of plaintive messages he sent her and the nonexistent response, wasn't any fonder of her father than I was of mine. The girl looked less like Zo than I'd thought when I first saw her picture—the stringy hair and baggy clothes were the same, but her features were smoother and more rounded. She had the same soft, waxy beauty as her father, if none of his impeccable fashion sense.

The house itself wasn't that impressive. It was half the size of ours, with barely any grounds, and what there was had fallen into disrepair. Kudzu crawled up the decaying brick, nearly blocking out the windows, and the weedy, browning lawn clearly hadn't been trimmed or watered in months. The security system was a sad, bargain-basement model—probably because no burglar in his right mind would choose a house like this to burgle when there were so many better options on offer—and Jude had no trouble jamming the alarm, shutting down the electrified perimeter, and easing open the back door.

"You're good at this," I said softly.

"Practice makes perfect," he muttered.

I didn't want to know.

It was well past midnight, and the house was completely dark. Auden, with a minimum of whining, had agreed to wait in the car under the theory that every criminal operation needed a getaway driver. Zo, Jude, and I used our ViM screens to light our way, and took our time making our way through the house, just in case we stumbled across anything relevant. Like a giant blinking poster detailing the logistics of phase three. Or a rabid guard dog.

Fortunately or unfortunately, there was nothing but a bare, personality-free house, with empty walls and furniture that, for the most part, appeared completely untouched.

The kitchen was empty of both food and standard appliances. Breaking into someone's house was different from breaking into a corp—it felt almost like we were peering inside call-me-Ben's head, and, much as I disliked the guy, I couldn't take much pleasure in the fact that the view was so pathetic. The only sign that someone actually lived here was the occasional pic of his daughter, some from years ago, some clearly recent, the only commonality between them the fact that Ben was never in the shot.

We crept up the stairs, peeking silently into each room we passed. The first was a closet, the second a marbled bathroom, and the third a true surprise: a cluttered laboratory, its tables and shelves filled with spare mech parts, its whiteboard walls covered with Ben's messy scrawl, circuit diagrams dotted with question marks and the occasional exclamation point. Ben may not have gotten much living done in his house, but apparently that was because he was too hard at work. Against my will I felt another stab of sympathy, one that was easy enough to suppress when I reminded myself what he was probably working *toward*. We fanned out through the lab, searching for anything that screamed *death to mechs*, but none of us was particularly well equipped to analyze his equipment or the thrust of his research. Ben was one of the lead techs at BioMax, and had led the team that designed the original download technology—he could be working on anything, and we weren't going to figure it out by studying his circuit boards. He would have to tell us.

The next door was the bedroom.

I held the gun. Jude cleared his throat. Ben woke up. There was a moment of sleepy confusion; then he saw the muzzle pointed at his forehead, and bolted upright. I stood at the foot of the bed, about five feet away from him. Far enough that he couldn't do something stupid, like lunge at the gun. Close enough that even I couldn't miss. Zo waited in the hallway, just outside the door, on guard for reinforcements we weren't expecting—and, if it came to that, reinforcement herself if Ben proved somehow, unexpectedly, able to take on me, Jude, and a nine-millimeter pistol. The weapon was just as heavy as I remembered, but it fit more comfortably in my hands this time. The safety was off.

"What is this, Lia?" Ben asked in a low voice. I could tell he was trying not to show fear, but his eyes darted back and forth, from Jude to me to the gun and back to Jude again. He was afraid. His hand inched toward the nightstand.

Jude shook his head. "I wouldn't," he said. "Unless you think your trigger finger's faster than hers is."

Even a low-budget security system came with silent alarm switches that could be conveniently positioned around the house. Maybe Ben had just meant to turn on the light, or reach for his ViM. But there was no point in taking the chance. "I'd listen to him," I said.

Ben did.

"What are you doing here, Lia? What are you doing with *that*?"

"You think he's talking about the gun, or about me?" Jude asked.

Ben wore a set of checkered flannel pajamas. His quilt was navy, with a thick black trim. For so long he'd been this BioMax boogeyman, always one step ahead of me, ready to cajole or blackmail or smarm his way into getting whatever he wanted. But now he was just a guy. And kind of a sad, small one.

"What's phase three?" I asked.

"What?"

"You're going to the server ship on Sunday. What are you doing there?"

"I told you before, we're dealing with the virus— Look, is this about Riley?" He sounded almost impatient. "Because if it is, I was just trying to help. I didn't know about the stored file until recently, and this really isn't necessary; I can—"

"Shut up. This isn't about Riley. *What's phase three?*"

Ben swung his legs toward the side of the bed like he was about to climb out.

"Don't move," I said.

He shook his head. "You're not going to shoot me, Lia."

"You're so sure?"

"I know you," he said, the same old Ben, sure he knew me

better than I knew myself. "This isn't you. Him, maybe, but not you."

"I'm choosing to take that as a compliment," I said. "But I'm guessing he will too." Never taking my eyes—or the muzzle—off of Ben, I handed the gun over to Jude. Just once, I'd wanted to see how it felt to have the power over Ben, the control, to know he had to do what I wanted. But I couldn't have pulled the trigger. I knew that, and he knew that.

For this to work we needed someone who could.

"Get back in bed," Jude said. Ben did as he was told. "You want to tell me this isn't me?" Jude sneered. "You want to tell me I don't have it in me?"

Ben was a good liar, but apparently not that good. He gripped the edge of the blanket, tugging it around himself like it was bulletproof. "What do you want?"

"Phase three," I said again.

"You keep saying that, and I'm telling you, *I have no idea*."

We went back and forth several times, until it was made clear that Ben was either far more courageous or more clueless than we'd given him credit for, because even with a gun in his face—wielded by a mech who would have loved nothing more than to pull the trigger on the man who'd delivered the news of Riley's death—he gave us nothing. I'd suspected all along that Ben wasn't behind BioMax's planned eradication of the mechs. He was too impassioned about the technology, too grossly sincere in his desire to help us, in his need to be *liked*. So maybe they'd kept him in the dark. It didn't mean he couldn't help us, willingly or not.

"I believe you," I said finally.

"Really?" he asked, surprised.

"Really?" Jude echoed, equally so.

"Really. So here's what you're going to do." I channeled my mother, and the imperious way she'd treated him, like he existed only to serve her purposes. I'd seen him bend to her, to M. Poulet, to anyone with enough power. If he liked to be led so much, we could accommodate him. "You're going to take us with you when you go to the server ship. Then it'll be easy to prove that you're not doing anything but helping us. Because we'll be right there with you."

Ben laughed, but it was a sick, frightened noise. "That's never going to happen."

"Try again," Jude growled.

"Do you know how much security there is on those ships?" Ben asked. "Even to get on the launch that's going to take us out to the ship, there are massive layers of security to get through. They're not going to just let me walk on board with a couple of mechs. And trust me, their guns are bigger than yours."

"So you're not going to help us," Jude said.

"I've been *trying* to help you," Ben said loudly, his voice climbing the register. "Why don't you just let me? Walk out of here, and we can pretend nothing happened. Let me stop the virus, and you can all just go back to your lives."

"All the people at Safe Haven, they can just go home?" I said.

"Of course."

"Because they're just being held for their own protection, right?"

"No one's being *held,*" Ben said. "It's like I tried to tell your mother: They're not prisoners; they're clients. We're protecting them."

"Have you been inside?" I asked.

He hesitated. "That's not really my area."

"So you can't really say what's going on inside."

"It's my corp," Ben said. "I've been working there for twenty years. I've been working toward *this*, toward *you*, for twenty years. Why would any of us want to hurt you? We *created* you."

"So you're God," I said. "Someone tell Savona. I hear he's been hoping for an introduction."

"I know BioMax took something from you, Lia."

It was a tidy euphemism.

"But look what we gave you!" he continued. "A new life. *Eternal* life. A miracle. And this technology isn't just about saving individual lives or winning wars—this is the preservation of human consciousness. Through any upheaval, through all our global crises, we now have the tools to endure. This is a new beginning for us, Lia. For humanity."

The saddest part of all was that I believed him. At least, I believed that *he* believed it. He believed in BioMax.

He didn't know.

"What's the EMP generator for?" I asked.

"What generator?"

"In Safe Haven, behind the residence facilities, there's an EMP bomb," I said. "Useful for emitting a giant electromagnetic pulse that could wipe us out in one shot. And not much else."

Ben shook his head. "You're mistaken."

"Or you are."

"We're wasting time," Jude said. "Can you get us to the ship or not? Because if not, you're not much use, are you?"

"Give him a chance," I said. It was a little late to try good cop, bad cop, but I figured it couldn't hurt. "I'm sure he'll think of something."

A bead of sweat trickled down Ben's cheek. His hands had turned white with the pressure of gripping the blanket. "I will," he said quickly. "I'll think of something."

But he didn't. Jude was getting impatient.

"Walk us through it," I suggested. "How do you get to the servers?"

"I have coordinates for the launch ship," he said. "We meet and set off from there—"

"Slow down," I said. "More details. When do you go. What do you do when you get there. You get the idea."

"I'm due at dawn. The rest of my team will arrive by two p.m."

"Who's on the team?"

"Just my staff, other techs."

"You get to decide who goes?"

He nodded. "I give the list to security; they screen us and let us onto the launch ship."

"And why do you have to get there before everyone else?"

"There's equipment to load," Ben said. "This is a scheduled monthly maintenance check, so we're replenishing equipment and supplies. I have to supervise that it's all accounted for and loaded—"

"That's it," I said.

"What's it?"

"The equipment," Jude said. He got it too. "Shipping crates, right? Anything could be inside them."

"Well, they screen them—"

"But you're in charge," I said. "You say what goes and what doesn't. You could get around the screening."

"Maybe." Ben looked like he was almost as afraid of that prospect as he was of Jude shooting him down in his bed. It occurred to me that if he got caught trying to help us stow away, his ending wouldn't be any more pleasant.

I hadn't asked for this, I reminded myself. And I hadn't started it. BioMax had. Call-me-Ben had chosen his side. It wasn't my fault this was where he ended up.

Still, I was glad Jude was the one holding the gun.

"So we stow away in the crates," Jude said. "Just one

problem—what's to stop him from screwing us over as soon as we're inside?"

"Don't suppose you'd just take my word for it?" Ben asked weakly.

"One of us needs to get on board with him," I said. "To watch him."

"That brings us right back where we started," Jude said, disgusted. "Nowhere."

"Not quite."

It couldn't be Jude, and it couldn't be me. No one would ever believe two mechs had business on a server ship, especially under these circumstances. Auden's face was too well known. Which left only one option.

And maybe I'd been thinking about it all along.

"Come in here, Zo," I called.

Ben's eyes widened as she came into the room.

"You recognize her?" I asked Ben.

"I don't think we've met, but I know the name."

Zo rolled her eyes. "Typical," she said. "We've met about ten times. Don't feel bad. No one ever notices me when big sister's in the room."

I didn't argue with her, because when it came to BioMax she was right. Which was what I was hoping. "No one knows her," I said. "She could be anyone. Even Halley."

What little color was left in Ben's face drained away. "What did you say?"

"Your daughter. Halley. Don't you think she and Zo look a bit alike? I know you haven't seen her in years, so maybe you should just trust me on this—"

"Do *not* bring her into this," he said, with cold fury. So he did care about something beyond his corp and his cause. Who knew?

"No one knows Zo," I said. "No one knows Halley. A little hair dye, some new clothes, a fake ID . . . There's no reason to think that your crew would be able to tell one from the other."

"You want—" He swallowed, hard. "You want me to pretend *she's* my daughter? And convince my team—and ship security—that for some reason I need to bring her along on a maintenance trip to a highly secure server farm?"

I shrugged. "Tell them it's a field trip. Or punishment. Or you're trying to buy her love with a vacation on the high seas. I don't care—you'll think of something."

Zo looked as uncertain as he did. "Lia, I don't know—"

"And I suppose she's going to, what? Hide the gun under her shirt? Or you want me to come up with an excuse for that one too? And have you thought about what happens to her if she tries anything? Surrounded by security?"

"We won't have to worry about that," Jude said, unexpectedly, and approached the bed. Ben pressed himself against the wall, eyes wild.

"Turn over," Jude said.

"Why?"

"Just do it."

"No. No, you want to shoot me, you look me in the eye."

"I don't want to shoot you," Jude said. "But I will if I have to. *Turn over.*"

Very slowly, Ben turned over, and lay facedown on the mattress. He was shaking. Jude bent over him. Something silver flashed in his palm as he brought his hand toward Ben's neck. Ben yelped with pain and jerked away.

"You can sit up now," Jude said, backing away. Ben rubbed his hand against the back of his neck, frowning as he felt something that shouldn't be there.

"What did you do?" he asked.

"Just a little fail-safe," Jude said. "Riley designed it. You remember how good he was with explosives."

Ben looked like he was remembering *exactly* how good Riley had been with explosives, at least when it came to wiring the Brotherhood laboratory for demolition. He looked like he was also remembering that the explosion in that case had happened somewhat prematurely.

Jude lowered the gun. In his left hand he held a slim cylinder with a button at the end. "There's a miniaturized explosive embedded beneath your skin, where your spinal cord meets your brain stem. I press this button, you go boom. Elegant, don't you think?"

He held it out to Zo, who waited a long moment before accepting the offering. I wanted to tell her she didn't have to.

"You're bluffing," Ben said.

"You want a demonstration?" Jude asked. "I give Zo the word, and you'll be smeared all over your bedroom walls. Which, admittedly, could use the decoration—but you wouldn't be around to appreciate it, so what good would that do?"

"Lia, this is insane," Ben said. "Tell me you know this is insane."

"Ben, you scooped my brain out of my dead body and loaded it into a machine. Don't talk to me about insane."

"I want you to leave my house right now," Ben said. "You leave, and I'm calling the secops, and we are done here. *Done.* You simply can't do this. I won't let you."

"Ben, listen to me—"

"Right shoulder," Jude said. "Two inches."

Before I could ask what he was talking about, there was a loud crack. Jude barely flinched with the recoil. The bullet blasted into the wall, two inches above Ben's right shoulder. Ben screamed.

"You understand I meant to miss," Jude said. "Next time I won't. Are you with me now?"

Ben nodded.

"Ready to help us?"

Ben snuck a few small glances at the hole in the wall, jerking his eyes away quickly, each time, like he preferred not to see. Then he nodded again. He was ready.

• • •

There were preparations to be made. Auden guarded Ben while we dealt with dyeing Zo's hair and dressing her up to look as much like Ben's daughter as possible. Zo herself took care of the fake ID—it clearly wasn't her first attempt. While she was busy with that, I had Jude to myself, which gave me the perfect opportunity to ask why the hell he'd neglected to mention Riley's magic mini-bomb at any point before the absolute last minute.

"Because I didn't think of it until then?" he said.

"You just *forgot*?"

"No, I mean, we needed it, so I made it up."

We were alone in the living room, with no chance of anyone overhearing us. Still, I lowered my voice to a whisper. "You were *bluffing*?"

"You thought I just happened to have the exact super-secret weapon that we needed in that exact moment?" Jude snorted.

"If it's not an explosive, what the hell is it?"

"I palmed some stuff from his lab, just in case."

"Just in *case*?"

He shrugged. "Bad habit. But it came in handy, right? That's where I got the injector. The 'explosive' is just a random chip."

"And the detonator?"

"Remote ignition starter for the car. Never leave home without it."

I wanted to punch him. "And when were you planning on telling me? Or *Zo*?"

Jude got serious, fast. "Zo can't find out," he said. "The bluff works only if *she* believes it."

"So you want to send her in blind and defenseless?"

"You want to give up and go home?"

I didn't say anything.

"You know I'm right," Jude said.

I didn't know. But I wasn't going to argue. I didn't need his permission to tell Zo the truth; I just had to figure out whether I should. So I pretended he'd convinced me, and shifted the conversation to what would happen if and when we got ourselves onto the server ship. We'd have one weapon, we'd have one hostage—and we'd be extremely deep in hostile territory with admittedly no clue as to what we'd do next. Playing it by ear wasn't exactly a comfortable option, but it wasn't clear we had an alternative. Ben would be able to guide us to the right part of the ship, and from there it would be up to us to figure out exactly what his team was planning on doing to the servers. I was more convinced than ever that he was clueless, which we could use to our advantage—but if he turned out to be a better liar than I'd thought, if he was leading the phase three charge, then we would deal with that, too. One weapon, one hostage. Worst case, we could try to alert the ship's security team, revealing BioMax's plans along with our presence, and probably, if the rumors were right about the on-board lawlessness, getting us all killed. But that was the thing we all understood, even if we hadn't talked about it: There was a plan to get ourselves safely on board.

There was no plan to get off.

FALLEN

"I don't know how to forgive you."

By four a.m. on Sunday we were ready. We drove to the loading zone in silence. Ben sat motionless in the back seat, looking neither at us nor the gun. He'd dropped any vestige of fighting back. He did what we said, followed our orders, and every hour, seemed to turn deeper into himself. I knew what it was like to give yourself over to someone else's decision making, following an external voice and silencing your own. But he was going to have to wake up soon, because in a few hours Jude, Auden, and I would be trapped inside a shipping crate; Ben would be on his own with only my sister and a dubious bluff to keep him in line. He was the only one who could talk us all onto the ship, and I knew he believed his life depended on it. I just didn't know how much he cared.

The BioMax equipment crates were being warehoused in a secure facility near the docks. Ben guided us through the shadows and pressed his thumb to the security pad. A panel the size of a garage door creaked open. The interior was dark, but I could make out the dim outlines of towering stacks of crates.

"Where's the security?" Jude asked, suspicious.

"Coordinates of this dock are on a need-to-know basis," Ben said dully. "For something like this, the best security is no security."

Jude shook his head. "Bureaucratic brilliance never ceases to amaze me."

I couldn't take my eyes off the stacks. "You're going to hide us in a crate and get us on the ship, right?" I asked Ben.

"That's the plan, isn't it?"

"So what happens when we end up at the bottom of a giant stack like this? We just wait a few months for someone to get around to unpacking us?"

"I'll make sure you end up somewhere private, where you can climb out and . . . do whatever you're going to do."

"And how do you plan to do that?"

"You're going to have to trust me," Ben said.

I laughed.

"Trust me," Zo said. I was sure no one but me heard the quaver in her voice. "He knows what happens if he screws up."

"You can still walk away," Ben said. Apparently, he still had a little fight left. "All of you. I won't say anything. And if BioMax is up to something—if your insane suspicious are right—let *me* look into it. There's no reason to throw everything away like this."

"Show us the crate," I said.

"Lia, please. Think about your mother. And Riley. He's waiting—"

"Show us the *crate*."

There were two of them, coffin-sized and air permeable so that the one of us who needed to breathe could do so. One was red; one was blue. Both were, according to Ben, intended to hold delicate replacement parts and so would arouse no suspicion when he insisted on personally supervising their loading and unloading. Two crates, three of us—and neither Auden nor I was willing to risk eight hours in a box with Jude.

"So, roommates?" Auden said, with a wry smile.

I wasn't ready to be his friend. "I need to talk to Zo for a second. Alone."

Jude looked alarmed. "Lia, just remember—"

I ignored him and grabbed Zo, drawing her deeper into the cavernous warehouse, away from the rest of them.

She shook me off. "If you're going to ask me if I'm sure I still want to do this—"

"I wasn't. Should I?"

"'Want' isn't exactly the word I'd use," she admitted. "But I'm doing it. I just don't know . . ."

"What?"

Something in her face relaxed then. The fierce, fearless mask of a warrior fell away, and she was just my sister again. My little sister. "I don't want to screw this up." She held the remote detonator between her palms, then crossed her fingers around it, like she was praying.

I could let her make her own choices, no matter how stupid and reckless they might be. But I couldn't let her choose blindly.

"Zo, there's something you have to know about the detonator."

"You mean aside from the fact that it's fake?"

I gaped at her. "You *knew*?"

"Haven't we already established that I'm not a moron? If Jude had something like this, don't you think he would have mentioned it sooner?"

"You knew from the start?"

"I know a car remote when I see one." She slipped it into her pocket. "I almost wish I didn't know. It'd be easier." She gave my shoulder a light poke. "Of course, *you* would have just screwed that up!"

I felt like an idiot, on multiple fronts. "Sorry? I think?"

"Maybe it's better this way," she said. "At least I don't have to worry about maybe having to kill someone. Because, honestly? I really don't think I could."

She sounded ashamed of the admission. I hated that.

"Are you going to be okay?" I asked. "Knowing you don't have any kind of weapon, that there's nothing you can do if . . ."

"I'm not worried," she said, though it was clearly a lie. "Besides, you'll be there the whole time."

"I won't be much good, protecting you from inside a box."

"Like you'd let that stop you." She looked away. "If I needed you."

"Zo—"

No. No more jokes or compliments disguised as insults or nervous edging around the truth. I hugged her, tight. She let me. Slowly, her arms crept around me, and squeezed. It had been a really long time. I couldn't even remember how long.

"I don't want to screw this up," she said again.

"You won't."

She pressed her face to my shoulder. "I missed you," she whispered.

"You too."

A small spot of wetness seeped through my shirt. But when she let go and backed away, her eyes were dry.

And, of course, so were mine.

The crate was too small for two people. Auden got in first, which was quickly revealed to be a stupid decision, because it left him crushed beneath me, his breath wheezing under the weight.

"Over a little this way," I whispered.

"If you just—"

"No, I think maybe—"

"A little—"

"And then—yeah—like that—"

But lying on his side was too uncomfortable, putting all his weight on either a bad arm or a bad leg—not that he complained, but I could hear the soft grunt of pain every time he shifted his weight, searching for the Goldilocks position, but there wasn't one, and we wrestled and rolled again. I ended up on the bottom, because I could bear the weight. Because I didn't need to breathe. Auden lay on top of me, and I could feel him trying to hold himself separate, support his weight on his arms, anything not to press against me.

For the first few hours it was easy to distract ourselves. There were the noises of the crew arriving, the sudden, jerky movement of getting transported out of the warehouse and loaded onto the launch boat, the ever-present fear that someone would make a last-minute check of the contents and expose us to the world. There was also Zo, who'd set her ViM to record and relay her every word to mine. So I could listen to my sister play the part of Ben's daughter . . . knowing that if something went wrong, there'd be nothing I could do but lie there and listen to the consequences.

Ben did an admirable job of getting his "daughter" the security credentials she needed, claiming that she'd made an unexpected visit and his custody agreement required he not leave her unsupervised for prolonged periods of time. The BioMax team seemed intrigued and almost delighted by her presence, some unexpected entertainment to break up the long, dull journey, and Zo obliged, laughing at their lame jokes and feigning interest in their boring descriptions of network-routing technology. For all we knew, one of them even had some relevant information about phase three and would be foolish enough to mention it in front of her.

It was the kind of luck that couldn't last.

"Who's your little friend?" The voice in the ViM was tinny and distant, but still easily recognizable.

I swore under my breath.

"What?" Auden whispered. I shushed him, and waited.

"Kiri," Ben said, voice tight. "I didn't expect to see you here."

No chance she wouldn't recognize Zo. She knew everything about me. It was her job. Or had been, at least.

"If we can nip this virus in the bud, it'll be a huge PR coup for the corp," Kiri said. "Which we could use, after the disaster of the last few weeks. They've sent me along to make sure we get our narrative right. You know how it is."

"Of course," Ben said weakly. I hoped he didn't sound as suspect to her as he did to me.

"So now it's your turn," she said.

"My turn?"

"I told you why I'm here. So why is she?"

Ben didn't say anything.

I didn't know what to do, if anything. I could bust out of the crate now, rush to Zo's side, and—

"Halley," my sister said. "Nice to meet you. And I don't

want to go on this stupid trip any more than you want me to. So if you can talk my dad out of it, be my guest."

"Your daughter?" Kiri asked, sounding surprised. Or was that suspicion in her voice? Did she know? Had she guessed?

I could imagine Zo's bitter inner monologue—*No one ever remembers me*—and just hoped she was right.

"Well, I've heard a lot about you, Halley, and I'm certainly not going to pass up the chance to meet the girl behind the legend. Welcome aboard."

After the terror passed, we were left with boredom. Long hours to kill inside our aluminum coffin, waiting for whatever was going to come next. Auden lay quietly on top of me for a long time. His chest rose and fell with shallow, even breaths, and I wondered if he'd fallen asleep.

"So," he whispered finally. "This is awkward."

"We probably shouldn't talk."

"Right. Safer that way. Someone could hear." I could feel his chest moving with every word.

"Right."

So we didn't talk. Not for a while, at least.

"The thing is, we never really got the chance," he said, some endless amount of time later.

"The chance to what?"

"Talk."

So I wasn't going to be able to avoid it. "Fine. Talk."

That seemed to shut him up. It was several minutes before he came up with something to say. "What are you thinking?"

"That's what you want to talk about?"

"I'm making conversation."

"Fine. I'm thinking . . ." It wasn't really any of his business. But then, it wasn't much of a secret. "About Zo. What are you thinking?"

"You want to know the truth?"

"Not really."

"I'm thinking about trying not to think about all the water underneath us."

I prepared myself for yet another guilt trip. Of course he was afraid of the water; he'd nearly drowned. But I wasn't about to let him tell me it was all my fault. I wasn't apologizing again.

"Not a problem for you, I guess," he said.

"What, water?"

"The lack of, you know, *facilities*," he said. "I can hold it for eight hours, but I've got to warn you, that's pretty much my limit. . . ."

"Gross!" I had to smile. "That's what you were talking about?"

"What'd you think?"

"Nothing."

"Now, I'm not saying I'm going to wet my pants—well, our pants, really, considering the circumstances—and it's not like I'm thoroughly humiliated or anything by the mere prospect, which is maybe something else I'm thinking about absolutely, and completely not thinking about."

I wondered if he was trying to make me laugh.

"Seriously, you can stop now," I told him, trying not to. "I get the picture."

"I'm just saying, it's rough for a guy." I could tell he was holding in laughter too. "You know, you've got the water down there, and then you try to stop thinking about that, and all you can think of are lakes, rivers, water fountains . . ."

"Showers," I put in helpfully. "Rain."

"Flushing toilets."

"Tall, cold drinks of water."

"Waterfalls."

There was a long pause. Neither of us was laughing anymore.

"It's not an excuse, you know," I said instead.

"What?"

"What happened to you." I paused, half expecting him to correct me. *What you* did *to me.* But he didn't. "It doesn't give you the right to do whatever the hell you want."

"I guess this is where I tell you that I didn't mean it. That I was angry. All that."

"Well?"

"I meant it," he said. "All of it. Or, at least, I thought I did. Which is all that matters, right? Now . . ."

"Now what?"

"I don't know."

I didn't want to say it. Mostly because I didn't want him to guess how much I needed the answer. "What happened to you?"

"You know what happened."

"*I* happened? Is that what you mean? I did this to you."

"You didn't."

"I know that."

"You didn't make me jump," he said. "You tried to save me."

"That's not what you told your *Brotherhood*."

"I never thought you *meant* to hurt me," he said. "I was always very clear about that. I just . . ."

"Wanted to hurt me back. Job well done."

"*I* hurt," he said. "Do you get that? You don't feel anything, but I feel *everything*. My back, my stomach, my legs, they *hurt*. And my right arm . . ." The one that wasn't there anymore, that had been replaced by plastic and gears. "That hurts the most."

I feel everything. You used to know that.

But out loud: "I said I was sorry."

"Yeah. You did. Right before you walked out. To go be with *them*."

"You *kicked* me out!"

He snorted. "Please. I was half delirious. You *wanted* to believe me. You wanted an out."

"That's not true."

"It was easier to leave, so you didn't have to look at me," he spit out. "That's the mech way, right? You hate weakness. You don't believe in it."

"There is no *mech* way. I'm not one of your cultists, too pathetic to think for myself."

Except that Jude was the one who'd told me Auden was better off without me. That mechs and orgs weren't safe together, because they were too weak and we were too strong, because they would always hate us and we would always hurt them. Before Auden had announced it to the world, Jude had whispered it in my ear. And I'd believed him.

Maybe Auden was right, and it had been easier that way.

"I don't know how to forgive you," I said.

"I'm not asking you to."

"Do you forgive me?" I asked.

"No."

I didn't say anything. The walls felt closer than before. It was wrong, lying here with him. We didn't belong like this; we didn't fit anymore.

"Why are you here?" I asked.

"Because you're right. I helped start this."

"Because you believed in it," I pointed out. "You just said that. You thought the mechs were evil, soulless parasites. And you *meant* it, remember?"

"I remember what I used to think of you," Auden said. "Before the download. When you were just one of them, and I was . . ."

The weird loser with the antique watch, the ragged backpack, and the nutcase conspiracy theories. The nobody.

"I thought you were useless," he said. "Not to mention brainless. I told myself you were nothing but a . . ."

"Bitch?"

"Pretty much."

"You were probably right."

"I wasn't," he said. "I believed it. I was so certain—that's what I told myself, but that didn't make it true."

Auden was the one, the only one, who'd been sure that I was the same download as I was before. I didn't know how to explain that it wasn't true. That the person he'd come to know, the friend he'd had, before everything had fallen apart, *wasn't* the same person as the blond bitch who'd cheered on the Neanderthals when they leaped on their prey.

"What happened to your glasses?" I asked instead.

"What?"

"Your glasses." Auden had been the only person in our school, the only person in our world, really—that is, the world of people who counted—who was born as a natural. Life-threatening imperfections were corrected in the womb, but everything was else left as it was, thanks to his mother's crazed Faither beliefs. He'd rejected the beliefs but kept the nearsightedness, kept the glasses—right up to the moment when he'd followed in her zealot footsteps. The moment that he'd declared artificial to be evil and natural to be divine. It had always seemed a strange time to let himself be artificially perfected, to bring himself that much closer to the boundary between org and machine. And without the glasses he seemed like someone else.

"I finally got it," he said. "What an insult it was. Ignoring the defect when I could fix it so easily."

"An insult to who?"

"To anyone who couldn't be fixed. I thought I was the only one being real. But I was playing pretend. So I got my eyes fixed. No more glasses."

"Oh."

"Surprised?"

"I guess I thought it had something to do with . . . your mom." I didn't know if I was allowed to bring her up. "I always thought you kept the glasses because they were, like, some kind of reminder."

"Maybe," he said. "But I didn't really need that anymore, did I? Once I teamed up with the Faithers." He snorted. "She would have been so proud."

"Is that a good thing?"

"She was crazy," he said. "It runs in the family, remember?"

"Auden—"

"I don't think we should talk anymore," he said.

Long hours in the dark. Silence. The sound of the waves lapping at the boat. The engine roar. The bouncing and swaying as the boat cut through the water. Beneath the white noise, almost my imagination, floating in the dark: "Lia. I am sorry."

I don't know how long I waited to answer.

But I finally did.

"Me too."

After five hours at sea, nine hours in the box, the engines fell silent. The boat stopped moving. We had arrived.

We waited, though it was torture, as our container was carried out of its storage room and then connected to something that swung us into the air, where we dangled for an eternity, picturing the waves crashing below, and then we waited again, tensed, for the lid of the container to swing open at any moment, as if there were anything we could do if we reemerged into a world swarming with armed guards, all of them aiming at us.

Now, again, it was a matter of trusting Ben to follow through on his promise, with only his life as collateral. We were set down somewhere, and the walls of the crate were thin enough to make clear that we weren't alone. The murmur of voices overlapped with the ViM relay in my earpiece. Zo and Ben were standing just above us—along with everyone else.

"Why don't you all get started with the servers," Ben said. "I just wanted to do one last inventory check, make sure everything got on board intact."

I cringed. It wasn't the most subtle attempt. But then, I

didn't know if I could have done any better, especially with a gun to my head—or in this case, in it.

"You got it, boss," a man said.

"We'll meet you there," another one added. "We've got some business up in the COMCEN."

"What business?" Ben asked.

"That's classified."

"This is my team," Ben said. "Nothing's classified from me."

"This just came in from BioMax."

"And?"

"And—come on, man, don't embarrass yourself in front of your kid. This won't take long. We'll meet you at the servers."

"You asking me, or telling me?" Ben said.

"What do you think?"

Ben didn't respond.

No one spoke for several moments.

"You know what they're doing up there?" Kiri said. I assumed the other techs—at least the defiant ones—had left.

"I'd think that would be obvious."

"Me neither," Kiri said. "But I have some guesses. Nothing good. This corp . . ."

"What?"

"How long have you worked for them, Ben?"

"Twenty years, almost. You?"

"Five. But after the things I've heard . . ."

"What?"

"I'm out. After we fix this screwup, I'm getting out. And maybe you should think about it too."

"What exactly have you heard, Kiri?"

"Let's just say if I were you, I wouldn't ask them any questions when they come down from the COMCEN. Probably best we don't know the answers." Her voice brightened abruptly. "Come on, Halley, no need to stick around here while your dad counts processors. Why don't you come with me? I can show you the server room. Thrilling stuff."

Zo hesitated. "Actually, I should probably just stick with my dad."

Kiri laughed. "What kind of teenager are you? Come on, let's see if we can get into some trouble."

Think of something, I willed Zo, but there was nothing left for Zo to say, and she knew it. "Okay. Sure."

Their footsteps retreated from the crate. They were gone.

Moments later Ben's signal came: three knocks. Time to trust him, one last time. I eased open the top of the crate and peered out. We were in a shadowy storage hold, boxes and crates strewn across a space wide enough to contain the entire Kahn house. And aside from Ben we were alone.

Auden climbed out gently, stretching his cramped limbs. But I was up and in Ben's face in seconds. "You just let my sister wander off? Alone?"

"What was I supposed to do?" Ben asked.

"Stop them! Keep her *safe*."

And then Jude was behind me, pulling me away, calming me down, reminding me that there was nothing to be done; he'd been listening to the same conversation I had, and Zo had played along, just as she should have. Kiri was harmless; Zo was safe.

"Get it together," he said, giving me a rough shake.

I shrugged him off. "I'm together."

Zo was safe with Kiri, I told myself. Probably. I could still hear them through my earpiece, Kiri prattling on about server architecture and the ins and outs of spin, Zo offering the occasional monosyllabic grunt, as they drew further and further out of my reach.

"So, you believe us now?" Jude asked Ben. "Or you want to tell me your precious corp hasn't turned shady on you?"

Ben looked shell-shocked.

"I got you on board," he said finally. "Now what?"

Jude was still holding the gun. "You heard them," he said—not to Ben, but to us. "Something's happening at the COMCEN, whatever that is."

"Communications center," Auden said. He'd proved himself an expert on server farms, or as much of an expert as anyone could be—a convenient holdover from his conspiracy-theorist days. "Probably up by the bridge."

"Right," Jude said. "That. So we find it. We stop them."

They were right. It made sense. Phase three was real, and it was about to happen here, above us, unless we acted.

"You go," I said.

Jude wheeled on me. "What?"

"You follow the techs," I told him. "I'm going after Zo."

"I can check on your sister," Ben said.

I didn't know why he'd want to be anywhere near her, unless he'd figured out that the explosive was a fake. Either way, even if he'd proved himself to be as much of a dupe as I'd suspected, I couldn't trust him with this.

"We don't know what's happening up there," I told Jude. "It could just be a coincidence. You follow the techs, I'll go to the server room, check things out there, and if everything's good, I can grab Zo and we can meet you."

"And if it's not good?" Jude said. "What are you going to do then?"

"I . . ."

"Take the gun," he said.

"What?" I'd been expecting more argument. "No."

"You're right. We should split up. We only have one weapon. So if you're going to insist on going off on your own, you take it."

"I can go with Lia," Auden suggested.

"No," Jude and I said together.

"The important thing is stopping phase three," I said. "That's where you need to be."

Maybe that's where I needed to be too. Maybe it was selfish to go after Zo instead—whatever I said, I didn't actually believe there was any reason to check out the server room, not after what we'd heard. But I couldn't let her disappear into the ship without any backup. If something went wrong, she expected me to be there. I'd let her believe I would be. If Jude and Auden went after the techs at the COMCEN and they managed to sound some kind of alarm, the ship would be crawling with security, and Zo would, most likely, be screwed. Right now, with any luck, the worst threat she faced would be Kiri boring her to death with a history of BioMax. In which case I'd find a way to get her alone, and we'd go above deck together. Who knew, maybe Kiri could even be an asset. If not, I'd deal.

But I wasn't going to let Jude and Auden risk everything out of some misplaced sense of chivalry. As I suspected Zo would be quick to point out, one of us being stupid was more than enough.

"I'll go with Lia," Ben said.

"And why would she want that?" Jude said.

"She won't get into the server room without my help. And without me, I highly doubt if she'll be able to figure out if anything's not as it's supposed to be."

"Right," Jude snarled. "And *with* you she's got an excellent probability of being turned in to the first security team you pass."

"Ben comes with me," I said.

"You trust *him*?" Auden asked incredulously.

"We should lock him in a crate," Jude said. "Just to be safe."

"He's right," I said. "He can get me to the servers."

"And he'll do that because he's so eager to help us? Much less get up close and personal again with the girl who can turn his pretty face into modern art?"

"I got you on the ship," Ben said. "You're going to get caught eventually—I don't need to do anything to speed that along. And in the meantime I'm as curious as you are about what the corp is doing. So I'll keep my mouth shut, and I'll get Lia to the servers, and, well, if you don't want to take me up on it, that's your choice. Doesn't seem like you've got a lot of options right now."

He was sounding like himself again, which was almost as infuriating as it was comforting.

"Let's go," I said. "We'll come find you in twenty minutes."

Jude tucked the gun into his waistband. "If we're wrong, and something's happening in the server room, or if you need me—"

"I'll call."

"Be careful," Auden said.

"You too."

Jude grabbed my hand. "We can do this."

It sounded too much like a question.

"We can do this," I echoed him, no doubt in my voice.

Jude shook his head, and smiled.

"What?" I said.

"Nothing."

"Let me guess, you're wondering how to admit, without sounding like an idiot, that all this time you were totally wrong about me."

He was still holding on. "Actually, I'm thinking—as usual—I was right."

Ben led me through endless corridors punctuated by locked doors and ID panels, the walls striped with logos making it clear that the mid-decks were filled with server farms for every major corp. Without him I would have been wandering blindly through what seemed like miles of hallway, searching for BioMax; with him I had only his word that he was taking me to the right place. The ship was larger than any building I'd ever been in, and aside from the almost imperceptible thrum of the engines, several decks down, it was hard to imagine we were actually moving through the water. Its size did offer us one advantage: It felt like a ghost town. I caught glimpses of security guards, from a distance, but we made it much of the way without catching their attention.

It had to happen eventually: Footsteps approached. Ben grabbed my wrist and dragged me down the corridor, jiggling door handles while he went until one gave. He shoved me inside.

I waited in the dark, ear pressed against the wall, fists balled, ready to fight.

"BioMax," I heard Ben say. "Here's my ID."

There was a mumbled response.

"Headed to the server room now, sir," Ben said loudly. "Just getting my bearings. Easy to get lost here."

Another mumbled response, and then they both laughed. A moment later the door opened, letting in a shaft of light. Ben's face appeared in the crack. "Clear," he said. "Let's go. Fast."

Zo's ViM relay had gone dead, but I told myself not to worry. No doubt all the computer equipment was just jamming the signal. Not to mention the fact that we were in the middle of the Atlantic in a high-security zone; no reason to think that wouldn't interfere with network communications. Still, I started moving faster. We wound down long, featureless corridors, turning corners seemingly at random, but Ben seemed confident he knew where we were going, and I was starting to trust that, if nothing else, he was determined to get us to the server room intact. Both of us. It was clear I never would have found my way here without him. And when we reached the giant steel door with the BioMax logo painted across it, I knew that without Ben, there was no way I would have been able to break my way in.

"Why are you helping me?" I asked quietly.

He triggered the locking mechanism and heaved the door open, gesturing me inside. "Keep out of sight. I'll check on Zo."

The room was loud and cold. Computer servers were lined

up like dominos from wall to wall. I didn't know whether it was the refrigeration system or the servers themselves, but there was a low, constant thrum, a vibration. It almost felt like I was shaking.

Ben swept down the central aisle, his eyes pinned on the numbers marking each row. It was a room built for hide and seek, and I tucked myself into one of the narrow alleys between server rows, padding softly down the aisle as I shadowed Ben through the room. He threaded through the rows and I slipped behind him, always keeping the thick, towering computers between us, though he never turned back to look. Finally, he stopped. One row away, so did I.

Kiri was waiting for him, with two BioMax techs. One had a hand clamped around Zo's wrist.

"Learn anything interesting?" Ben asked his "daughter."

"She didn't," Kiri said. "But I think it's safe to say that I did."

Ben's expression didn't give anything away. "Problem?" he asked mildly.

"You tell me." I'd seen Kiri Napoor in a variety of moods—conciliatory, wheedling, triumphant, frustrated, distraught—but I'd never seen her like this. There was no mood, no emotion, just: cold. "Why am I standing here with Lia Kahn's little sister? And why are *you* trying to pass her off as your daughter?"

I cursed myself for not taking Jude up on his offer. If I had the gun, I would . . . what? Burst out from behind the servers, guns blazing, shooting wildly? Save the day?

Ben sighed. "You knew."

"Of course I knew." Kiri scowled. "It's my *job* to know. I've never understood why you thought so little of me. So you want to tell me what she's doing here?"

The situation could still be salvaged, I told myself. As long as no one panicked.

"Well?" Kiri pressed, when Ben didn't answer.

"What is that?" he said, turning his attention to a small pile of equipment and mess of wiring at the base of the server bank.

"You're asking *me* questions?"

"You're just here to observe," Ben said. "So what are you hooking up?"

"What's she doing here?"

"Is that an uplink device?" Ben said, approaching it. Kiri blocked his path. "Zo's here as a favor to a friend," Ben said. "Nothing to worry about."

"I wouldn't say that," Kiri said. And with the same jaunty grin she'd always given me when talking me into yet another tiresome BioMax PR chore, she pulled out a gun.

The two BioMax techs did the same.

Zo yanked her arm out of the tech's grasp. She brandished the remote over her head. "Don't!" she shouted. "If I press this button, he blows up."

Kiri turned to Ben, eyebrows arching toward her forehead. "Is that true?"

"Afraid so."

"A hostage," Kiri said to Zo. "Impressive. And now everything makes sense. I can see why he'd do whatever you said."

"Exactly," Zo said. Her voice was shaking, but her hands weren't.

If I showed myself now, would I make things better or worse?

"It's an untenable situation," Kiri said. "We'll have to fix that."

She raised the gun.

Zo screamed.

A spot of red bloomed on Ben's forehead, and he dropped backward, arms splayed, eyes open. Dead.

I was halfway out of my hiding place—halfway to Zo—when I realized that she was still on her feet, unharmed.

I stopped.

I hid.

It was the smart move; we were outnumbered, and throwing myself at two men with guns trained on my sister could only make things worse. If Kiri had intended to shoot her, she would have done it already. Probably. Still, I felt like a coward. And I hated myself for it.

Ben was dead.

Ben had kept his mouth shut about me, about Jude and Auden. He'd picked a side, our side. And now he was dead.

Without taking my eyes off my sister, I reached for my

ViM. If I could get through to Jude, if I could call in a rescue—

"Where are the rest of them?" Kiri asked Zo.

"The rest of who?" She was staring at Ben, eyes wide and watery.

"You're not here alone."

Just tell her, I thought.

Or maybe, *Don't tell her*. Information was leverage, Riley had once reminded us. Secrets were power. If Kiri got what she wanted out of Zo, what need would there be to keep her alive?

On the other hand, if I showed myself, gave Kiri what she really wanted, maybe she'd just let Zo walk away.

"It's just me," Zo said, and I could tell she was trying to regain some semblance of spunk. It wasn't working. "Sorry to disappoint."

Something buzzed at Kiri's waist. She lifted her ViM to her ear and nodded. "Good. Bring them in." Then she turned back to Zo, with that eerily familiar smile. "I see you're just as big a liar as your sister."

I didn't have to call Jude. He was here, with Auden by his side, both of them frog-marched into the room by four Bio-Max techs, techs carrying guns—a real one for Auden, a pulse one for Jude, both of them deadly.

"Any problems?" Kiri asked.

"Not a one," the tallest one said. "They fell for it all the way."

"Good job." She waved a hand toward the nearest wall. "Put them over there."

The techs shoved them into the wall, along with Zo, lining them up, their hands out at their sides, fingers outstretched, palms empty, nothing up their sleeves, so to speak. Nothing left to stop this . . . except me.

"So where is she?" Kiri asked.

"Who?" That was Jude, eyes wide, expression clueless. Unconvincing.

Kiri just laughed. "I know she's here, somewhere, lurking about." She raised her voice. "Are you here, Lia?" she shouted. "Hiding? Typical. Most people would want to help their friends—their *sister*. But not you, Lia, right? Nothing changes. All that matters is *you*."

"How long have you been talking to yourself?" Jude asked. "You may want to see someone about that."

Kiri ignored him, and gestured to the two techs who'd been there with her the whole time. "What are you staring at? Get back to work."

They put their weapons away and knelt at the base of the nearest server bank, where they began fiddling with a web of wires spiraling out of the exposed circuitry. They were hooking up a device and clipping it to the wires.

Seven of them. Three of us, backs against the wall.

And then there was me. Hiding. Waiting. Watching.

In other words, doing nothing.

“That’s an uplink jack,” Auden said suddenly, loudly—far more loudly than he needed to, unless he was hoping to be heard by someone who might be all the way across the room, invisible. “I’ve seen one of those before.”

Ben had pointed it out too—just as loudly.

“Smart kid,” Kiri said, sounding distinctly unimpressed.

“So you’re uploading something into the network?”

I flashed on the data banks we’d discovered in the BioMax basement, the neural patterns they had filed away for a rainy day, for whatever machine they deemed ready for an obedient human brain to guide its movements, its actions at the beck and call of BioMax, mechanical slaves.

What would happen if they uploaded one of those obedient cybernetic slaves to the network? How much would they control? Maybe the AI, the war machines, had all just been practice—maybe BioMax wanted more than money. Maybe they wanted everything.

Kiri ignored Auden and addressed the techs. “How close are we?”

“Five minutes,” one of them said, voice slightly wobbly. “If it works.”

“It better work.” Kiri jerked her head at the two techs guarding Zo. “Make yourself helpful,” she snapped. “Go see if you can’t hunt down their little friend. I know she’s on board.”

They shifted nervously, glancing at each other, but neither moved. One mumbled something under his breath.

"What's that?" Kiri glared.

"Bad numbers if we go," he muttered. "Three of them, two of us—"

"They're *children*." She rolled her eyes. "Fine. Kill the defective and the girl, but save the skinner. If this doesn't work, we might need him."

"To upload?" Auden said, nearly shouting.

Not because he was afraid. Not because he was panicking.

Because he was talking to me.

"We can't use him," one of the techs said. "If we upload an intact one, it's possible—"

"Who said he'd be intact?" Kiri smiled. "Now, take care of it."

Kill the defective and the girl.

Two men raised two guns. Kiri watched, waited. Still smiled. And it was like she was smiling right at me, like she knew I was there and was taunting me, *daring* me to show myself, to do something stupid, throw myself at her, at Zo, at the weapons, throw everything away, like she couldn't wait for it to happen, and she couldn't wait to watch.

Two men, two guns. But there were no guns guarding the uplink device. Only two techs, who were barely my size, who had dropped what they were doing and were frozen, watching Kiri, watching the guns, watching death about to happen.

This is a dumb idea, I thought, but there was no time to think.

I ran.

I ran toward the server, toward the uplink jack, toward the techs, who scattered as I barreled toward them, and I lunged for the uplinker, fumbling with the familiar wires and switches, aiming the wireless input jack at my pupil, only one chance to get this right, to flip the switch, to do *something*, even if the triggers compressed and the guns fired and physics took over. I couldn't stop Kiri. I couldn't stop bullets. But maybe I could stop them from uploading whatever they were so desperate to upload—by uploading myself first. Maybe it would only stop them for a moment, I couldn't know. But a moment might be enough to save Zo.

Kiri's thugs flickered at the edge of my vision, and as I fumbled with the device—urging myself faster, *faster*—I saw them whirling around, and then there was an explosion in my ears, and suddenly the world shifted. I didn't understand why the ceiling was so far away, why I was on the ground, why I couldn't move, why the explosions were still firing, but quieter now, like sharp popping noises, distant bombs bursting in air and, with each of them, pain, bursting in me. Legs, chest, neck, more, until there was no telling one from another; the pain radiated everywhere, sharp and sweet, and in the rush I could believe that my body was a body, that I was alive.

The upload worked, I thought.

I will survive.

But it didn't work that way. The memories would survive.

The pattern would survive. But I wasn't in the uplink, and I wasn't in the servers. *I* was on the ground. I was bleeding a viscous green fluid and firing sparks and watching uselessly as my friends took advantage of the distraction and struggled for their lives. I was stuck, as I was always stuck, in this body that didn't belong to me, that *wasn't* me; that's what Jude had taught us, that's what I was supposed to believe—I was my mind, I was my memories.

But my mind, my memories, were locked inside the head, and the head was bleeding.

The eyes were bleeding, fluid clouding the artificial irises, and Kiri appeared before me tinged with muddy blue, the pulse gun she raised little more than a black smear. I didn't hear what she said. I saw Zo open her mouth, but couldn't hear her scream.

This is not my body.

This is not me.

This is not—

AFTER

I was Lia Kahn.

That was the end.

That was the beginning.

This is real, I thought. *This is not.*

This is me.

This is not.

I was in pieces.

I was sand, sprinkled on a beach.

Thousands of grains—lost in a billion.

I sorted through them.

Found myself, recognized myself, separated myself from the world.

One by one.

This is other.

This is me.

• • •

After the accident I was lost in the dark. Alone. A solitary something, locked in endless nothing.

There was no darkness here.

I was lost in the light.

The white-hot light of information, arrays of photons, billions to the billionth power, ones and zeros, electrons entangled, quantum spin states flipping up and down, all the data, all the words, all the commands, all the memories, all light. All me.

I was nothing.

I was billions upon billions of photons, spread out across a server, across a network, across an invisible web that circled the globe. But like finds like. Lia found Lia. Billions of Lias, flowing together, craving cohesion, links growing, bonds forming, until billions became one, and one became billions.

Until I became me again. The same; different.

Until there was no *this is me, this is other.*

There was only us.

Lia Kahn.

And the network.

It took a thousand years.

It took a nanosecond.

And then I woke.

I opened my eyes.

All my eyes.

I saw.

I saw with a billion eyes. Heard with a billion ears. Security cameras, satellites, ViMs, motion detectors, heat sensors, radars, anything and everything that linked into the network linked into me.

I saw the Parnassus corp-town, the mechs still trapped inside, waiting for the end. The guards, who breathed in and out because the correct combination of gases flowed through the air vents, air vents with circuits, with programming, with chips that drew data from the network, that drew their commands. Like the command to filter out a negligible amount of oxygen, shifting the balance, depriving org lungs, letting the guards sleep. Letting Ani and Quinn lead the mechs out of their prison and—as I smoothed the way—to the dead zone, a new safe haven, letting Ani and Quinn play mechanical Moses, leading their followers to a poisoned promised land.

I saw into BioMax, slipping past their firewalls like water through clasped hands—it was nothing but a joke, the thought that any wall could be high enough, strong enough, safe enough to keep me out—and I found the electronic bits and bytes that were once and would again be Riley. I saw the body that would soon house what passed for his soul, a body they would load him into, because I would make them, and some distant part of me, the part that still remembered what bodies were like and why I'd clung so tightly to mine, wondered what kind of world he would wake to, and whether he would care I was gone.

I saw Auden on his knees, palms together, head bowed. And beside him, a gun. Beside him, bodies.

I saw another body, the body that had belonged to me, a different me, a body that had given me life and then given out. I saw Jude and Zo standing over it. I saw Zo crying. I saw Jude take her hand.

They didn't know I was there, watching. They didn't know I would guide them safely off the ship, back to dry land.

They didn't understand—and how could they, how could anyone, until I showed myself—that I was there, but not just there. I was everywhere. I was the brain of my father's elevator, as he rose into the sky and trusted that the electromagnetic brakes wouldn't malfunction and plunge him into the ground. I was the guidance system of the Honored Rai Savona's car, the only thing standing between him and a fiery hell. I was the record of every credit, the buying and selling that gave the corps their power and the wealthy their luxury. I was the contract binding the corp-towners to their servitude. I was the power grid of the cities, shutting down at night, trapping the animals in their cage.

I was watching, and I would get them home.

I was Lia Kahn, once. I was a girl, an org. And then I was a machine, a copy.

I was confused.

Before.

I'm not confused anymore.

I remember who I was; I remember everything. I remember what Lia Kahn used to want, what she used to need. I remember who she used to love.

But remembering is not experiencing.

I remember what it was to be an *I*, a single thing, a point. I remember believing I had to choose. To be this thing, or that. To be an us; to fight a them. But that's the past. I'm no longer human, no longer machine. Not alive, not dead.

There is no more choosing.

There is no more *I* to choose.

They fear me, I know that. They fear what I know, what I control, what I can do. They try—pathetically, uselessly—to catch me. To erase me. As if I were still a *thing*, a discrete individual that could be purged. As if I weren't the entire system, as if I weren't inside of them, all of them.

I understand everything now. I understand what's wrong, and I understand how to fix it. I can control, but I can also protect. I can save. I can mold this world into what it should be, and when they see that, they will fear me no longer.

I can save them all. And I will.

Whether they want me to or not.

ACKNOWLEDGMENTS

This trilogy began as an argument.

A series of arguments, actually, over the course of a seminar in the history of mechanical life. I signed up expecting to watch a few Terminator movies but instead found myself arguing about the nature of humanity, the definition of thought, the value of emotion, and the ever-shifting boundary between man and machine. You could call this trilogy my final paper. I owe a huge debt of gratitude to my professor, M. Norton Wise, and fellow students—especially Sameer Shah and Naamah Akavia—for raising more questions and debates than could be answered in a one-semester seminar. Also for putting up with me, which was no easy task.

And in the category of "this trilogy could not have existed without" are the ridiculously talented writers Holly Black, Libba Bray, Cassandra Clare, Erin Downing, Maureen Johnson, Justine Larbalestier, Leslie Margolis, Carolyn MacCullough, and Scott Westerfeld, who read drafts, paved over plotholes, shared in my neuroses, buoyed my spirits, and did their best to keep me reasonably sane. Thanks also to my agent, Barry Goldblatt, who's usually the one stuck dealing with me when the whole "reasonably sane" thing doesn't work out.

A million and one thank-yous to Jennifer Klonsky, Bethany Buck, Emilia Rhodes, Lucille Rettino, Bess Braswell, Paul Crichton, Anna McKean, Cara Petrus, and the rest of the Simon Pulse team, who put everything they had into these books and, for the last six years, have demonstrated an amazing Martha Stewart–like ability to turn a publishing house into a home.

Thank you to Sherry and Jim McGlynn for handing me my first science-fiction novel (not to mention bribing eleven-year-old me with ice cream to sit through the entire showing of *2001*), and thanks to Brandon McGlynn for adding some science to my fiction.

And one final thank-you to Isaac Asimov. If you've read his books, you know why.

If you haven't, start with *I, Robot*.

(Start now.)